A BULLET FOR BILLY THE KID

A BULLET FOR BILLY THE KID

A WESTERN TRIO

WILL HENRY

FIVE STAR
A part of Gale, Cengage Learning

GALE
CENGAGE Learning™

Detroit • New York • San Francisco • New Haven, Conn • Waterville, Maine • London

GALE
CENGAGE Learning-

Five Star Publishing, a part of Gale, Cengage Learning.

Set in 11 pt. Plantin.
Printed on permanent paper.

LIBRARY OF CONGRESS CATALOGING-IN-PUBLICATION DATA

Henry, Will, 1912–1991.
    A bullet for Billy the kid / by Will Henry. — 1st ed.
        p. cm.
    "A Five Star western"—T.p. verso
    ISBN-13: 978-1-59414-725-8 (alk. paper)
    ISBN-10: 1-59414-725-6 (alk. paper)
    I. Title.
PS3551.L393B85 2009
813'.54—dc22   2008039750

First Edition. First Printing: January 2009.
Published in 2009 in conjunction with Golden West Literary Agency.

Printed in the United States of America
1 2 3 4 5 6 7 12 11 10 09 08

CONTENTS

FOREWORD
BY JON TUSKA

Henry Wilson Allen was born in Kansas City, Missouri. After attending Kansas City Junior College for two years, he drifted West, working at odd jobs until he ended up in Los Angeles. He worked for a newspaper for a time and then found employment in 1935 with a company manufacturing animated films. Two years later Allen was hired by M-G-M as a junior writer in their short subjects department. It was first in midlife that Allen decided to try his hand at the Western story. *No Survivors* (Random House, 1950) was his first Western novel. It was published under the byline Will Henry because Allen did not want anyone in the film industry to know he was writing novels (something he later dismissed as a wrong-headed notion). While numerous authors of Western fiction before Allen had provided sympathetic and intelligent portrayals of Indian characters, Allen from the start set out to characterize Indians in such as way as to make their viewpoints and perspectives an integral part of the story he had to tell.

Allen's second novel was *Red Blizzard* (Simon and Schuster, 1951). Harry E. Maule, who had become Western fiction editor at Random House in 1940, rejected it. When another publisher accepted it, Allen's agent, August Lenniger, had Allen adopt a different pseudonym, reserving Will Henry for novels published by Random House. The second byline was Clay Fisher. It is probable that what Maule detected in *Red Blizzard* was Allen's tendency to impose an often superfluous historical framework upon what remained in essence a traditional Western plot. However, in view of Maule's rejection of this second novel, Allen's reaction—only natural under the circumstances—was to believe that he was able to write two totally different kinds of Western stories without himself being certain as to just how and why one was distinct from the other. Every time Maule rejected a novel, it became a Clay Fisher. In the event, there is really no difference between a Will Henry and a Clay Fisher novel except as an indication of the whimsies of Harry E. Maule's personal taste. Allen's next Will Henry novel was *To Follow a Flag* (Random House, 1953), an expansion of "Frontier Fury" that appeared in the magazine, *Zane Grey's Western* (9/52). It was the magazine story that served as the basis for the film, *Pillars of the Sky* (Universal, 1956) starring Jeff Chandler and Dorothy Malone. In either form this story is as much a straight action narrative as the next Clay Fisher title, *Santa Fe Passage* (Houghton Mifflin, 1952). However, this latter book was also an expansion of a short novel Allen had previously written for the magazine market and that now appears in this collection for the first time in its original form. It was the magazine version of the story that served as the basis for *Santa Fe Passage* (Republic, 1955) starring John Payne and Faith Domergue.

Frequently Allen could be intimidated by historical sources. He might add merely a dramatized floss to an historical account, such as his reworking of James D. Horan's version of Jesse James in *Desperate Men* (Bonanza Books, 1949) in the Will Henry novel, *Death of a Legend* (Random House, 1954). In *Reckoning at Yankee Flat* (Random House, 1958) by Will Henry, Allen provided a fictional account of the Henry Plummer gang. Since Professor Thomas J. Dimsdale wrote *The Vigilantes of Montana* (1866), this story has intrigued novelists. Allen may have been more meticulous than many of his precursors in depicting the actual historical events, but he could not succeed in bringing Plummer himself to life, relying instead on quotations from people who had known or seen the man. Yet, curiously, in the much later *Summer of the Gun* (Lippincott, 1978), with no historical context to intimidate him, Allen was able to create a truly vivid character in the gang leader Fragg, whose fictional personality is much closer to that of the historical Henry Plummer than the ambiguous shadow in *Reckoning at Yankee Flat*. Of all his attempts at straight fictional biography, perhaps only *I, Tom Horn* (Lippincott, 1975) can be judged a complete success. Indeed, it is more than that. It is a masterpiece, perhaps most fully realized not in the motion picture based upon it with Steve McQueen in the title rôle but in the full-length audio version from Recorded Books, Inc., as read by Frank Muller.

In general many of Allen's best novels deal with the failure of the frontier experience, the greed, the rape of the land, the apparent genocide, novels that end tragically because, in the history of the American West and given the premises built into these plots, such an outcome is inevitable. In this group belong two of the novels for which Allen won Spur Awards: *From Where the Sun Now Stands* (Random House, 1960) and *Chiricahua* (Lippincott, 1972). Also worthy of inclusion are *The Last Warpath* (Random House, 1966), an inter-connected series of tales about the Cheyenne Indians, illustrating how Allen was basically a short story writer whose novels are often a patch-work of novelette-length sequences fused together but able easily to stand alone, and *Maheo's Children* (Chilton, 1968), a story of Preacher Nehemiah Bleek and his Indian orphans set against the background of the Sand Creek massacre. *The Gates of the Mountains* (Random House, 1963) is a highly romantic retelling of the Lewis and Clark expedition and is clearly not in quite the same class as these others, despite its having also won a Spur. The shortcomings in this last title, however, apply to an extent even to Allen's best novels where the use of historical sources tends usually to be somewhat improvisational. *Maheo's Children,* in fact, was first intended as a straight historical narrative to be published under the byline Henry W. Allen and Allen submitted it to Don Ward, at the time an editor at Hastings House, a publisher of Western history books. Ward sent a section of the manuscript to Mari Sandoz (who herself published several not altogether reliable historical accounts with this same publisher) and her reactions were contained in a letter dated July 26, 1964 to Don Ward, reprinted in *Letters of Mari Sandoz* (University of Nebraska Press, 1992) edited by Helen Winter Stauffer. "The foreword or introductory bit tells one right off that the author knows nothing of the Cheyenne religion," Sandoz commented. ". . . All Allen offers here is the usual uninformed white man idea of sun, rain, and earth gods. Living up on the Tongue [River] even a few days should have taught him better about the Cheyennes. If not, Allen can read, can't he?" The books Sandoz cited, however, were by George Bird Grinnell with their openly favorable view of the Cheyennes and biased portrait of the Pawnees. Obviously Allen once more felt intimidated by historical sources and, therefore, turned this attempt at straight history into a fictional account intended now for a young adult audience. It was possible, therefore, to restore Allen's original text for this book, included under his first title for it, "The Legend of Little Dried River", in *Frontier Fury: A Western Duo* (Five Star Westerns, 2007).

The appeal of Allen's historical Western fiction to some critics has been his political and social perspectives. Betty Rosenberg in her Introduction to the Gregg Press' library reprint edition of *From Where the Sun Now Stands* in 1978 wrote: "The information . . . for realistic and honest novelization of the Indian wars was available. Lacking was a novel-reading audience willing to accept tragedy in place of romance. Such an acceptance would force the reader to recognize that Indian cultures and ways of life are sophisticated realities and their destruction wanton evil; that the invaders' Manifest Destiny was a blatant hypocrisy, an excuse to cover the theft of land and commercial exploitation; that missionary activities were a tool of subjugation; that the imposition of an Anglo culture upon the Indians was an unwelcome curse." The subject of this novel is the war against the Nez Percé Indians in 1877 and their subsequent defeat. These Indians did have a long tradition of peace and friendliness with the whites and in their terrible passage from Idaho through Montana to reach Canada, in which attempt they failed, they did not harm a single white woman or child because, in the words of the Nez Percé first-person narrator of the novel, "we had lived too long as brothers of the white man. Even in our last hours, we could not kill and mutilate his loved ones." As the 1960s progressed, such a sympathetic posture would become politically correct in viewing *all* of the Indian nations and tribes which, in its way, overlooked what made the Nez Percé stand out as victims and made this episode in their relations with Anglo-American culture such a poignant tragedy. For all of that, in Will Henry's *MacKenna's Gold* (Random House, 1963), Allen characterized the frontier buffalo soldiers as having "the hot blood of their savage African ancestors running wild in them"—an image right out of James Warner Bellah's *Sergeant Rutledge* (Bantam, 1960). Yet he also gave a powerfully vivid and sympathetic portrait of black Isom Dart, based on an historical character, who was born a slave and who found a new life as a freed man on the frontier in *One More River to Cross* (Random House, 1967).

After *Summer of the Gun,* Allen found it impossible to write another novel, although he was urged to do so by editors. After 1980 his memory began increasingly to fail so that by 1990 he would confess that he could no longer keep together the threads of any story. He stopped typing and his last letters to me were hand-written. We had begun corresponding in 1978 when he wrote to me following a favorable review I had written about the Gregg Press' reprint of *From Where the Sun Now Stands* in the *West Coast Review of Books.* Over the years, we must have exchanged 200,000 words with each other, often writing on a weekly basis. We also visited, and he showed me his little writing house where he worked (it was his original home in Encino, before money from motion pictures based on his work allowed him to build a much larger home on the same expansive lot). I shall always miss his spiritual companionship. He was a good friend, and I am old enough to know how few of them one has in his lifetime.

Over the years, Dorothy, his widow, has searched for unpublished material among his papers, while I sought to collect all of his Western fiction published in various magazines. Except for a futuristic novel set in the Arctic in the 21st Century, in which the United States and the Soviet Union are still grappling for political and territorial advantage, this present collection marks the end of the trail. For me it is sad, because a new Will Henry story, or a magazine story that has not otherwise appeared in decades, has always been an event to be celebrated, and it has been a pleasure for me to see my old friend return for encore after encore in the Five Star Westerns.

"I am but a solitary horseman of the plains, born a century too late and far away," Allen once wrote about himself. He felt out of joint with his time, and what alone may ultimately unify his work is the vividness of his imagination, the tremendous emotion with which he invested his characters and fashioned his Western stories. At his best, he wove an almost incomparable spell that involves a reader deeply in his narratives, informed always by his profound empathy for so many of the casualties of the historical process.

★ ★ ★ ★ ★

THE FOURTH HORSEMAN

★ ★ ★ ★ ★

I

In the mind of the weary horseman, pausing atop the rimrock, eyes slitted to the westering sun, there was no confusion. He *knew* where he was. *Peaceful Basin,* the boy had told him. *If you make it away, Frank,* he had said, *head west for the basin. Look up Old Jim Stanton. . . .*

Lifting the alkalied corners of his mouth in a grimace, the stranger contemplated the nether passage of the Mogollon Rim. The trail was slashed into the raw rock as though some old fearsome god of the Navajos had thrust his skinning knife into the bowels of the basin's walls and ripped upward to their pine scalp lock in one angry belly slice. But the boy had said it was the only break in the rim for sixty miles, and a man could take it or leave it. Clucking softly to the bay stallion, he sent him down the first pitch of the granite decline. The hour of easy choices was long gone for Frank Rachel.

The old man put down the axe and stepped away from the chopping block. He looked up the valley, squinting against the glare of the early sun. Shortly he moved behind the corner of the corral fence, reappearing seconds later to peer through its peeled logs, the axe replaced by a rusty-snouted .45-70 Springfield carbine. Eyes narrowed, he watched the approach of the solitary rider.

After ten seconds of study, he was no more pleased than he had been when he put down the axe for the Springfield. He had spent enough of his grown life watching distant dots across the mesa jog up to turn into solitary, hard-eyed horsemen to know the cut of this one now turning off the valley trail and in toward his ranch. He sat a horse like all of them, like a lean sack of loose oats. His long legs reached straight for the ground in the let-down stirrup leathers. Cradled under the offside knee was the omnipresent Winchester. Slung across the cantle were the trademark sougan and slicker, encompassing in their slender girth all that the world held personal to the man straddling the low-horned roping saddle. He fitted all right, and yet he didn't. There was something missing: a standard item that should have been there but was not. Then the old man had it—in a land where a man would as soon mount up without his Levi's as he would without his six-gun, this one rode without a Colt.

"That'll be far enough!"

The flat statement caught Frank, making him curse. Damn it, he hadn't seen the old coot. He pulled the bay in, sat waiting.

"I'd like them hands crossed on the horn." The old man stepped around the fence corner, the big bore of the Springfield wandering the newcomer's belt buckle.

Frank nodded, let the reins slide.

"They're crossed. You Stanton?"

"A name's a name," said the old man.

"Mine's Frank Rachel."

"One's as good as another."

"Try Johnny Fallon, then." There was an edge of grit in the dry dust of the suggestion. The old man held.

"World's full of Johnnies, mister. Franks, too. . . ."

Frank kneed the bay, quartering his offside toward the rancher. Covered, by the motion, his left hand slid from the horn into the onside saddlebag. "Catch!" he called, flipping the weapon.

16

Again the old man held. His eyes caught the sun flash of the big revolver as it turned in the air and lit in the dust at his feet. But his hands did not vary their grip on the carbine or his eyes leave the big horseman.

"Where'd you get it?" he said.

"Kid by the name of Johnny Fallon give it to me. 'You'll need a passport for Peaceful Basin,' he says. 'Use mine.' "

"What else he say?" Frank saw the rim frost edging the old man's eyes.

"Not much." He shrugged. "Man doesn't waste wind with a Forty-Four rifle slug in one armpit and out the other."

"Lungs?" The frost broke to the quick pain of the question.

"Both. He was already bled out bad when I rode onto him. Lasted maybe two hours."

"How come you to ride onto him, mister?"

"I'm ridin' the high line down from the north. . . ."

"Figured that." The interrupting nod was short.

"Don't break in on me, old man." The return nod was shorter. "It ain't polite."

"Go on. . . ."

"It's about dark. This kid is maybe a mile up on the posse that's tailin' him and bad hit, plain enough, by the way he was sacked in the saddle. I seen where I could get to him before the posse did . . . providin' he held out and the daylight didn't."

"You got hid out all right?"

"On a hogback ridge." Frank nodded. "The posse had only to bottle both ends and wait for sunup."

"The boy go hard, mister?"

"Not too. He was dream talkin' toward the last. About the basin here, and worryin' as to the posse grabbin' me for the job he had done."

"Some bad of a job?"

"Some. Train, east of Tucumcari. Busted a mail sack. Still

had some of it on him. Registered stuff. They'll never learn. I put it under the rocks with him. Smoothed our tracks and got out of there before moon up."

"Trouble then?"

"Likely. One of them hit the ground too soggy. The rest of them run me till daybreak. I lost them in the *malpais.*"

The old man chucked his head. "Them lava beds is hell on posses." He said it as though he had been there. "That about it, son?"

"About," the big rider agreed. He scowled, hawking the alkali dust from the back of his throat. The cottony spittle lanced the dust alongside the gun at the rancher's feet. "I'm near talked out, old man. Your turn."

"He was my sister's kid," Stanton said simply. "Feed's in the shed yonder. Water tank's past them big oaks. Grub'll be ready when you are."

"Suits me." Frank was turning the bay stud with the nod. "A man does better with his belly full."

"Either way, he does," replied the old man cryptically. "Whether it's lead or beans he's got it full of."

The greasy slabs of yearling loin beef and the pint ladles of re-fried red chili beans evaporated under the big rider's wordless assault. Old Jim Stanton took the opportunity to size up fully his self-appointed guest. It was a sizing up well calculated to put the thoughtful chill of reconsideration on his hasty approval of the dead Johnny Fallon's pearl-handled passport. He was a big devil, bigger by something more than you had spotted him for, riding up. Over six feet tall by half a hand, the three-inch hike of the Texas boots put him to towering up like a White Mountain pine. Even so, he was built, as Old Jim liked to put it, all of a piece. When you got over the surprising heft of him, you got around to the face. Old Jim had been looking at rimrock all his life. He knew it when he saw it. He saw it now in the narrow face of Frank Rachel.

The eyes caught you first, and for a moment you could not recall them. Then, of a sudden, you had it. When you did, the hair fell into place and you had everything about him—and just what it reminded you of. In the natural course of frontier events it was not given to many cowmen to see a *real* one. Oh, plenty of the Mexican or mountain variety, with their little heads, dainty faces, and house-cat manners. But a *real* one now!

Old Jim Stanton had seen one. In a flea-carnival wagon over in Albuquerque the summer of 1869. He had stood and watched him a full hour. Those eyes had been as yellow and clear as the bottom of a sand pool in the Verde at low water, and as quiet, too. Yet restless and never still, at the same time. *Let me out,* those eyes had said. *Open the door and let me out. I'll be your friend for life.* Then, sweeping across the cage bars, over your head to the distant peaks of the Sangres, they had whispered: *You do it and I'll smash your head like an eggshell. I'll knock you down on the first jump and kill you on the second. I'll be gone, and ever gone, and you the fool for letting me out.*

The old man hunched his shoulders as to a draft felt only by him. His eyes flicked to the stranger again, pausing on him only long enough to note the heavy sweep of the ash-blond hair, the dried-straw droop of the bleached mustaches. It was all there: the yellow, restless eyes, the stiff roach of the wheaten mane, the motionless wide line of the dark-lipped mouth. Maybe human, maybe otherwise. It made a man's hide crawl, either way. You looked at the big rider now and you knew it. You had let a lion into your house.

II

Peaceful Basin lay dark and still, waiting for the moon. It came, lipping the rim with silver, spilling over into the basin. The men built fresh cigarettes and talked, first, as Western men will, of livestock.

"Stock winter through pretty well here?" The big rider spoke softly, the way a man does who has lived much alone.

"You ain't asked the half of it!" It was a topic dear to the old man's heart. "Down here in the basin she's half the time open from October to April. Cattle do fine, no matter."

"Hosses too, I reckon." The talk shifted easily from cattle.

"There ain't a better hoss country. Lots of mineral in both grass and water. I got the only native bunch in the basin, growed by somebody here ahead of me. The Apaches burned him out, whoever he was. The bunch run wild till me and the boys brung them in with salt and sugar. You never seen such mares, mister!"

He had not missed the careful way his companion followed each word once the talk swung to horses. And before that he had not missed the blood-fine lines of the bay horse the big man rode. Or the fact that he was an uncut stud. He concluded now, his statement a direct question for all its casual ease.

"Not many rides a stud. And none I seen so far, a blood stud," he said.

There was a long pause, but when the stranger answered, a man knew he had not been hungry only for the beef he had just put in his belly. Or solely for the smoke he now held so long and gratefully in his lungs.

"Old man"—he dragged deeply on the cigarette—"if we could see the whole blessed world spread out in this moonlight, right from where we're settin' on this stoop, we couldn't see another blessed thing rightfully belonged to Frank Rachel. He's all I got . . . man, beast, or woman." He hesitated, dragging again. "He was took from me once. Legal bill of sale stole and blotted." Again the hesitation. "I seen you cuttin' trail on my face color. What would you say if you was asked?"

"Color's fresh," said Old Jim slowly. "You're old to the sun but it's new to you these past days. Somewhat and of recent late, I'd say, you ain't been in it."

"You'd say right." The bitterness stained like acid. "Two years, old man. Fed out of a pan, night and mornin'. Walkin' the bars all day long, lookin' just one way all the time." The cigarette flipped spinningly across the yard. "They left the cage door open one night. I got the bay back and burned the blotted bill." He shrugged.

"You left a receipt, I reckon?"

"Paid in full," said Frank. "Eyes wide, boots in place."

"Hossflesh comes high with some. You paid plenty."

"I paid what was askin'."

"But killin' a man?"

"I bought cheap there." He looked at Stanton. "If anything ever again happens to that stud, you remember that."

It was a clear threat, plainly out of time and place so far as Old Jim Stanton could see. The old rancher merely nodded. "I'll remember it, son." His voice dropped. "What is it you wanted of me that you ain't told me? I smell trouble, boy. You put the ache of it in my bones."

"I'm tired of runnin'. I want to turn around and rest, that's all." The admission came openly, no hint of harshness in it, but only a suppressed loneliness that cut deeper than any hard talk. "You're right about me and trouble. A man's got an eye and a face for it and it's goin' to look him up every time. You meet some jasper and you nod and say good mornin', and he backs off and says that's a god damn' lie, and there's your trouble. I been meetin' that kind all my life. It's been a fight . . . thumb in the eye, knee in the guts, Colt slug in the belly . . . ever since I was a kid. I ain't never had a friend."

"Friends ain't born, they're made," said Stanton abruptly. "Your kind never takes the time."

Frank eyed him a long time. "I'm aimin' to take it now," he

21

said at last. "I want to stay here in Peaceful Basin, and make a friend if I can. I want to get down off my hoss and stay down off of him from now on. You know what I mean?"

"I've been there," said Stanton softly. "It's why I came here myself."

"You'll let me stay then . . . ?"

There was an intense, humble appeal in the words and Stanton felt himself wavering. "By God, son, I'd like to, but. . . ."

"Old man, you let me, *I'll be your friend for life.*"

The chill of the words and the sudden light in the pale eyes struck Stanton. *Let me out,* those other eyes had said. *Open the door and let me out.* He shook himself, not wanting to look back to those eyes. "I just can't do it, Rachel. I can't pay the hands I got."

"I don't want money!" The excitement grew in the soft voice, thrilling the old man with its strange, lonely rush. "I want *mares!*"

"Mares? God A'mighty, what for?"

"For me and the stud. A mare a month and found. I'll work that way for a year. Don't put off on me, you hear?"

Stanton felt himself suddenly and compassionately moved beyond the uneasy borders of the fear put in him by the gaunt rider. "I hear," he said. "A mare a month and found. Your pick of the bunch."

Hearing himself say it, he did not care. He felt, all at once, like throwing an arm around those spreading shoulders. Like putting a friendly hand to that broad back to let the rider know he had a home at last. Then, even as the impulse struck him, the old rancher was taking a second look through the evening darkness, seeing the tall rider ease, cat-like, to his feet and move away. He knew now that the impulse was a fool one, and false. He was thinking suddenly, as the stranger thanked him and started for the shed with the big stud, of just one thing: that red and yellow carnival wagon over in Albuquerque thirteen years ago, and of those gold-flecked, amber eyes looking through him and beyond him to the last far peaks of the Sangre de Cristos, high and blue and lonely up back of Santa Fé.

III

The next morning the old man awoke to find his "lion" gone, the "cage door" of the horse shed swinging idly open to mark his passage. He was in the midst of a heartfelt sigh of relief when the soft voice hit him from behind.

"Guess who?"

He came around, not liking to be Indian-stalked any better than the average Arizonian, and nettled, too, that he could be. "Not Frank Rachel," he said acidly. "That's as sure as sheep-dip stinks!"

"A name's a name." The stranger lounging easily in the shed door made rare use of his hard grin. "You said it yourself."

"Well, it's a new day," grumped Stanton irritably. "Where do we go from here?"

"Up the valley first. I want to meet your boys. Then that Apache burn-out where you got the mares."

"And . . . ?"

"A look at the whole basin from up on top somewheres. A man's found a hole, he likes to see how to get in and out of it, likely."

"Likely," growled Stanton. "Let's ride."

The three JS hands, according to what little filling in the old man had given him on the long ride up Cherry Creek to their line camp, were brothers and half-blood Modoc Indians. Originally from northern California, they had come to the basin two years ago, in the fall of 1881. There was quite a clan of them, including their father, a young sister, the wives of two of the brothers, and their several small children. The new hand would see, the old man had grimly predicted, that the half-breed brothers were *hombres duros*—real hard men. The forecast proved as right as rim ice in November. The minute Frank laid eyes on the JS crew, he saw.

Sizing them, as he and Stanton rode up to their noon fire, he quickly figured that, squaw-bred or pureblood, these three would do better to side with than against. The old man introduced them as Ed, Jim, and John Fewkes, his own companion, for lack of more honest information, as Frank Rachel.

They acknowledged the newcomer with a mutual, calculating nod. Ed Fewkes said: "Get down and come in." John, the youngest brother, added simply: "We seen you comin'. Help yourselves." Jim Fewkes said nothing and, not having said anything, looked at Frank, long and slow.

While the old man was questioning them on the progress of their stray gathering, Frank poured himself a cup of coffee and watched Jim Fewkes. This required no particular sense of judgment. Of the three, the middle brother was plainly the one to watch. Peculiarly handsome, as were all of them, Jim Fewkes fascinated a man where the others only caught his eye long enough to warn him, then let go of it.

Where they were dark, he was darker. Where their eyes were slightly oblique and of that murky green frequently seen in the Indian cross-breed, his were slant as a Mongol Hun's, and of a peculiar turquoise brilliance that defied the memory of any quite like them. And he moved around in a shadowy way that put you to watching his feet, and to nodding to yourself when you did. Where his brothers used the standard Texas boots, Jim Fewkes wore a set of soft-tanned Apache moccasins under the cover of his regulation Levi's.

Frank's regard was being returned, in kind, not alone by Jim but by Ed and John Fewkes. Seeing it, Frank made a mental note. They watched a man hard and close but there was no challenge in that watching. There was no invitation to get cozy, either. Just the kind of watching one strange wolf-dog will give another when the meeting is unavoidable and the trail passably narrow.

Frank felt the satisfaction of this grow quickly. The Fewkes boys had looked him over, and he them. Nobody had felt called on to make a show of it. Each and all, apparently, had seen what they had seen—and bought it.

Long after he and the old man had left the noon fire, he found himself thinking about Jim Fewkes. There was gnawing inside the big rider, the empty pangs of a hunger that would not be put down. Not having felt it before, a man could not identify it for sure, but he could guess at it. Maybeso, being that green-eyed half-breed felt the same way about it, and nothing meanwhile went wrong to spoil it; he and Jim Fewkes were going to be friends!

IV

Winter came to the Mogollons, glistened briefly up on the higher rims, fell swiftly away under the early March sun. At the JS, preparations were begun for the spring branding. Frank knew that if he were to take over the Apache burn-out and get his horse ranch going, he would have to be about it.

Old Jim Stanton had insisted on his taking his twelve mares in advance. He had known it had been the former's stiff-backed way of paying off the debt of Johnny Fallon's gun. Accordingly he had simply nodded—said: "I owe you one, old man."—and gone about his picking.

Perched now atop the split-log rails of the home pasture, soaking up the April sun and surveying his sleek-coated mares and the proud-necked bay stallion, Red Boy, he heard the rusty scrape of the bunkhouse door behind him. Watching, he saw Jim Fewkes move to the work stock corral, shake out his loop, and snake it, underhanded, over the head of his blue roan.

Frank slid off the fence, saddled Red Boy, headed the mares, and drove them out of the pasture. Jim joined him below the ranch house, kneeing his roan alongside the stallion.

"I got a cute way up to that burn-out," he said. "Figured I'd ride with you."

"Figured you would." Frank nodded. "I'm obliged."

The morning was well gone when they topped out on Apache Bench. The last part of the way had been up a four-mile gorge so bad and cut-up underfoot that half the mares were going sore-footed by the time they got out of it.

"There's another way," Jim said. "You come up the south slope past Diamond Butte. It's easier, but it's longer. There'll be a time you'll want to remember this one."

Frank looked across the waist-deep winnow of the bench grass, across the scattered heads of granite that with park-like regularity lifted their piney crowns above the level of the mesa top. South, the still snow-capped crests of the Sierra Anchas thrust up against the raw blue of the spring sky. To the west the naked rock of the Mazatzals bulked, hot and dry. Eastward and into the north shouldered the heavily timbered scarp of the Mogollon Rim and beyond it, tumbled range on tumbled range, rolled the Sierra Blancas.

Ahead of them a short mile, sunlit and still under the noon-high light, lay the charred ruins of the ranch house. The corrals, yet standing and in good repair, lay behind the rocky rise upon which the forgotten settler had built not wisely but exceedingly well. It was a place of the wildest beauty, well fitted by a stupendous Nature to stir the souls of lonely men.

"We're home." said Frank Rachel softly. "Let's move in."

His companion nodded and they moved off quickly. Jim Fewkes watched the big man riding ahead of him. He had not missed that *we* where a man might have said *I.* He wondered if his fellow rider had meant anything by it. And if so, just what?

In the back-of-beyond country, a man takes a long time sizing another man. Peaceful Basin was behind the back of beyond. Jim Fewkes had sized Frank Rachel for six months. But he shook his head, putting down now again what he had from the very first: the strange, belly-warming tug this big devil put to work inside you. *Not yet,* he thought. *In another six months . . . maybe. But not yet.*

The six months came and went. Fall again lay, crisp and sear, over the Mogollons. Frank Rachel had worked his year for the JS; the happiest, best year he could remember clean back to his bitter boyhood. The mares were his, the Apache Bench ranch house rebuilt plank for hand-sawed plank. Down the bench, sun-bright and glossy against the gray of the grass, his twelve mares stood in tail-switching contentment to the suck of Red Boy's first crop of foals. All was well in Frank Rachel's world.

Coming out of the feed shed, bucking the oat sack, he grinned at Red Boy, watching him curiously over the top rail of the stud corral. He went into the box stall, filling the feed bin with the rolled oats. Behind him, the big stallion moved in, putting his nose playfully under Frank's arm and bunting him hungrily aside.

Frank cursed him with clear satisfaction, put a hard knee into his belly, and moved him over, then squeezed along the logs past the nervous sway of the satiny rump. At the last minute, the stud threw his quarters into the logs, playing at the daily game of pinning the man. Frank was ahead of him, already squeezed clear. He hit him whackingly across the rump with his Stetson. The big horse humped, tucking and swerving his haunch into the opposite wall with shed-jarring force. He rolled his eye whites wickedly, neighed harshly. It was the rest of the game, and the man cursed him with hard-grinned fervor.

Still, it was not the sound of the stud's eager challenge or of the man's gladly answering profanity that followed the latter back out into the sunlight. It was another sound, quick and clean and good, and startling in its unexpected richness. It was the first time in five years that Frank Rachel had laughed.

He built his smoke, looking long and thoughtfully across the mile-high mesa of his domain, his mind going back over the six months that had passed since Jim Fewkes had first brought him here. He had left the JS shortly before the last fall gather, his place taken by two new hands, Tom and Judd Graden, lately drifted into the basin from Globe. Old Jim had been glad enough to see him go, and the others had not been too dewy-eyed about it, either. For his part, he had borne up under the grief of the parting without too much difficulty. It had been only Jim Fewkes who had worried him.

The half-breed had not said a word. Had not even looked up from peeling out his roan's frog. Had just let him ride away. Then, when Frank was a mile up the trail, he had waved after him—just once. Frank had answered that wave eagerly. And had held the bay stud in to see if Jim would acknowledge the answer. He had not, and Frank had turned for Dry Cañon, figuring his year-long hope of making a friend was dead and gone. But a week later to the day—it was a Sunday like this one, he remembered—the roan had ambled up out of the cañon. And this time, when he had waved, Jim Fewkes had waved back. And more. When he had come up, he had slid off his roan in that Indian-quick way of his, stared you back for a length of time that made you wonder if he wasn't meaning to knife you for your year of trouble over him. Then he had stuck out his hand, stiff and awkward as a cigar-store Mohawk's. After that, no Sunday failed to pass but what the rat-tailed roan stood hip-shot in front of the Apache Bench cabin. And with the swift, succeeding weeks Frank found what he had sought above all else.

He had found it in the silent stalks for table game in the brush lands under the mesa's edge, in the wild rides along the main rim, cat hunting or bear running with the dark-faced half-breed. And in those briefer, happy times across the night fires. Those times when the coffee can kept moving until it was drained of the last black dreg and the rushing spells of talk tumbled out, as only they can between men who are at last alone with the night and the stars and the soft wind in the grama grass and with two bellies full of a word-hunger many a long year in the building. In all these things, then, had Frank Rachel found himself, and found that other thing for which he had so long searched in lonely vain—*a man to be his friend.*

V

There was peace at last in Rachel's heart as he sat that final Sunday in the sun along the south side of his ranch house. He had found a home and a friend. What more might the world hold for a lonely man? The thought of a woman stirred briefly in him. It pulled in his lean belly and put the little muscle tremor to running his jaw, the way it always did when he was in a tight and seeing no way out—save back of a gun. He shook his head. No. Women meant trouble and trouble meant killings. Both were far behind for Frank Rachel. He had unhooked his guns. He would live in peace.

The whistle of a mountain quail broke his reverie. He grinned quickly, recognizing Jim's familiar signal. Lounging away from the wall, he waved at the approaching horseman.

Jim Fewkes came on. There was no return of the wave. He brought the roan hard up and stepped down off of him, letting the reins slide.

"What is it?" Frank asked quietly.

"Trouble," the half-breed answered. With the three words given and the one taken, peace and contentment were not to come again for big Frank Rachel. "How many head you figure we should have cut out for the old man's Fort Apache Army contract?" The reference was to the JS fall roundup.

"Contract calls for four hundred. You should have cut six, easy. Why?"

"We cut three hundred and ten. The old man was short ninety head and lost the contract."

"Who filled?"

"The Graden brothers."

"The who . . . ?"

"You heard." Jim kept it short. "Tom and Judd Graden. I caught them, drivin' at night. Said they were workin' for a new outfit, seein' as how Old Jim was goin' under."

"You couldn't see the brand, likely. Did they call it for you?"

"JT on the left hip. Smooth crop, left ear. Crop and half un-derbit on the right."

Frank looked at him. "Where's the brand book for this basin stuff?" he said softly.

"Prescott."

"Red Boy's full of oats," said Frank.

"So's his old man," grunted his companion. "What you get-tin' at, Rachel?" The half-breed never called him Frank.

"Just this, Jim. You ever see a finer day for a ride?"

"Can't remember one. Where to?"

"Prescott, likely."

A grin flickered and was gone.

"Great minds. . . ." Frank nodded, and turned for the stud corral.

"Hold up now." The half-breed's words checked him. "Pres-cott's a three-day ride comin' and goin'. No use both of us makin' it, is there?"

"Maybe not. What's on your mind?" Frank had not missed the undue urgency in his friend's voice, was puzzled by it. Jim answered him quickly.

"The Gradens left me to think their new owner is a Globe man. I've sent Ed and John down there to check. That don't leave nobody at our place to look after the women and kids exceptin' our old man. I want you to go down there and stay till I get back. Rachel"—he dropped his voice—"there's somethin' stirrin' down there in the basin. You can spend them three days looking under the dust it's raisin'. You follow me?"

"The Graden place, eh?"

"Yeah. They'll be the rest of the week gettin' back from Fort Apache. You'll have plenty of time."

Seeing the way it was going, Frank shrugged, hard-faced. "I'll ride down and look after your folks. That's for you. And I'll smell around the Graden place. That's for Old Jim Stanton. But past that I'm cashed out, you hear me, pardner? You tail my drift?"

Jim nodded, letting it out softly. "You ain't buyin' no chips, happen us and the Gradens comes to a call. That it?"

"That's it," Frank said.

"It suits us." The turquoise eyes were slitted. "Us Fewkes takes care of our own. We was first in the basin ahead of the Gradens. Likely we'll be the last behind them."

"It figures." The dry grin returned as Frank threw the saddle on the bay stud. "Say, Jim!" The question, called after the already cantering Fewkes, sounded like an innocent afterthought. "What's your sister's name?"

The half-breed spun the roan, apparently not buying any innocent afterthoughts that morning. "Libby." The single word carried short and unqualified across the mesa between them.

"Libby what?" Frank was still grinning.

"Fewkes," called the other, his voice monotone-flat. "She's a blood sister. See you remember it, *hombre!*"

Frank swung up in the saddle, sat staring after him until the roan disappeared past the ranch house rise. It had been a warning. A man could not take it otherwise. But how meant? Was Jim telling him to look *after* the girl? Or *out* for her? Or had it been just the way it sounded? To look neither out nor after her, and not even *at* her!

He shrugged again. Play them the way they fell. Only tinhorns picked them up before they were all down. "Stretch it," he said grimly to the haunch-swinging stud. Then, grunting it: "You got a woman, you got trouble. You don't spell them no different."

VI

He passed the first of the Fewkes' cabins at sunset. He knew it for young John's place, standing a short distance up the valley from that of the elder Fewkes. Minutes later, he was checking the bay stud and studying the main cabin frowningly. His friendship with Jim had not broadened to include the rest of the family. He had never been here before.

The ranch lay in a crescent of low ridges, the open side of the crescent to the southeast. There were three buildings: a one-room ranch house, a cook shack, a hog shed. The beaked bridge of Frank's nose wrinkled. If there was one thing a stockman hated to see better than he did sheep, it was pigs. And he was seeing pigs. A whole herd of the oil-shiny, slobbering filth eaters. He shook off his disgust, deliberately jumping the bay stud into them, sending them squealing and grunting in rage. Then the cabin door was scraping open.

"You'll be wantin' somethin', mister?"

It had to be Jim's old man. You could see that in the way he handled the ancient Winchester.

"I'm Rachel," he began.

"We know that," old John Fewkes interrupted. "What you want here?"

"Jim sent me. He's gone to Prescott. Said maybe you'd have me around till he gets back, seein' Ed and John are away."

"They're always figurin' their old man needs a wet-nurse. Get down." There was nothing of peevishness in the old man's remark. Frank nodded to himself. Likely he and old John Fewkes would get on.

Inside the cabin he met the Fewkes women: Lydia, the old man's wife; Mary, young John's wife; and Bess, Ed's sullen, black-haired woman. Jim, he knew, was unmarried.

The supper was put on the table: fried fatback, heavy corn pone, home-jarred turnip greens, stale back-stove coffee. They ate in silence, Frank shortly following the old man back out into the dusk of the ranch yard. They built their smokes and sat in continued silence over the first, deep lungfuls. Presently the old man hawked and spat.

"Likely Jim told you about the girl," he said unexpectedly.

"Likely." Frank nodded, watching him. "Where's she at? She ought to be in. Jim said there was some trouble here in the basin. Or the smell of it, anyways."

"Jim smells trouble farther than most. We ain't got any trouble. Lib's up to Stanton's, buyin' a mare. She's horse crazy, that girl. Some plain crazy besides."

"How you mean?" Frank asked.

"She don't like it here. Hates the loneliness, she says. She's a bit-tosser, don't curb worth a damn. Never did. 'Course, she's only comin' seventeen. Might settle down later on. I doubt it. Anybody that don't call this basin for God's front yard is a little off. Wouldn't you say, mister?"

"I reckon I would."

Old John shrugged. "What more could a man want? Or a

woman, either? You got everything here. Wood, water, grass, game, no Apaches since 'Seventy-Nine. You can stretch your elbows and not punch nobody in the ribs doin' it. You got peace and you got quiet." The old man paused, as a man will when he is taken with the thought he has already said too much. "Now where's your trouble in all that?" he concluded defiantly. "God damn it, Jim's as crazy as the girl!"

"Maybe," said Frank. "How about the Gradens?"

"There's no trouble with the Gradens," rasped the old man quickly. "They're both good boys, hard workers, too. Don't talk much, neither. Not as much as some. . . ."

"I hear you, old man." He grinned the acknowledgment. "A man gets lonely up on the bench."

"Talk brings trouble. It brings it quicker than anything else. I'm goin' in." Frank sensed the quick resentment, wondered at it even as the old man was turning for the door. "You can set out here. The girl will be along directly."

The door had scarcely closed on the yellow lamplight when the soft voice hit him from behind. He came off the bench, turning and crouching.

"Jumpy, aren't you, stranger?"

He felt the thrill of the satiny voice, tried to make out the shadowy figure it was coming from. "I didn't hear you comin'. You don't make much noise, girl."

"Oh, hell, mister"—her easy naturalness slid over the word pleasantly—"an Indian never makes any noise. You ought to know that by now."

"I ought," he said, the continuing nerve tingle of the low voice racing up his spine. "You sound enough like Jim. Move out and let's see how you look."

That was the first time he heard the laugh, the throaty melody of it enough to put the short hairs of a man's neck on end. And back of the laugh came the girl, stepping into the patch of light from the cabin window.

"My God . . . ," was all Frank Rachel could manage.

A tall girl, she was as dark of skin and hair as her brothers. In the soft light he could make out the straight, short line of the nose, the full curve of the mouth, the angularity of the high cheek bones, the bold tilt of the chin. She laughed again then, the wide lips dark and glistening over the flash of the white teeth. "You're doing your share of the looking, mister. Just let me know when you're done."

"I'm done," he said, letting the last of the held breath go. "Your turn, I reckon." With the growing grin, he stepped forward into the lamplight. She did not answer, just looked. He grew nervous, cursing inwardly. "Well, seen enough?" He tried putting a lightness into it he did not feel.

"Too much, mister." There was that heat-lightning smile again. "You're not my kind."

Smile or no smile, it set a man back. It was said in a level way that made it sound like it was not meant to come with a smile in the first place. "You always get what you want?" He couldn't keep the belligerence out of it.

"I aim to mostly. How about you, mister?"

That question meant only one thing. She was calling him straight out. No man could miss it. "I don't want much," he said flatly, her boldness rattling him. "I ain't lost no women, if that's what you mean. Leastways, no *little kids.*" He meant it nasty and he said it that way. It had just occurred to him that Old Man Fewkes had said she was only coming seventeen.

She stepped close into him then, the wash of the lamplight limning the wanton mold of her body, the wicked upturn of her lips. There was no mistaking the invitation. No misreading the weave of those hips as she moved toward him, nor the deliberate back-flinging of the shoulders that brought the firm tilt of the breasts suddenly hard forward and upward beneath the thin cling of the cotton shirt.

He swept one long arm behind her, his free hand sliding up to bury itself in the tumbled blackness of her hair. She let herself come into the embrace, her dark head turning to seek the eagerness of his lips. Then, as his wide mouth met hers, she twisted away from him with a low cry. He saw the flash of the clean teeth and felt the quick pain of them against his neck. He saw and felt, too, the ringing slap of her open hand slashing across his cheek. Then he was hearing the throaty laugh across the lamplit stillness.

"You shouldn't play with little kids, mister. You're too big!"

With that she was gone, the soft closing of the cabin door leaving him alone in the Arizona night. The lamp in the window faded quickly and went out. He stood a moment more, then turned away with a bitter curse.

A man could not know yet, what kind of trouble was building in the basin for the rest of them. But he already knew the cut and color of his own. Just as sure as Chiricahua signal smoke went straight up, he had been right in the first place. Trouble for Frank Rachel was named Libby Fewkes.

VII

He rode slowly, following the main trail up Cherry Creek toward Parker's Store and the crossroads, his thoughts far from Tom and Judd Graden and Old Jim Stanton's disappearing cattle. His mouth still burned from the half kiss Libby Fewkes had torn away from it. The lean pinch was still in his belly and the feel of trouble lay heavily within him. He would scout the Graden place, wait and have his talk with Jim, then ride for Apache Bench and stay there.

He threw the stud off the trail, kicking him up the low ridge that flanked the Graden place to the south. At the top of the rise, his scowl deepened. Yonder there in the moonlight, not a quarter mile from the crossroads and the store, lay Judd and Tom's spread. It was not much, even for a two-bit homestead: one-room ranch house, open-face hay shed, bare pole corral, water tank, and piped spring. There was no stock in the corral and none wandering loose. The cabin stood dark.

He clucked to the stud, sending him down the ridge. From the size of the fire bed centering the corral, a man knew considerable hide had been burned here, and not long ago. Likely they had used a running iron, but if they had not. . . .

They had not. He found the iron in the shed, his finger quickly tracing the cold rim of the brand. The scowl faded under the frost of the grin as he swung back up on Red Boy.

"Hike it, hoss. Beginner's luck, old son. We got the one spot to an ace-high straight workin' here. Just wait'll we play it on friend Jim!"

Ed and John rode in late Tuesday afternoon, Jim at dusk Wednesday. After a silent supper had been wolfed down, the half-breed motioned all of them outside. With the Durham spilling carefully into the cupped rice papers, the game got under way.

"What'd you find in Globe?" Jim struck his match.

"Not a damn' thing." Ed made his light in turn.

"It figures," Jim grunted. "I done a little better."

"How so, Jim?" John's quick question struck Frank as a little nervous.

"This so," said Jim. "There's a JT registered in Prescott, all right, and not to no Globe man. It's to Judd and Tom Graden."

"That's a damn' lie!" Ed broke in heatedly.

"I reckon you know better than that, Ed."

"Meanin' what?" The older brother's demand was blunt.

"You tell me," said Jim, voice flat and soft. "I come past Old Man Stanton's on my way in. He told me he tailed that bunch of beeves the Gradens was drivin' to Fort Apache to fill his order. He seen you and John ride in to side their fire, Monday noon."

"You'll eat that, by God!" Ed's crouch and set were quick, but not quick enough. Frank was between the brothers, his move too swift to forestall.

"Wait up, Ed. I got cards in this deal, too. Jim's called and I'm standin' pat. You can kick over the table or throw in your hand. You, too, youngster." The dark nod went to John.

"I pass," said Ed, stepping slowly back. "Jim's bluffin' and you're holdin' deuces."

"John?" The youngest Fewkes stood silent. "Last chance, boy. Lay them straight up or it's no shuffle," Frank warned quietly. "I ain't backin' no play to sandbag Old Man Stanton. How many you want?"

"I'm out, Frank." John dropped his eyes. "It's Ed's play."

"It is," said Jim Fewkes, moving into his brother. "Turn them over, Ed."

"And don't try to draw out on us," added Frank softly.

Ed folded suddenly, his answer coming as easily and uncovered as though he were admitting he had forgotten to close the back house door. Jim and Frank looked at him a long three drags. It was Frank, finally, who flipped his cigarette away.

"You was in it with them, then," he said. "On a deal to lift the old man's stuff and register it four ways."

"More or less." Ed shrugged. "Me and John run the stuff in. Judd and Tom done the blottin' over to their home place. Them boys will hog the whole basin, given time. You'll see, by God! John and me just figured to throw in with them and hog right along on equal shares. What the hell would you have done?" he concluded defiantly. "Or you, by God, Jim?"

"It's done," was all Jim Fewkes said. "It can't be undid." He paused, slit-eyed. "But if either of you ever touches another JS beef, I'll kill you."

"If I don't beat him to it," said Frank, "he will."

The brothers said nothing, and Jim concluded, dead-voiced: "I'll talk to the old man. It won't make it right, but at least he'll know it ain't us Fewkeses if his JS stuff keeps disappearin'."

"Yeah"—Ed nodded slowly, no remorse in his Indian-deep grunt—"and I'll talk to Judd and Tom Graden. Old Stanton's stuff or not, I'm aimin' to get my cut on that Fort Apache bunch."

"*We'll* talk to them," amended John thoughtfully. "I'm real curious about that JT over to Prescott."

"Don't forget what happened to the cat," growled Frank disgustedly. With the words he moved toward Red Boy.

"What cat?" Young John's query showed cool indifference, and no degree of shame whatever.

"The curious one," nodded the big rider, swinging up on the stud. "He got kilt."

"Go to hell." The younger man grinned. "I've shot my share of cats, mister. Them Graden toms don't scare me none."

Frank pulled the stud in. His offside hand slid down and under the stirrup leathers, easing the iron free.

"Think it over," he advised softly. "And here's something to think it over on."

With the words, he tossed the JT iron toward them. He saw it arc and turn in the moonlight, and heard the muffled metal ring of it as it struck the thick dust of the yard. He waited only until Jim reached to pick it up and lit the match to examine it. Then he turned the stud away.

VIII

The following Sunday brought no mountain quail whistles from Dry Cañon. Another week passed, and another. Still the cañon was silent and Frank waited no more for the familiar signal. It was clear now that the split over the lifting of the JS cattle was going to cut between him and Jim as sure as it had between Ed and John and the Gradens. He had ridden with a running iron under his own stirrup fenders. Half the cattle spreads in the West were started that way—by the hands stealing the owner blind. Likely in his day Old Jim Stanton had re-run a brand or two. By siding Jim in backing Ed and John down, Frank had done what he could for the old man. And it had cost him Jim's friendship. He did not blame Jim and his brothers but it was now more than ever clear to him that he did not want any more cards in the deal.

The fourth Sunday following his showdown with Ed and John and while he was cleaning Red Boy's box, the big stallion whistled with sudden fierceness. Hayfork in hand, Frank stepped to the box door, his eyes swinging toward Dry Cañon. She was riding a classy little sock-foot sorrel, hazing three loose mares ahead of her, and, if a man had thought she looked like something in cabin lamplight, it was simply because he hadn't seen her in broad daylight. Watching her pull up at the corrals and swing down off her pony, a man could only step back into the shadows of the box, hoping she had not seen him. And she had not.

She walked toward the stud corral, eyes fastened on the nervous pacings and head flingings of the bay stallion. Frank watched her go. He felt the warning pulling in of his belly, tried to clamp off the quick tremor of the jaw muscle. It was no use; his belly went right on pulling in. Frank fought down the dark impulse, broke his gaze from the girl. Where in God's name was a man's pride that he would be peep-tomming like this? Sure, he was woman hungry. But not for this woman. Not for Jim's *little sister*, for God's sake!

When he stepped from the box, the peculiar amber paleness of his eyes had cooled, the old brief grin was lifting the wide mouth corners.

"Lookin' for somebody, girl?" He saw he had startled her, was pleased when she admitted it.

"Hello, Frank." She was immediately cool. "You sneak around pretty quiet yourself."

He knew she was talking about the way she had come up on him in the dark outside the Fewkes cabin. Somehow, it nettled him. He made it short, wanting suddenly to have her get away from him, and far away.

"What brung you up here, girl? Them mares you got?"

"Maybe. . . ." She had come up to him, face upturned, lips curving to the slow smile, a peculiar intensity in the turquoise eyes. "Maybe not. . . ."

He stepped back, getting angry now. Damn her anyway. Every look and word she gave a man seemed to mean just one thing. "I don't want your mares. Nor you neither," he said thickly. "You get them and yourself out of here. Far out! And fast!"

She moved after him. "The mares are for Red Boy. That's all right, isn't it, mister?"

"It's all right," he said stiffly. "I'll bring them down. I want to see Jim anyways. Now fork that sorrel!"

With the warning, he swung his back to her, stepped again into the box. Seizing the hayfork, he thrust it savagely into an opened bale, shoved the fragrant hay over the clean floor. He gave her time to be well started, then cursed and dropped the fork. She would be well across the bench by now. A man couldn't blame himself for taking one last look. He turned, eyes widening.

She was still there.

She moved toward him through the open door, stopping so close to him that the thrusting breasts came lightly into him—so close that the perfumed tumble of her black hair touched his jaw—so close that the woman smell of her came up and around

41

and over him, smothering him with its thick excitement.

"Frank. . . ." The slender softness of the hands slid up his chest, the moving hips coming forward with the reach of the arms, the breasts firmly against him. "Frank . . . finish that kiss."

He seized her, pulling her into him. She writhed savagely with the embrace, her teeth finding his neck, her body twisting, her voice whispering thickly.

"Frank! Oh, *hombre!* *¡Hombre!*"

He twisted with her, smashing her gasping lips apart, his only answer a wordless growl, deep, brutal, primitive, filled with a savage hunger five long years in the fasting. . . .

The following Sunday found him hazing the mares back down Dry Cañon. He pulled into Jim Stanton's JS by noon, watered the mares, had coffee and a short talk with the old man. Things had been moving in the basin.

Judd and Tom Graden had refused to deal Ed and John Fewkes in. They had backed their play with four new hands, the Bivins brothers who, with their father, Old Mark Bivins, had for three years been running a big-loop spread in the upper box of Cañon Creek. The Bivinses were Texas gunmen and open rustlers; their appearance as Graden "hands" simply pointed up Ed Fewkes's hard prediction that Judd and Tom were intending to take over the basin, wall to wall. But all thoughts of Judd and Tom went quickly under as the old man's continuing words picked up the track of another Graden—one Frank had never heard of, let alone seen.

"Name's Garth." Old Jim scowled. "Big devil and a slick dresser. He ain't a cowman, you can lay. Rides a good horse and wears his guns tied down."

"Where's *he* been at all this time? I thought there was just Judd and Tom and that kid brother of theirs." Frank was referring to young Billy Graden, a nineteen-year-old boy lately arrived in the basin.

"So did everybody else," grunted the old man.

"They're sure gatherin' the clan." Frank nodded. "What's this new one look like, in case I should meet him?"

"Looks to be maybe a gambler or well-off cattle buyer. City-slick anyways, and got some money apparently. Fast shuffle, short gun, easy dollar . . . you know the kind."

"I've seen a few," said Frank. "What's he done to get hisself talked about in the basin? Shot up Charley Parker's Store or run off with somebody's best girl?" He put his hard grin back of the remark, but the old man failed to return it.

"He ain't shot up the store," he said slowly.

"Meanin' what?" Frank was eyeing him now.

"Meanin' somebody's best gal maybe, I dunno. . . ."

"By God, not Libby Fewkes?"

"Who else, son?" He said it carefully, seeing the quick, bad light shooting in the pale eyes.

Frank stood up. "Where's he at?" he asked softly.

"I'm goin' to tell you somethin', boy." The old man ignored the question. "You can like it or lump it. You stay clear of them Gradens and them Fewkeses, alike. There's only one good one in the lot of them, and that's Jim." He saw the big rider's eyes narrow, did not miss the soft menace in his question.

"Where's that leave Libby, old man?"

"It leaves her out," said Old Jim Stanton quietly. And having said it, he stood up. He saw the sudden clenching of the big fists, watched the pale eyes flare and go dead. "She ain't right for any man, Frank," he added gently.

It was the first time the old rancher had called him by his first name. Frank dropped his eyes, said dully: "Get on with it."

"I ain't never married," Old Jim began. "It's her kind is the reason I ain't." He paused, letting his gaze find the top of the rim and hold there. "I was twenty-eight"—he nodded—"and so hot in love I couldn't think nor work nor eat. All I could get my mind on was that hellcat face of hers and all I wanted to get my hands on was that twistin' body." He paused again, his eyes coming back to Frank. "The date was set, the ring bought, but the bells never rung. A man come up the river from the gulf towns . . . this was in Texas, better than forty years gone. . . ." His voice trailed off with the shrug. "I know that kind, boy. They can be sixteen or twenty-six or forty-six. They're all alike and you can tell them. They've eyes that look at a man like he was naked. Every time they move it's in a way the average woman couldn't learn in a million years of tryin'. It's somethin' born in them and that they can't help. But it's somethin' that's poison to me and you and to all men like us. Boy"—his voice slowed as the gnarled hand found the broad shoulder—"that Libby Fewkes is pure poison for you. Happen you get a good enough dose of her, you're dead."

Frank Rachel looked at him for a long, slow breath. Then he swung his eyes downvalley toward the Fewkes Ranch, letting another silence grow. "I'm already dead, old man," he said at last, and turned away, not looking back and not returning Old Jim's hesitant call and wave of good bye.

He never came again to the JS; he was to see Old Jim Stanton only once more.

IX

The Graden place had changed. He checked Red Boy on the ridge, easing himself in the saddle. Two new hay sheds and a closed box stall had been added. A bunkhouse adjoining the cabin was under construction. Clearly the Gradens were spreading out. He clucked to the stud, putting him down the ridge. Outside the cabin he pulled up, sat waiting, knowing they had seen him.

Presently Judd came out. He made no show of the Winchester, just cradling it thoughtfully.

Tom loomed behind him. "Howdy, Rachel," he said. "Get down and come in. Where's your Western hospitality, Judd?"

"You never know about him." Judd hunched his shoulder toward Frank. "A man can't rightly tell if he's aimin' to shoot or shake hands."

"He ain't aimin' to do neither," said Frank. "He's aimin' to talk."

Both brothers looked at him. "Get down and come in," repeated Tom. "We got coffee on. I been wantin' to talk to you, too."

They went inside and pulled up chairs, Judd pouring the coffee. Frank and Tom did the talking.

"What's on your mind, Rachel?"

"Trouble."

"Well, we got plenty of that," said Tom bluntly. "You want some of it?"

Frank eyed him. Tom was different from Judd. He was broad-jawed, big-nosed, wide-mouthed, and had a pair of lake-blue eyes as cold as snow water. He always looked at a man, smooth-faced and quiet, as he was looking at Frank now. Ed Fewkes had been right. Brother Tom *was* the one.

"I don't want none that ain't rightly mine," Frank answered. "That's why I'm here."

"Fair enough. What's your deal?"

"There's big trouble buildin' in the basin. I figure it's mainly between you and the Fewkeses. I got my own dirt to worry about. I'm sayin' you Gradens stay shut of me and I'll stay shut of the Fewkeses. You don't stay shut of me, you ain't begun to learn what trouble is."

"Sounds like a threat, Rachel. Is that the way you mean it?"

"It's the way."

They eyed each other, Tom breaking first.

"It's a deal. We'll leave you alone."

"You will, all right," grunted Frank, "but that ain't the whole of my deal."

"What else you want?" Tom pushed back his chair.

"Garth Graden. . . ." He tailed it off, coming to his feet with it. "Where's he at?"

"Out ridin' with a female friend." Tom shrugged, watching the big rider's hands.

"You mean a *lady* friend, don't you, mister?"

Tom held. "If I'd meant lady, I'd have said it." He nodded quietly. "He's with Libby Fewkes."

Frank hit him in the belly, doubling him over. As he came forward, he smashed at his jaw. Missing the chin, the blow glanced across the cheek. Tom went into and over the rickety table, coming back up on one knee, shaking his head dazedly. Frank moved in on him, and with the move he heard the forgotten Judd's slow voice.

"I wouldn't, Rachel. . . ."

Frank came around, stepping back from the steady point of the Winchester, facing them both. "That's two men have said that about the girl," he grated. "The next one gets killed. You hear me?"

"We hear you," said Judd. "Now get on your hoss."

"Wait a minute." It was Tom, moving around the broken table, wiping the blood from his face. "You shouldn't have hit me, Rachel. You'll find that out. But that's between you and me. We made a deal that covers others. I say it still stands. Think it over."

He *was* thinking it over. He had made a fool move, the kind that had had him in trouble all his life. If he had had his guns on, Tom Graden would have been still on the floor and staring wide, instead of standing there offering him a second chance to hold on to what he had finally made for himself here in the basin.

"I'll take some and leave some," he said at last. "Our deal stands . . . for you and Judd and me."

"How about Garth?"

"Libby and me is goin' to be married," said Frank harshly. "Anybody that thinks different has got a short hour to saddle."

"Don't push it, Rachel. Garth's not the marryin' kind. He's just messin' with the girl. I'll talk to him."

"Talk takes time. I ain't got any. You see him before I do, you talk to him. Otherwise you won't need to." He was through the door, stepping up on the stud, jerking him around, pulling his soft mouth cruelly. "If he's got to Libby," he snarled, "he's already dead!"

They stood in the doorway, watching until the bay stallion had topped the ridge and was gone. Then Tom Graden turned.

"He's the one, Judd. Always remember it. He'll go over to the Fewkeses when the time comes."

"He will, and the time's comin'."

Tom returned Judd's look, nodding. "Likely you're right. But nobody, Frank Rachel included, is startin' my war before I'm ready for it. We got to move fast now. We should have told Garth about Frank and Libby."

Judd shrugged. "If Garth's aimin' to take a cut at the girl, knowin' about Frank wouldn't have stopped him. You know Garth." He paused, eyeing his older brother. "And if he is aimin' to take a cut at her, you already got your war, Tom, ready or not."

It was coming dusk when he rode down on the Fewkes' cabin. The door stood open and the lamp was turned high. He recognized the tall figures lounging by the woodpile, rode over, and got down, his question uneasy.

47

"What's up, Jim?"

"Choose your pardners." It was the hard-voiced Ed answering him. "The dance is on."

"Don't riddle me none. What's happened?"

"Lib's gone," said Jim.

It hit him behind the knees, put the sink in his belly clear to his toes. Still, when his words came, they were as quiet as Jim's. "That Graden bastard . . . ?"

"Likely," grunted the half-breed. "She's been seein' him."

"She's no good," snarled Ed. "Never was. Pap always said she'd end up runnin' off with the first son-of-a-bitch showed her a twenty-dollar gold piece."

"I'll kill him!" rasped Frank, not hearing Ed, his mind already far from any of the Fewkes brothers.

"You'll have to catch him first." It was still the cynical Ed. "They're fast mounted and long gone."

"I'm ridin'," snapped Frank, swinging the stud.

"You can't ride four ways, Rachel." It was Jim now. "They could have hit for Prescott, Globe, Holbrook, or Phoenix. There's no tellin'."

"You three makes me four! You tellin' me you mean to set by and see your sister took?"

"She wasn't took," said Jim softly.

"You don't know that, god damn it, Jim!"

"I know Lib. . . ."

It was all he said, but the way he said it, slow and without the bitterness of the others, heavy and tired and clearly hurt, took the fight out of Frank and made him think.

"Will you look after the mares up on the bench, Jim? And see to them till I get back?" he asked quietly.

"You still goin after them, *amigo?*"

"As far as the trail reads."

"You can read that trail without ridin' it." The half-breed's words were still gentle. "She don't want you, Rachel. You ain't her kind. She can't stand loneliness, never liked it here, never wanted to live here. She's gone now. Maybe she'll be happy where she's went. Leave her go. Leave her find out."

"I'll kill him," was all Frank Rachel said.

"And what about her?" Jim caught his eye with the low question.

"I'll bring her back, if she'll have me and will come. I said I loved her."

"I reckon I do, too," said Jim Fewkes quietly. "But you'll not bring her back here. She's made her bed and she's got into it with muddy boots."

"I'll not bring her back here." His words were as soft as Jim's but they seethed with the bitterness in them. "And I'll not come again myself. Not while she's alive. . . ."

"And what about when she ain't?"

"When she ain't," said Frank Rachel slowly, "and if there's a Graden mixed into it, to the last brother they got, this basin will bury him." He paused, swinging the stud with the vicious curse. "And with his god damn' muddy boots on!"

X

The spring of 1884 came, and the early golden fall. The first year passed and with it passed Jim Fewkes's somber prophecy. Libby had not returned to the basin and Frank Rachel had not found her. He had been close behind her again and again, but each time he was an hour or a day or a month too late.

He rode on. Santa Fé, Taos, Las Vegas, Silver City; it was always the same. Yet, no, after Silver City, not quite the same. After that there was no more track of Garth.

He heard of her again, in Albuquerque, and months later in Tularosa. He lost her there and it was almost fall again before he picked up the trail in Tucson. From Tucson the track led to

Tombstone, and there it ran out.

Everywhere in Tombstone the questions and answers were the same: dark girl? Queer blue eyes? Tall, mean-built, quiet? Yes, she had worked the Oriental for a spell. Then the Crystal Palace and the Bird Cage. Where was she now? Still in town? Who would know, or care? A man forgets that kind as soon as he's done with them. But she was gone from Tombstone, as she had been from every town before it. Frank had gotten that from Big Minnie Bignon. Yes, she had worked for her. Called herself Lib Garten. or Grayton, something like that. Hell, no, not as a chippie. In her condition, mister? Sick? Of course not, you damned fool. Sure, I kept her here till the kid came. Yeah, it was a boy. Born dead, too, better luck for her. Gone? Sure she's gone! That was in August. This is September, sport! Say, mister, was that girl a damned half-breed of some sort? Me and the girls often wondered. She never talked. . . .

Tombstone broke his heart. He quit then and went back to the bench.

The winter of 1886 passed and spring ran into summer. He went to the basin only for supplies. At first the ranchers spoke to him but a man who won't answer back is soon enough let alone. Jim came occasionally to the bench, or sometimes rode part way with him from Parker's Store. But by late summer the big rider's moroseness began to wear even on the loyal half-breed. It was clear Frank did not want to see or talk to anybody, not even him. Jim came no more to the Apache Bench ranch.

With October wearing away into November and November following swiftly into the first crisp snows of December, Frank Rachel began his fourth lonely winter on the bench. He knew now that Jim was done with him, and the deep hurt already in him grew uglier.

He had ridden the complete loop again. He was right where

he had been when he had first checked Red Boy on the rim to gaze down into Peaceful Basin. It was a lonesome road stretching away down Dry Cañon and into the silent valley now. A man didn't have to look very far down it to see where it was leading him. Maybe another year, a month, a day, maybe even another hour. It made no difference. There it was and a man could see it, stark and hard and lonely as always. Lying there. Watching him. And waiting for him to come to it. The end of the trail again.

A week before Christmas—Frank never forgot the day; it was a Sunday like always—a mountain quail whistled from Dry Cañon. He ran from the hay shed, waving the fork and yelling. He threw the fork away, grabbed his hat off, and waved that. Then he just stood there waiting for Jim to ride up.

Rounding the lee of the ranch house knoll, Jim saw him and swallowed hard. Hair grown shoulder long, driving in the heavy wind, standing there bareheaded in the whipping snows of the ranch yard, twisting the old black hat in his hands—yeah, it did something inside you when you looked at him. It made you feel sudden lonely, in a way that hurt you bad, way down below your heart. And it made you slide off your pony and plow toward him through the snow, hardly able to wait to get his hand in yours.

"Hello, Frank. Merry Christmas. . . ." It was the first time the half-breed had ever used the name. It came out strange and awkward, stumbling a little. But it came, and it came backed with his lean brown hand.

"Jim! By God, it's you, Jim!"

"Yeah." The thin rider grinned bashfully. "Now lay off poundin' me and help me get these hosses into the shed. They'll chill standin' in this wind."

Frank looked more closely at the spare mount Jim had led in across the bench. "Why, that's Libby's sock-foot sorrel, pardner!

What's the idea?"

"Little Christmas present." His companion grinned. "Forget it. You got a couple of hoss blankets handy?" They were in the shed now, and Frank brought the blankets, as the half-breed added fervently: "I hope to Christ you got a pot of coffee on!"

"Sure, pardner. Fresh made this week." His own grin was working now. "God A'mighty but it's good to hear a man's voice again. Even yours!"

In the ranch house they shucked out of their wolf-skin coats, kicked the snow out of their boot arches, bellied up to the pine table. Jim Fewkes came straight to the point.

"I ain't playin' Santa Claus, Rachel. It's more trouble in the basin. The Gradens swore out warrants for rustlin' against Ed and John. They got most the ranchers on their side. There's been gun play."

"How so?"

"Old Jim Stanton's got a new foreman, feller named John Gilliom. He's roundin' up Old Jim's stuff for final sale. The old man's pullin' out. They've rustled him blind."

"Still the Bivins boys workin' on the q.t. for Judd and Tom?"

"Still. But this Gilliom jumped Ed when he was out lookin' for a fresh-stole bunch of JS beef. Accused Ed of it and Ed downed him. That started it."

"Kill him?"

"Just broke his leg. Held wide a-purpose. But the war's on. I can't hold Ed and John no longer. And I don't aim to. It's why I'm here."

Frank sensed he was getting to it now, asked slowly and with eyes hardening: "And why are you here, *amigo?*"

Jim matched his hard stare. "Ed's made a deal that will knock them lousy Gradens clean back to Ioway or wherever the hell they come from. It's a long shot but will pay off in high numbers if she hits."

"How long a shot, Jim?"

"Long as they come."

"I'm listenin'."

"Sheep!" rasped the half-breed.

"You gone crazy, Jim? You can't mean it serious! Not bringin' *sheep* into the basin, you can't!"

"All the same, I do. Me and Ed and John. We're askin' you in."

"You're askin' the wind. I don't hear you."

"You're either in or out, Rachel. Nobody stays neutral, not with woollies comin' over the rim. You know what that is."

"I've been there," grunted Frank, and fell silent. Presently he asked: "Who's puttin' up the sheep?"

"Skaggs Brothers, up to Flagstaff."

"They're big boys. They'll play rough."

"I'm grooved now. We ain't meanin' to play for chalkies."

"When you aimin' to start bringin' them in?" He asked it easily and quietly, Jim's answer, just as easy and quiet, pulling him clear off his chair.

"We shoved the first bunch over the rim in September."

"God A'mighty, three months ago."

"More or less."

"Anybody we know killed yet?"

"Not one. The Bivinses and some of the Hash Knife boys from up on the rim run a couple of big bunches over the cañon edge on us. Another bunch was clubbed and shot while they stuck up the Navajo herder. We still got better than two thousand head on graze, and nobody hurt serious. Tom and Judd seem to be holdin' off for some reason. We ain't heard from them."

"A man never hears the slug that hits him," said Frank grimly. "What are you Fewkeses gettin' out of the Skaggs deal, the sheep berries?"

"Fifty-fifty down the line. If we get by with it, we'll have more honest money in two years than the Gradens made crooked in five."

"I'll bury you nice," grated Frank, coming to his feet. "Under that hog wallow back of the big oak. You'll make tough acorns."

"Soft ones make bad bacon. You ain't answered me, Rachel. What cards you playin'?"

"Who's callin', Jim?" It was deadly soft.

"I am." The answer was softer still.

"So what you think I'll do?"

"Throw in with us."

"You figure I ain't got no choice?"

"I figure you ain't."

"You figure crazy. I ain't changed my mind none." The coffee cups were on the table now, the black pot empty, the talk pulling swiftly to its close.

"You'll change it."

"Don't crowd me, Jim." The pale eyes began to ice over. "There ain't nothin' left in this world that would take me back into that basin."

"There is, Rachel. You're forgettin' somethin'." Jim's eyes caught his and held them. "Somebody, I mean. . . ."

Frank was on his feet, leaning across the table, eyes wild. His voice came, hoarse and hollow and deep. His hands gripped the pine planks until the knuckles cracked. "Jesus God, Jim . . . you don't mean Libby?"

Jim Fewkes nodded, his slant blue eyes for once warm. A man couldn't miss the pain and loneliness and sudden wild hope his words had put into the big rancher's hoarse cry. Not even if he was half Indian and hard as a dry-oak wheel hub. He had not before begun to guess what the girl had meant to Frank Rachel. But he wasn't guessing any more. Now, he knew. And he knew what his next words would mean to his friend. "I found her," was all he said. "I know where she is."

XI

"Where?"

The single word dropped into the silence as Frank, the wild light fading from his eyes, let go of the table and sank back into his chair.

"Back at the Bird Cage."

"How come you to find her, Jim?" His mind was clearing now, his voice steadying.

"I never did quit lookin'," said the half-breed simply. "When I heard from you she had been in Tombstone, I figured she'd come back sooner or later. It's the biggest camp short of San Francisco, and, when a girl's down like that, she either works or dies hungry. Lib ain't the dyin' kind."

Frank stood up, facing him across the table. Jim took the big hand, clearly embarrassed.

"For hell's sake, Rachel, it ain't nothin'." He dropped the hand quickly. "Just go and get her. It's why I brung her mare. Pack and get. I'll watch your spread. If you rustle your behind, you can be home by Christmas."

"Christmas. . . ." Frank let the word fade, his hand taking the half-breed's arm, his pale eyes holding on the dark face. "Merry Christmas, Jim!"

He was gone then, the door sucking shut behind him, the building howl of the blizzard smothering his tall form before he was halfway to Red Boy's box stall.

He pushed the horses hard, raising the lights of Tombstone about 11:00 p.m. the second night, that of the 13th. Shortly before midnight, he was riding down Allen Street. At the corner of Fourth he turned in at the O.K. Corral stable. Putting the horses up, he told the boy to strip them, rub them down, throw a feed of hot bran and rolled oats into them, have them ready to go in an hour.

The Bird Cage was two blocks up Allen, cornering it at Sixth Street. The hurdy-gurdy of it nearly stampeded him. He downed three straight whiskies at the outer bar, then signaled the houseman. The latter sidled up, disdainful of his rough, out-country rancher's clothes.

"How'll you have it, friend? Plain or fancy?"

"Fancy, and *pronto*. I ain't spendin' the winter here."

"Box Five, inside, friend. Anybody will show you the stairs up to the boxes. Any preference in girls?"

"Lib Graden. . . ."

The houseman looked at him. "She ain't the best, friend. I could send you something a mite fancier."

The big hand slid to him, seizing the high roll of the cutaway lapel. "You send Lib Graden, *friend.*"

"Lib Graden coming up. Box Five." The houseman backed off hurriedly, not liking what he saw in the pale eyes. These damned cowmen were all alike—hell on whiskey and women and wanting both before they were five minutes out of the saddle.

Frank squeezed into the main auditorium of the ill-famed Bird Cage and looked around. The huge room was jammed with drunks and with half-naked women. It was crowding midnight now and the place was going full blast. On the stage down in front, a chorus row of six girls, all black silk legs and pink-skin breasts, was kicking and yelling and poking feather-trimmed behinds into the customers' admiring faces. Somewhere a damned tin-pan piano and a Mexican cornet were murdering a bastard musical offspring sired by "Camp Town Races" out of "Oh Susannah".

He spotted the staircase and pushed toward it. Inside Box Five, he trimmed the gas lamp, turning it far down, and stood back by the entrance curtains to wait.

She came in soundlessly, not seeing him, sank to the red plush settee, sat staring at the floor. Frank's belly pulled in, his heart settling in him like a thrown stone in deep, cold water. She was not yet twenty, but the work of ten years had been done in the last three. About her whole person was an aura of sickness and despair. And more. Of lostness and desolation and abandonment. And of misery that would have broken the heart of a rock. As he watched her, his chest tight with the ache of his held breath and headlong memory, she coughed hollowly. The cough built wrackingly behind the crumpled soil of her handkerchief, became a spasm, subsided. The dark stain of the flush spots over the gaunt cheek bones spread with telltale swiftness, carrying ominously even in the gloom of the gas lamp.

Frank, his face as white as hers, moved away from the wall. The one word, deep and soft beneath the muffled, brassy intrusions of the Bird Cage's midnight revelry, broke the stillness of the box.

"Libby. . . ."

She stiffened, then turned, the turquoise blaze of the slant eyes fierce and wild as ever. She rose slowly, hands pressed to the bareness above her dress top, as though she sought, unconsciously, to shield it from him.

"Lib, it's Frank. I've come to take you home, girl."

"Frank . . . oh, God . . . Frank Rachel!" He saw the tight quiver break across the compressed line of the lower lip, and saw the quick-welling glitter of the tears before she turned half savagely away.

He stood, not daring to touch her, the ache in his throat swelling unbearably. "Did you hear me, Lib? I said we're goin' home."

The shoulders straightened but she did not turn. Her voice came haltingly and tear-thick, all the old magic of it building in him, tearing at him, taking his heart back across the lonely years. "Frank . . . oh, God, Frank, you don't know me any more. Go away . . . go away!" The cough came again, breaking her plea, wracking the thin shoulders.

He took her then, gently and tenderly as a child, holding her to him until the spasm died and the labored breathing grew still. The big hands ran beneath the black hair, smoothing it back, lifting the tear-stained wetness of the face. He kissed her on the forehead, awkwardly, almost shyly. His arm came around her and he turned, with her, for the curtains. For a brief moment the old grin softened the edges of the grim mouth.

"Come on, Lib girl. You shouldn't play with these big kids. You're too little. . . ."

It was the 24th of December, a black night and with the wind rising again, when they cleared the junipers below the ranch house knoll and got their first sight of the Apache Bench cabin. They pulled in their horses, sitting them in wordless wonderment.

Through the starlit stillness of the Arizona night, the candles winked and glittered behind the frost-rimmed casement of the single, small window. Their lights danced gaily along the awkward dangle of the tinfoil strips, peered flickeringly among the clumsy puff of cotton batting festooning the tiny cedar's limbs. Even the lopsided Star of Bethlehem, tin-snipped from the rolled-out side of a tomato can and girded on to the topmost twig with a rusty cinch of baling wire, managed to respond to the struggling spirit of the occasion by assuming a dignity not inherent to the crude form given it by Jim's talents with the tin shears.

"My God," Frank breathed. "It's a Christmas tree. Old Jim's gone and put up a tree for us. First one I ever seen on Apache Bench," he concluded happily.

"It's the first one I've ever seen any place," said Libby Fewkes quietly.

He looked at her then, seeing the swift glitter of the tears against the frost rime of the wolf-skin collar. Kneeing Red Boy, he moved to her side. He leaned over and kissed the wet cheek, circled the fur-clad shoulder, pulled her to him.

"Now, don't cry, honey. We're home, girl, you hear me? There's no more trouble for you and me in this world, Libby."

She nodded, snuggling to him, and he paused, tightening the circle of his arm. His voice dropped, with his lips and the tender kiss. "Merry Christmas, Missus Rachel."

XII

The winter of 1887 was the happiest time of Frank Rachel's life. Libby seemed to mend rapidly in the high air and clear sun of the bench and Jim came regularly from the basin to make their Sundays perfect. By agreement, Libby's presence on the bench was kept a secret, and by equal agreement Frank and Jim rarely discussed the situation in the basin. The trouble there was growing but insofar as Frank knew or cared, only sheep had so far died in the Peaceful Basin War. Jim, declared an equal partner in the Apache Bench horse ranch by Frank's insistence, was their only contact with the valley, and he never talked unless asked. And he was seldom asked.

In March Jim took Red Boy's first crop of three-year-olds to the spring sale in Phoenix, realizing a record price for green colts. The big stud's fame was growing swiftly and that growth should have bid fair to predict a safe and certain future for Frank Rachel and his hard-earned hopes. It was not to be.

With the raw, cold winds of March, Libby's cough, nearly gone the past months, began again. By April the wracking convulsions had become constant and the torn squares of bed sheeting, pressed fiercely to her tortured mouth and always hidden from the hovering Frank, had begun to show the angry, bright red stains.

But May and the first, soft breath of the Tonto spring brought a seeming hopeful rally to her weary flesh and spirit. She was shortly able to be outside and sit in the warmth of the ranch house porch, watching Frank work the green colts. During this time the sucking foals, invariably fronted by their arch-necked sire and backed by their concerned dams, made a play yard of the area around the porch. Libby never tired of hand feeding them the lump sugar and dried apples that Frank grinningly supplied. By month's end the bay stud had become such a pet and pest that Frank mock-seriously sought Libby's permission to build a box stall wing on the cabin, that she might pass him his sugar during the night—"Happen the silly bastard should get lonesome in the dark."

Libby had laughed at that, for the first time in weeks. The throaty happiness of the sound put the quick hope springing again in the big rancher's breast.

With the spring of 1887 safely passed and summer running swiftly along, a man could begin to feel he was going to win, was going to lick that damned cough and everything that lay behind it.

It was the first week in August—a Sunday, with Jim due to whistle any minute from Dry Cañon—that it happened. Frank had gone out late, after fixing Libby a holiday breakfast of fried venison. As he started across to the corrals, his grin was as light as the lift of the morning breeze in the new grass. But the lightness died aborning as his glance leaped across the yard to the emptily swinging door of Red Boy's box stall.

He ran, awkward in his haste and the pinch of the Texas boots, to the deserted box, scrambled from there to the top rail of the corral fence, eyes sweeping the bench north and south. It was as empty as the box.

No need to whistle the stud in. Or to ride down and scout for him in the junipers toward Diamond Butte. A man knew his horse and he knew the heavy sink of his heart within him. Red Boy was gone.

They sat at the pine table, he and Jim, stirring the sugar into the coffee, talking low and quick and dry-lipped as men will when they are too angry for loud words. By the open porch door, Libby rocked silently in her chair, not hearing them, not knowing they were there, her eyes finding only the deserted run of Red Boy's corral, her ears alert only for the shrilling whistle of the stallion's neigh.

Jim Fewkes cursed again, growling his answer to the man across the table. "Whoever has got him, Rachel, they'll spread it in the basin that it was us Fewkeses did it."

"They'll have to spread it pretty thick for me," grated Frank. "I reckon you know that."

"Thanks." The nod was short. "But that ain't gettin' us your hoss back. And from the looks of Lib we'd better get him back."

"She ain't talked since I told her he was gone," Frank said it as if he was alone in the room.

"It's what I mean," said Jim quickly. "Folks sick with that damn' lung fever can't take no bad setbacks."

"Lib'll do, she's been gettin' better." Frank was still talking to the room.

"She ain't." Jim dropped his voice. "You're so close you can't see it. She don't weigh a hundred pounds. I seen our mother die of it. She got better, too. . . ."

"Lib'll do, I said!" The anger of fear was in the outburst. Jim sensed it for what it was.

"Sure." He shrugged, watching him. "Leave it go at that. Likely she will. Happens we get the hoss back. . . ."

Frank looked at him, voice suddenly steady again, pale eyes

flaring. "I'll get him back," he snarled.

"*We'll* get him back," amended Jim softly. "But not settin' here."

"Let's ride," said Frank Rachel.

"In the words of my mother's people," murmured the half-breed, getting up, "my ears are uncovered."

"After you, chief." Frank reached his hat off its wall peg, swept it sardonically toward the door. He followed Jim out. At the corral, he said: "You got any spare Forty-Four Winchesters? I'm low."

"Enough," grunted the half-breed. "It only takes one in the right place."

XIII

They cut the stud's sign south of the home pasture, following it down over the south rim past Diamond Butte. On good ground where they could read it clearly, they made out five sets of shod prints overlying the familiar twisted right rear hoof mark of the bay stallion.

"It figures," said Jim presently. "The four Bivins boys and Anse Canaday."

"Anse who?"

"Canaday. New foreman for the Gradens. Half-brother to the Bivinses. A Texan and a gunfighter like the rest, weasel-faced, sneaky buzzard, laughs like a girl. . . ."

"Skinny, gopher-jawed, bad cast in his left eye?" Frank took up the description, interrupting the half-breed. "I knew him in Texas. Let's get along."

For several miles the track lay, plain and easy, shortly giving Frank the belated idea and opportunity to catch up on his local history lessons.

"Say, Jim"—he grinned—"how's the war goin'? Made your million yet? Seems like I ought to get a cut on your share of them sheep, seein's how I'm splittin' with you on the hoss ranch."

"It's a deal." His companion's expression did not alter. "You got a shovel?"

"Meanin' I'll need one?"

"To scoop up your half." The other nodded. "You was right. All I got comin' is six months of piled-up sheep berries. The Skaggs pulled out, weeks gone."

Frank nodded, stumped as usual by the half-breed's incredible taciturnity. "For good, you figure?" He asked it idly, covering his amazement.

"Bad or good, they won't be back. They lost upwards of two thousand head shot and clubbed before it was done."

"Sorta leaves the Gradens settin' a better saddle than ever, don't it, pardner?"

"It does," the half-breed grunted. "Yonder's Cherry Creek. And nothin' but naked rock beyond."

"Yeah, here's where we lose them. You can't run no trail on raw granite, no matter you're half Injun."

"I don't need to run no trail." Jim's slant eyes narrowed. "You'll see, *hombre*. Kick up your hoss."

"He's kicked," growled Frank.

Ten miles below the Bivins place on Cañon Creek, they cut Red Boy's sign again. Nightfall found them a half mile below the ranch, the sign still holding. They rode cautiously forward.

The cabin stood dark, no smoke lipping its sheet-metal chimney. In the corral were five used-up ponies, still lather-caked and sweat-warm.

"What you think. Jim?" The question came only after a long pause.

"I don't like what I think. Your hoss is gone," he answered softly. "What you want to do?"

"Stay here and kill a man." The reply came just as softly.

"Who'll look after Lib meanwhile?"

"Who else?" Frank stared at him through the dark.

"If you don't show by tomorrow night"—Jim nodded—"I'll bring her back down to the basin."

"I'll show. Get goin'."

"Look sharp," said the half-breed. "Them Bivinses is bad medicine."

"I'm scared to death," grunted Frank. "Hop your butt."

Seconds later, he was alone. Jim's disappearance from the corral was as soundless as the Apache moccasins that carried it out.

Frank rigged a lead line for the five horses in the corral, swung up on his own mare, headed into the night. He was careful to keep to the soft ground of the creekbank, leaving a clear trail. Two miles downstream, he cut into the rocks, tied the horses, bellied down to wait.

Dawn came early, crowding 4:00. And crowding 4:30, the light still murky and bad, came something else.

He heard his man coming before he saw him. Then he was seeing him, seeing the familiar silhouette, thin, high-shouldered, Texas-straight in the saddle. He let him get just past the rocks, then shadowed out on him.

"Bivins . . . !"

The horseman, Winchester in hand as he had ridden up, fired from the horn, into the sound of the voice. He never got his face up to follow his shot. The big .44 slug took him under the breastbone, ruptured out his back, knocking him off the far side of his horse. The horse reared, smashing the body into the trail side rocks. It fell free, slid into a pile of granite chips, not moving.

Frank waited in the rocks. Hearing no sound from the ranch in answer to the gunfire, he moved down to the body. Turning it over, his eyes widened. It was the old man, Mark Bivins.

He studied him a minute, face muscles twitching. Too bad. The poor old coot had probably had nothing to do with it. Still, it made no difference. He was as dead as he was ever going to be. There was no use letting him lie around to brag about it. First light was coming fast now. It was high time to get the hell shut of the Bivins' backyard.

An hour later he paused to let the horses blow on the main ridge. Far below he could see the flyspeck dots of the Bivins cabin and corral. The corral was still empty. No smoke showed above the cabin chimney. Nodding, he swung off the mare, hoisted the old man's body off the led horse.

Yonder crack in the caprock would do fine, he decided. Coming to its edge, the second nod flicked briefly. If they looked for their old man now, they'd be a long, lonesome time finding him.

He watched as the slack body bounded and twisted off the sides of the cleft, crashing and disappearing in the heavy choke of scrub far below. He looked down a moment, then grunted with the third and farewell nod.

"Like father, like son. You should have raised Anse better, old man."

XIV

It was midday when Frank topped out on the bench and rode toward the Apache Bench buildings. Jim came out of the cabin as he was putting up the mare. One look at his face was enough.

"Lib?" Frank asked shortly.

"Yeah, she's bad. Ain't let up coughin' since I got back. Won't eat and ain't been to sleep."

"Pull the saddle on the mare." Frank was turning for the

cabin, his face white. "Stay shut of the house for a spell, you hear, Jim?"

Outside the cabin door he paused a moment, head down, hand on the latch. Then he opened it and went in. She lay motionless, eyes closed.

He watched her a long time, then said softly: "Libby. . . ."

"Frank. . . ." The eyes remained closed. "Don't put off on me. Red Boy's gone."

"Don't talk now, Lib. We'll get him back. You'll see."

"I won't. . . ." She shook her head, the pause building endlessly. "Frank. . . ."

"Yeah, honey?" He caught the change in her voice, the hollowness of it putting the frost suddenly hard and deep in his belly.

She turned to him, taking his hand, crushing it to her cheek, the sharp fright in her voice twisting in him like a knife. "Frank, I'm sick. Awful sick. And scared . . . scared to death. I'm going to die, Frank."

He felt the parched heat of the cheek burning his hand, and then the quick scald of the tears. He took her to him, holding the frail body close.

"Libby, Libby, don't talk like that, baby girl." The thin arm tightened about his neck and he let the final words come with a fierce softness, his eyes looking far past the dark nestle of her head, far past and out and across the lonely sweep of the bench. "It's like Jim said, Lib honey. You ain't the dyin' kind."

Libby Fewkes died on the early morning of August 9th, 1887, five days almost to the hour following the disappearance of the stallion, Red Boy. She went in her sleep and peacefully. She was asleep when Frank went out to feed the weanlings; she was still asleep when he returned minutes later. He called her name three times before he realized she would never awaken.

He didn't look at her again, nor cover her face. Catching up the little sorrel mare, he threw the saddle on her, cinching it tightly for the double carry. He returned to the cabin and dressed Libby in her old clothes—in the worn fray of the cotton shirt, the faded blue of the denims, the soft-tanned cling of the Apache moccasins—the way he wanted to remember her. He rode with her in his arms, light and easy as a child. In the whole of the long ride down the bench and up the steep trail of the backing wall—the trail that led to the look-out spot where he had taken her those sunny winter days to look down upon their beloved bench and its sleek, grazing horses—he did not look once at her.

On the outer jut of the look-out, under the shelter of the lone, twisted juniper, he halted the mare. Hesitating only a moment, Frank nodded. It was the place: high and wild and lonely—like herself. No visitor would pass here but the wind, no caller come save the winter snows, no sound break beyond the long clear note of the blue mountain quail.

He worked quickly, lifting and shouldering the big granite boulders each into its reverent and careful place. When he had done, he stepped back looking down upon their rough pile. He bared his head, the big hands twisting at the stained brim of the black hat. He said it quickly then.

"Good bye, Libby girl. You know I loved you. God bless you, and God help me. . . ." He turned away, his head swinging up to let his eyes sweep across the timbered silences of the basin below. The last words came so low the wind scarcely caught them: "And God help every Graden in that basin. . . . You killed her," the savage whisper raced. "You killed her sure as you'd done it with a knife. You hear me, Tom? You hear me, Judd? You hear me, all you Bivins bastards?" The short laugh was ugly, chilling. It was unsteadily deep, profaning the stillness of the time and place. "You hear me, Garth Graden, wherever you are? Get your god damn' muddy boots on. I'm comin' down there now."

Back at the ranch, he worked quickly. What he could do for the colts was soon done. Beyond that it would be up to them. There was still plenty of summer hay standing on the bench. Little Tonto Creek ran some kind of a trickle even through August and September. The spring foals were rising three- and four-months old and could move fast enough to stay clear of prowling bear and lion. The grown stock was all grass fat. Likely they would all make it through.

He was not long in the cabin. The floorboards behind the Buck's range came up quickly; the heavy bundle was lifted out. He looked at them, his first sight of them in four years, bringing the unconscious talon-like set to his big hands. He belted them on, easing them deeply into the oil-soaked holster pockets, his hands coming into the cold touch of their butts like those of a lover long hungry for the touch of the wood and the steel. The rest of it was soon done.

It was perhaps two minutes later when he smashed the glass well of the table lamp over the firebox of the range. When he turned away, the first racing lick of the flames was flaring up the dry cedar walls.

Half an hour after the sorrel mare had braced her forehoofs for the first steep pitch down the head of Dry Cañon, all that remained of the Apache Bench ranch was what had been there before Frank Rachel: the staring emptiness of the abandoned sheds and corrals, the blackened stone of the cabin's chimney, the gaunt ribs of its granite sills.

XV

The five men, riding down the ridge toward the Graden cabin in the early moonlight of August 9th even softened by Luna's mellow glow, would have required the West's favorite term for such as they. They were all bona-fide hardcases. Harp, Clint, Simm, and Jake Bivins rated the label with little argument— Anse Canaday, without any at all. In front of the cabin they halted their ponies, legged off of them, left their reins trailing. There was no knock at the door and they filed in hard-faced and without formal greeting to face Tom Graden.

"It's been a week, Tom. We're done fooling around." Harp did the talking but it was Anse who Tom Graden watched. "We've covered the basin. Nobody's seen him."

"Give it time, Harp." Tom remained seated at the table. "Old Mark's been gone a week before now."

"Time's up, Graden." It was Anse's thin voice. "We found Pap's hoss in Rock House Cañon this mornin', saddle still on and cinched to ride."

"He could have been throwed. It happens every day."

"Not this way, it don't." Anse's reedy voice rose, then dropped. "The bit was pulled and the reins tied up so's the hoss could graze."

"All right." Tom Graden's slow words were suddenly far from soft. "So somebody shot the old man. We don't know they did, but we'll say it. And on top of sayin' that, we'll say this. . . ." He paused, letting them get set for it, moving away from the table and into Anse. "We've licked the Fewkeses and drove the Skaggses' sheep back up on the rim. We've done it without one white man gettin' killed. You know my orders. They haven't changed none . . . no killin'. That goes if you find your old man tomorrow with six slugs in his back and Jim Fewkes's knife carved in his belly. You understand that, Anse?"

"All right . . ."—the other's scarred mouth twisted to an empty grin—"so I understand. Anything else, *Mister* Graden?"

"There is. See you remember it." There was no answering grin. "Judd tells me somebody run off that bay stud of Frank

Rachel's. I ain't namin' no names. But Rachel's the last man I want pulled into this basin trouble. Happen you put off on me once more, Anse, you're done here. Is that clear?"

"Why sure, Mister Graden, clear as the skin on a school-marm's shank." Anse's woman-high laugh broke jarringly.

Harp Bivins added his hard grin to his half-brother's laugh. "Let's ride, Anse. *Tempus,* as the book feller says, is figetin'."

"So am I," drawled Clint.

"Double for me," said Simm.

"It's close in here," observed Jake. "Smells a little high. I need air."

The five riders filed out, climbed on their ponies, kicked them into a hammering gallop up and over the ridge. Tom Graden watched them go, his face expressionless.

"Live by the sword . . . ," he finally said to himself, and turned and went into the cabin.

The five horses swung south of Parker's Store and the cross-roads, moving closely bunched in the moonlight. At Cherry Creek their riders pulled them up. Anse broke the silence that had been thickening since the parting with Tom Graden.

"You don't suppose Mister Graden would mind if we took one more little look for Pap, do you?" he asked pleasantly.

The big-shouldered Harp took the matter under sober consideration. "Why, now that you mention it, I don't suppose he would. Let's get along."

"Where to?" queried the unimaginative Jake. "We done been every place in the basin."

"Yeah," echoed the slow-witted Simm.

"Save one," amended Clint, his mind moving at the quicker pace of Anse's and Harp's.

"By God, the Injuns!" ejaculated Jake, proud of the speed and brilliance of his deductive powers.

"Let's get along," repeated Harp unsmilingly. "I could use a little sleep before the shootin' starts."

"Me likewise," seconded Clint. "It ain't healthy to be heavy-eyed when you got your sights full of half-breed bucks."

"It ain't." Anse nodded succinctly. "Nor to be heavy-footed, neither. We'd best leave the hosses at John's place, happen he's not home, and work down afoot. Then hole up around the place and wait for daybreak."

"You ain't just whistlin' 'Dixie'," drawled Harp. "Let's ride."

"We're gone," said Anse. "Hold the hosses to a walk once we're clear of the crick. That damn' Jim could hear a cinch buckle squeak in a six-foot snowstorm."

"Upwind," added Clint dourly.

"And with earmuffs on," concluded Harp.

Frank crossed below Parker's Store and took the eastbank trail about 9:00. He rode slowly, continually casting the trail ahead. Back home on the Texas border they had called this a Comanche moon. A man had been early taught to keep his eyes and ears open when it was lighting up the country.

At young John's place he held up for five minutes, watching the silent cabin and the open moonlight of the corral. At the end of that time he went on in, satisfied the cabin was deserted. But it was those saddled horses in the corral a man wanted to get a closer look at. When he had had his look, Frank knew where his work lay. He never forgot a man or the horse he rode. In that bunch of ponies were some he remembered. Harp's roan, Clint's buckskin, Jake's and Simm's two raunchy bays. . . .

The main Fewkes cabin lay dark and quiet, only an occasional sleepy grunt from the hog pen giving it life. Still, a man knew better. Somewhere out ahead of him were five men and as many rifles. He had one easy choice. The only way up to the cabin was along the pasture fence upwind of the hog pen. Presently, easing through the tall grass of the fenceline toward the old juniper at its cabin side corner, he grinned. That thicker shadow at the base of the old tree looked to be nothing more than a field boulder. But field boulders seldom wore wide hats—and never snored.

Simm never knew what hit him. For the historical record, it was Frank Rachel's 1873 Winchester butt, solidly planted behind his left ear. Twenty crouching steps later, the big rider slid into the cook shack. If the sleeping arrangements at the Fewkes place had not altered, he should find Jim bunked in here by himself. They had not, and he did.

"Lost your way, stranger?" The polite inquiry came question-marked with the shove of the Winchester into the Rachel kidneys.

"Yes, sir." Frank grinned. "I'm lookin' for little Jimmy Fewkes and I'm a good friend of his."

"Why, you god damn' fool, I could have killed you."

"You pays your money and you takes your chances," said Frank. "Roust out Ed and John, the war's on." Quickly he gave the half-breed the story. Minutes later, Jim was back with Ed and John.

"Lead off," he grunted to Frank. "It's your war party."

The four men drifted past the hog pen, slid silently along the pasture fence. At its corner Frank paused, checking Simm. The big man had not moved and he hit him again to guarantee he wouldn't.

"I ought to scalp the son-of-a-bitch," rasped Ed, half meaning it.

"Save it for Anse," said Frank, meaning it all the way. "He's the prime pelt in this pack."

"I'll skin Harp for mine," muttered Jim. "Always like to take the biggest cub in the litter."

"It don't leave me much," complained John. "Jake's half bald and Clint's mangy. But"—his grin picked up—"beggars can't be choosers."

"They can't," growled Frank. "See you stay to the high stuff along the fence, and keep your butts down."

"Look who's tellin' us Injuns how to belly-sneak tall grass," John murmured sarcastically.

Nobody answered the youngster's mock-serious jibe. His grin fell away as he turned to follow the others down the moon-black fenceline.

XVI

Leaving John's corral on the "borrowed" Bivins horses, Jim Fewkes got his first good look at Frank Rachel. He and Frank had had few secrets in their lonely association. Jim had never seen the short-barreled .44-caliber Peacemakers but he had known about them, and about their owner's hard promise that had put them under the floorboards of the Apache Bench cabin. Seeing them now, he knew before he spoke what had brought them out.

"Lib's gone." He broke his eyes from the Colts, holding his voice guardedly down. "When?"

"This mornin', Jim."

"Quiet?"

"And peaceful. She never woke up."

"It was the stud hoss bein' stole that done it." The half-breed's words went bitter. "Most of it, anyways."

"It was Garth Graden done it . . . all of it!" A flat, ugly deep-ness underlay the slow rise of the denial. Jim's nod came as he reined Harp Bivins's roan around.

"Likely we're both right. We'll collect double."

"Double or nothin'," Frank said. "Let's ride."

"Hold up a minute." Jim's wave checked him. "Ed . . . John. . . ." The low call brought the two horsemen alongside

Jim, quickly giving them the later facts of Libby's life. When he had finished, the two brothers were silent.

"I never said it," muttered Ed at last, "but I sure missed the girl. I missed her a lot."

"And me," added young John simply. "How do we ride it from here, Jim?"

"We'll head for Will Mittelson's. He's away to Globe and he won't mind us usin' his place for what I got in mind."

"He sure won't," said Ed. "He's lost his share of beef to the Bivinses. I reckon you're aimin' to leave them a clear trail."

"Clear as the crick bottom," grunted Jim. "They'll smell Rachel's rat along about daylight. Time they get horses out of our pasture, they should be along to Mittelson's for noon dinner. Any objections?"

"Suits me."

"And me."

"How about you, Rachel? You mind shuckin' out a free feed for the Bivins boys?"

The big rider shook his head. "Not me," he said thoughtfully. "I'm thinkin' about somethin' Old Jim Stanton told me, the first hand-out he give me when I rode into the basin."

"How's that?" asked Jim quietly.

"He said a man does better with his belly full . . . whether it's beans or lead it's full of."

Ed Fewkes's grin spread wolfishly. "Somethin' tells me"—he turned his pony with the slit-mouthed opinion—"Anse and his big brothers ain't goin' to like our brand of beans."

Frank swung his pony to follow Ed's. Jim and John kneed their mounts in behind his. "A man never likes it in the belly," he said unsmilingly.

It was twenty minutes past high noon Saturday, August 10th, when Harp Bivins pulled his horse off the Mittelson Ranch road below the house and headed him in across the meadow toward the cabin. With him were Anse, Clint, Jake, and Simm and three newcomers, John Payton, Tom Tuckman, and Bob Gillespie. The newcomers were all Hash Knife cowboys from the Aztec Land and Cattle Company, former allies of the Gradens in the clash over the Skaggs brothers' sheep. Payton was a Texas gunman of considerable reputation who had headed the Hash Knife forces in the sheep fights. The three had met the Bivins group by accident, joining up with it to "see the fun." It was a day and time when no self-respecting gun hand ducked the chance to hear lead fly under the least of circumstances. When known "sheepmen" were involved, what was an ordinary pleasure became a happily anticipated duty. None of the group had any idea Frank Rachel was with the Fewkes men.

Now Harp rode up to the silent cabin, halting his horse in front of the low fence that surrounded it. Flanking him, right and left, sat John Payton and Anse Canaday. The others—a little nervous even at eight-to-four, where those four were three Fewkeses and an unknown "friend"—unconsciously kneed their mounts back, graciously giving their three leaders working room. The cabin remained silent, no sign of life showing in or around it.

Harp shifted uncertainly, looking at the others. Anse laughed nervously. Payton scowled. The rest of them looked away.

"Hello, anybody home?" Harp's inquiry showed an understandable trace of nerve edge.

The cabin's silence held.

"It's me, Harp Bivins. Answer up in there."

The door swung open, framing the precise, forward step of Jim Fewkes. "I'm answerin', Harp. What you want?"

It had seemed like a Sunday school picnic five minutes before. Suddenly it was not so hilarious. The silence built and still Harp could not find his words. John Payton, dark-faced and tense, kneed his horse a step forward.

"We was wonderin' could we get some noon dinner . . . ?"

"No, sir." The answer was ominously civil. "We don't keep no hotel here."

Once more the silence held. Tom Tuckman, the second of the Hash Knife cowboys, broke it awkwardly. "Is Mister Mittelson here?" It was a simple stall.

"No, sir." The careful civility of Jim Fewkes's voice did not shift. But the worn barrel of his Winchester did. "He done rode off somewhere."

Nobody spoke. Not a man moved.

Tuckman, not stalling now and patently wanting to break it off, laughed uncertainly. "Well, boys, we can ride on down to Voseman's and get our dinner. . . ."

"You'll get it here, you bastards!" None of them had seen the big man move around the corner of the cabin. "You come for it here and you'll get it here. Make your moves."

"Frank Rachel!" Anse Canaday let it out as though it had been driven out of him by a fist in the belly. He held a minute, white-faced, then suddenly jerked his horse back and around. In the same instant John Payton flashed his draw.

Frank cursed, in the last second cheated by Anse's whirling mount. He threw down instead on Payton. The leap and roar of his right-hand gun shaded the Texan's, but the smash of the .44 slug missed the Hash Knife gunman, quartering through his horse's paunch.

Harp had not yet moved for his guns when Jim Fewkes's Winchester bellowed in echo to Frank's Colt. The tremendous weight of the rifle's long bullet smashed into Harp's face, shattering the nose, ranging upward and blowing out the base of his skull. He sprawled lifelessly in the dust at the same moment John Payton's horse was going down.

Blending Frank's and Jim's fire, Ed and John, shooting from

the cabin window, levered their Winchesters into the rearing tangle of the cattlemen's horses. Tuckman was hit, the heavy slug ripping through his right lung, knocking him half off his mount. Bob Gillespie, driving his horse free of the tangle, was shot through both arms and the right thigh. Payton, freeing himself of the pinning weight of his dead pony, was coming to his feet.

Jim snapped one at him, the bullet taking away an ear, plowing on across the jaw. The Texan stumbled over his horse, shaking his head to free it of the blood. Frank shot him in the belly, four times. He twisted, staggered two steps, fell over Harp Bivins's torn body.

The rest were by now safely away, galloping across the meadow. Anse had never been in it. Clint and Jake were unwounded. Simm had taken a clean flesh wound in his left side. Bob Gillespie, last away as he sided Tuckman to keep the lung-shot Hash Knife cowboy in the saddle, was badly hit and bleeding profusely.

Two men were dead. One, Tuckman, clearly done for. Two others, Gillespie and Simm Bivins, were wounded, the former dangerously. Payton's opening shot at Frank had chipped the cabin's corner logs. One of the general wild shots had splintered the doorjamb alongside Jim Fewkes. Those two foot-wide misses provided the sole degree to which the avenging Bivins forces had made good their lethal intent. The entire affair—from Harp's call to the silent cabin, to the echo of the final shot fading against the towering face of the Mogollon Rim—had taken less than a full minute.

Harp Bivins was the first white man officially to die in the Peaceful Basin War. His death blood-stamped the beginning of the ugliest vendetta in the remembered history of the frontier.

XVII

The killing of Payton and Harp Bivins was the torch. The flame it set spread through the basin. What had been a desultory sheep and cattle war became a flaring outbreak of personal violence. Every scarred boulder and twisted piñon in Peaceful Basin hid a man of one side from the trail rider of the other. Every man rode armed, when he could not avoid riding at all, and the order of the day was shoot first and turn the body over for identification afterward.

Many of the newcomers left the basin at once, a few of the old-timers slipping out unnoticed under the dust of their departures. Among these, Old Jim Stanton was the first and most notable. The old cattleman paused only long enough to pay one last respect to the lonely rider whose destiny he had from the beginning so grimly foreseen.

Frank saw him coming and called into the cabin. "Old man, fetch Ed and Jim. Yonder comes Jim Stanton."

Old John Fewkes came out, peered at the advancing horseman, went without argument toward the cook shack. He was back at once, his sons trailing him, the omnipresent Winchesters in hand.

As the old rancher rode up, Jim inquired briefly: "What brings you downvalley, Mister Stanton?"

"Come by to see Frank, mostly." Old Jim was curt. "I bid him into the basin. He can bid me out of it."

"What you meanin'?" Frank moved forward with his question.

"I'm leavin' the valley, son."

"I heard you was some time ago. What's got you started so sudden?"

"I reckon you know some of it. I come by to give you the rest."

"Such as?"

"I just come from a meetin' at the Gradens'. Every cattleman in the basin is up there. Tom's still tryin' to hold them but he ain't goin' to make it this time. That cussed Canaday is talkin' wild. You boys got a fair start if you want to use it."

"We're beholden, old hoss." Frank eyed him, frowning. "Why'd you do it now?"

Stanton shrugged, looking uncomfortably away. "I never felt I'd paid you off for sidin' my sister's boy. Figure it that way."

Frank stepped up to his stirrup, his heart telling him why the old rancher had come.

"It don't figure that way," he said simply. "Gimme your hand."

Their hands met, the older man clearly embarrassed. He broke the clasp quickly, picked up his reins, wheeled his gelding. "Be careful, boy." He nodded. And then, softly: "I wish you was goin' with me, Frank. . . ."

He went out of sight around the creek bend as they watched, not looking back or turning to wave. It was the last Frank Rachel ever saw of Jim Stanton.

Minutes after the old man had left, John Fewkes, who had been guarding the trail from Mittelson's, raced his mare up to the cabin to report the approach of Anse Canaday's vigilantes.

"Ed, John. Get the canteens." It was Jim snapping the orders. "Throw some beef in a bag." As his brothers ran to carry out the instructions, he turned to Frank. "We'll head for Rock House Cañon. There's an old Hopi pueblo up there built on a rock shelf forty feet high."

"Any water up there?" Frank swung his horse.

Jim nodded. "Spring at the foot of the shelf."

"At the foot . . . ?"

"Yeah. It ain't perfect."

"Any way out for us, say come dark tonight?"

"Down the shelf."

Frank grabbed the canteen Ed handed him, pulled his horse

aside as the latter and John legged up. "I know a cañon that's goin' to have a new name before we're done with it."

"Like what?" suggested the half-breed.

"Like Rock Hearse," replied Frank evenly.

"I always said you should have been an Injun," grunted his companion. "You got a great sense of humor."

Five minutes later, topping the hogback behind the Fewkes' pasture, they had their last view of the clearing below. And the clearing had its final look at them.

"They seen us," Jim said.

"One of them things," added Frank. "Let's go."

Noon came and was sweated under. The heat under the cliff house wall was intolerable, that on the cañon floor little less. The men on the shelf panted and cursed and watched the naked shimmer of the rocks below.

By 4:00 the water in the last canteen was gone and by six their thirst suffering became unbearable. Then, just before dusk, they observed some hopeful movement in the downcañon camp of their besiegers. It became shortly apparent that the bulk of the cattlemen were returning to the basin for supplies, their main need no doubt the same as that of the thirst-crazed defenders. The tiny rock pool of the spring at the base of the shelf was the only supply for either camp, and it lay under the guns of both.

By full dark the men on the cliff knew they were finished. It was get water or die—and get it before the moon came up. They had an hour, maybe a shade more.

"I'm goin' down," croaked Ed. "We're dead anyways."

"Hold up, *paisano.*" Frank retained his grip on the canteens. "I got a better idea."

Swiftly he sketched it for them, Jim nodding as he went along, Ed scowling, John blank-faced. It was a desperate proposition but they were desperate men. Even so, when he had finished, Ed's query was immediate and acid.

"Yeah? Then what? You miss the guy that's watchin' the spring and the whole gang downcañon opens up on you two. Then me and the kid sets up here all day tomorrow suckin' pebbles and watchin' the bottle flies blowin' you and Jim down there."

"I said it ain't guaranteed." Frank shrugged. "But neither is God." Then, after a significant pause: "Anybody thirsty?"

Jim went first, sliding over the lip of the shelf. Behind him, stocking-footed, moved Frank. Two endless minutes after that, Jim was at the spring filling the canteens. Twenty feet above him, Frank crouched against the face of the shelf, Winchester tightly cheeked, muzzle trained toward the spiked silhouette of the yucca plant behind which lay the cowboy the cattlemen had posted to guard the spring. He waited for what seemed an eternity for the prearranged signal from Jim—the "accidental" banging of a canteen against a trailside rock. At last it came. And with it came the spit of the orange flame from the base of the yucca.

Frank fired then, holding low and levering four shots. He saw the shadow straighten up, twist violently, fall back behind the yucca. He was up then and running, hearing the slide and scramble of Ed and John behind him on the shelf trail and seeing, ahead of him, the looming blur of Jim's form. As the alarmed voices of the downcañon camp began to call back and forth across the darkness, Jim passed out the refilled canteens, along with some cogent advice.

"We'll go on out, afoot. They can never follow us in the dark and we can get hosses later."

While he talked, the others drained their canteens, Frank holding half of his for the half-breed. He handed it to him and Jim drained it. When he had, he sailed it across the cañon. It hit bangingly on the far wall, bounded and rattled to the granite floor.

"It'll give them somethin' to stalk," he vouchsafed. "Let's drift."

Shortly they were at the cañon's mouth and Jim turned north, skirting the piled boulders and deep brush of the main ridge. He moved fast, knowing they would need the rest of the night to reach their destination, north of Mittelson's, on foot. The others followed single file and wordless, needing all their breath to hold to the half-breed's swinging dog-trot.

Within the hour the moon rose, white and glaring, spilling its clear wash into the narrow gorge of Rock House Cañon. By its light, the seven horsemen picked their careful ways through the boulder litter choking its mouth, their progress as grimly silent as had been the flight of their intended quarry. Silent, too, was the eighth horseman, his body sagging across the saddle of his led mount, the awkward flop of the shattered thigh bone that had bled him to death before his companions could move him bumping and jolting the flank of his nervous horse. The nameless cowboy who guarded Rock House Spring that night was the third recorded white man to die in the Peaceful Basin War. The unmarked headstone of that simple fact has remained his only epitaph for sixty-odd, forgotten years.

XVIII

On the third day following the Rock House fight, Frank, on guard above the cliff path leading to their hide-out, saw the two horsemen far below. One of them, stick-straight and familiar, was Old Man Fewkes. The other was a stranger.

Frank sent the quail whistle up the mountainside and shortly Jim came down to join him in the look-out. Studying the horsemen below, his eyes harrowed.

"It looks like Jim Hook," he growled.

"Who the hell's Jim Hook?" Frank matched his frown.

"Deputy for Sheriff Perry Odens over in Apache County. *Es hombre malo. . . .*" He tailed off in the *patois* Spanish of the territory, scowl deepening. "I'm goin' down."

He watched Jim slip down the mountainside and halt the horsemen. Old John Fewkes at once dismounted, giving Jim his horse and beginning the precipitous climb up the hide-out trail as his son talked swiftly with the deputy. It was a short talk, Jim riding off with Hook before the old man reached Frank's side. Frank's question brought acid, instant answers.

The Apache County deputy had given Old John a long yarn about having a warrant for Judd Graden and wanting to talk to Jim about it. He claimed to have been in the basin over a week, waiting to jump Judd when he could catch him alone. The whole thing smelled as high as a ten-day dead horse to Old Man Fewkes, and trouble was as bound to come of it, he grumbled, as the sun was due to sink in the west. With that he bid Frank a scowling farewell, slid back down the mountainside, headed south on foot.

The hours seemed to drag without end but dark came at last, and a nervous hour later Jim Fewkes followed it in. His report was as short as it was sinister.

"Where the hell you been?" demanded Ed querulously. "We thought for sure Hook had double-crossed you,"

"He for sure did," snapped Jim. "Me and you and John and Frank and everybody in the basin that's sided us. He's killed Billy Graden!"

The silence held while in the minds of each of the listening men the bleak implications of Jim's final words raced. Billy Graden was just past twenty-one and the barrel-apple choice of Tom Graden's proud eye. He was a good-natured, popular, hard-working boy who had never in any way been mixed into the basin trouble. None of the silent men on the mountainside had the least doubt what his killing would be called, nor what its occurrence would bring about. It would be called murder. And it would bring Tom Graden raging out into the open at last.

Frank was the first to speak. "How'd it happen?"

"It ain't sweet, so I'll make it short," grated Jim. He talked fast, telling them about the warrant, about Hook's refusal to show it to him, about his subsequent suspicion and trailing of the deputy.

"So, after leavin' me," he continued, "he swung a wide circle and hid out in some brush alongside the Payson trail, where it crosses north of the Graden meadow. I hid out on a ridge higher up and waited along with him. Late in the afternoon I seen a horseman comin' from the direction of the ranch. I seen it was young Billy and let down some then, figurin' Hook would never make a show against the boy." He paused, growling the rest of it savagely. "I was that close above them I heard every word of it. Hook kicked his hoss out in the trail as the kid rode up. He had his gun out. He said . . . 'I want you, Graden. I got a warrant.' I reckon the kid didn't know Hook. But he knew a gun. He went for his own. Naturally he never got it out."

"That all?" asked Frank.

"I wish to hell it was, but it ain't. The kid's hoss bolted for the ranch and he hung onto him. I dusted for home and run smack into a JT hand crossin' the ridge to see what the shootin' was about. It was Joe Ellensburg. He didn't see Hook, only me."

"Ain't that sweet," drawled Frank, pale eyes narrowing. "Now where the hell do we go?"

"Out on the basin floor!" It was Ed snarling the answer. "Jim might have been tailed. I don't want no more hole-in-the-wall hide-and-seek. We camp in the brush on upper Cherry Creek till we get a chance to make it to the cabin and get hosses."

"Ed's right," muttered Jim. "Let's get a move on."

"After you," rasped Frank angrily. He continued cursing under his breath as he followed the three half-breed brothers down the narrow trail. He had had about enough of this infernal Apache sneaking around. Damn these crazy Indians anyway! The time was fast coming, if it had not already arrived, when they would, all of them, have to stand and make a showdown of it. To the dangerously trained hands and deeply hurt heart of Frank Rachel, that time could not come any too soon. In the big rider's belly, as he trailed the Fewkes brothers across the valley floor, the old pinch was growing.

XIX

Billy Graden was shot on the 17th. He died the following night at the Graden Ranch. His last words to his grief-stricken older brother were: "Why would they want to kill me, Tom?"

Now Tom Graden seized belated control of both his own hired gunfighters and of the so-called "honest" cattlemen who made up the Graden side. Terror swept the basin anew. The outburst of feeling that had flared following the killing of Harp Bivins paled by contrast. The Fewkes men and Frank Rachel were doomed as surely as though by a constituted court of law. Their sentence was death: Tom Graden their judge, prosecutor, and self-appointed executioner.

The fact that Jim Hook, not Jim Fewkes, killed Billy Graden was not known until Hook returned to his St. Johns office over a month later. By that time the Fourth Horseman had already thundered across Peaceful Basin's "dark and bloody ground."

It was the morning of August 23rd when a scout rode into the Graden Ranch to report seeing the brothers and Frank Rachel leaving the old Fewkes place just before daylight. Within minutes the Graden forces, headed by Anse Canaday, were riding for Old John Fewkes's cabin.

They had not gone a mile down the Cherry Creek trail when they met, head-on, with another even bigger and more determined group. When the sheriff and deputy sheriff of Yavapai County rode into you, backed by a twenty-man posse, you pulled in your ponies and waited.

" 'Mornin', Canaday." Billy Mulvehey, the Yavapai sheriff, did the talking. "Where you bound?"

Anse thought a moment, then simply growled: "After the Fewkeses. What brings you?"

"More of the same. I've got bench warrants for every one of them."

"For what?" asked Anse sourly. "Runnin' sheep?"

"For the murders of Harper Bivins and John W. Payton," answered Mulvehey evenly. "Any objections?"

"None, Sheriff." The crazy laugh broke quickly. "Let's go!"

"There'll be shootin' when I say, and not before," said Billy Mulvehey, and swung his pony. The thirty horsemen splashed across Cherry Creek, turned south, kneed their ponies into a high lope.

They got onto the trail at the Fewkes Ranch, followed it northward until late afternoon. By that time and from the way their tracks lay, Mulvehey was convinced that the fugitives were heading for the old Navajo Trail and Holbrook, probably to stock up on ammunition. Knowing the old trail was the only break in the north rim, he announced his intention to camp astride it and await their return. Camp was made.

At 8:00 that night, with the supper fire banked and the last cigarettes being built, the sound of a shod horse was heard along the upper trail. Seconds later, the horseman rode into the reach of the firelight.

Mulvehey kept it quiet, making no move with his Winchester. "I've got a warrant for you, Frank. You're under arrest."

"Save it, Sheriff. I got a friend wants to see you."

"Name of Jim Fewkes?" asked the officer.

"Didn't catch the name, Sheriff. You comin'?"

"You've got a friend, Frank. Any objections to me bringin' one?"

"Pick your man." The big rider nodded. "My pal don't like to be left alone. He's scared of the dark."

"I imagine," murmured Mulvehey. "Leg up, Jules."

"Bring the warrants," said Frank. "My friend's purely human. He'll want to see his name in print."

"I'll show it to him. Lead off."

"That you, Rachel?"

The low call came out of the darkness, checking the shadows of the three horsemen.

"It's me. We're comin' in."

"Who's with you?"

"Billy Mulvehey, like you wanted. And Jules French."

"Come along in."

Mulvehey swung down, asking softly: "That you, Jim?"

"Yeah. Hello, Billy. We heard you was comin', and with warrants for the lot of us. I got a deal."

"You heard right. That Jim Hook gets around."

"Hook's my friend . . . same as you," said Jim slowly.

"Leave me out of it," replied the officer. "What's this Anse tells me about you pluggin' young Billy Graden?"

"Hook done it."

"All right, we can check that. What's your deal?"

"Show me the warrants and we'll come in on one condition."

"Name it and maybe you can have it."

"You get out warrants for all the Gradens' bunch and pull them in first, and we'll come in peaceful."

"Otherwise?" Mulvehey eyed him through the dark.

"Otherwise, unpeaceful," grunted the half-breed.

Billy Mulvehey was afraid of no man, Jim Fewkes included. But it was a way out. And he was up for reëlection. His question went to his silent deputy: "What do you think, Jules? It might work."

"Same as you, I reckon. I don't see no better way."

"All right, Jim"—he turned to the waiting half-breed—"it's a deal. Twenty-four hours after I take the Gradens, you be at your old man's ranch. All of you."

"Ed and John and me," corrected the half-breed. "I can't speak for Joe Boyce or Billy Beshar or the others."

"They'll come in. I ain't worried about that. Frank"—Mulvehey wheeled on him—"what about you?"

"I'll be there." The big rider nodded. "Providin'. . . ."

"Providin' what?" The officer's voice tightened.

"Providin' I get Garth Graden meantime."

Mulvehey looked at him, nodding thoughtfully. "I'll buy that. The odds favor me."

"They do," grated Frank, his voice suddenly harsh and deep. "I reckon you can find your way back?"

Mulvehey swung up. "I reckon. So long, Jim."

"So long, Billy."

"See you, Fewkes." Jules French heeled his pony to follow Mulvehey's. "So long, Rachel."

There was no answer. Frank and Jim had disappeared. The two officers looked at one another and shrugged. Guiding their ponies out of the blackness of the piñons, their shadows were quickly lost in the downtrail darkness.

XX

The following morning the posse broke camp, Anse and his followers having left in anger the previous night when Mulvehey returned without Frank Rachel or Jim Fewkes.

Frank had wanted to trail Anse but Jim had insisted they stay with the posse until it left the basin. Now they were shadowing it, seeing from its direction that Mulvehey apparently meant to ride by and check the scene of the Bivins and Payton killings at Mittelson's ranch. The posse arrived at the ranch shortly before noon of the 24th.

Desolation and the smell of death were on every hand. The cabin had been burned to its sills, only a sifting pile of wind-blown ashes marking its site. A solitary pig and half a dozen forlorn chickens wandered the emptiness of the yard. Two dead horses lay sun-swollen and fly-blown beyond the cabin sills. And beyond the horses the raw scars of two new graves were loosely covered with piled rocks. Even as the posse approached, a big dog-coyote and his whimpering mate, drawn by the decomposition already invading the shallow sepulchers of Harp Bivins and John Payton, left off their impatient pawing at the frustrating stones and slunk away.

Mulvehey and his men did not open the graves, nor did they linger in the vicinity of their brooding silence. Minutes after they had ridden up, the Yavapai sheriff led his men away, their direction west by north, for Parker's Store, Payson, and Prescott.

On the wooded ridge south of the ranch, Jim Fewkes cursed viciously. "It's that lousy Anse did it! You was right, Rachel. That's why he snuck away last night."

"The hell with it," said Frank. "Whoever done it is goin' to say we was the ones. Let's get outta here. That place down there gives me the willies. I don't like the smell of a dead man."

The half-breed slid back down off the ridge and stood up. "You should have thought of that before you chose your life's work," he said frostily.

Frank returned the bleak look. "I'm not funnin' with you, Jim. I got a feelin'." The half-breed waited, saying nothing, and he went on. "Jim, you know how a dog will sometimes take to howlin' before his master or even just anybody in the house or maybe a neighbor or anybody he knows is goin' to die?"

"Sure," said the half-breed quickly. "I seen them do that myself. What's that to do with you?"

"I got that feelin'," said the big rider somberly. "One of you is goin' to die."

"Hell, it don't take a nose like a death-smellin' dog to figure that out." Jim's guttural voice was Indian-deep. "I got you beat. It ain't one that's goin' to die. Nor two, nor six. There'll be a dozen men dead before another month. Let's get along, *hombre*."

Frank chucked his head, saying no more. But as he followed the half-breed back toward their Cherry Creek camp, his pale eyes were set and expressionless, showing no feeling. Inside of him the dog was howling, and it would not stop.

For the next five days they kept to the brush while an endless shift of scout posses, kept night and day in the field by Tom Graden, scoured the valley in search of them. Then, suddenly, on the sixth day, they saw no more scout parties. Two more days crept by and then, on the evening of September 1st, a quail whistled a little too loudly downstream of their hiding place. Jim answered the whistle and minutes later two men drifted up through the creek brush on foot.

They were William Jacoby and Joe Boyce, Fewkes partisans, neither of whom Frank knew. No time was wasted on introductions. The discourse that followed was close-cropped and entirely ominous.

Garth Graden was back in the basin, had taken over the leadership from Tom. The rumors at Parker's Store said that the new leader planned forcibly to remove the Fewkes women and children to Holbrook and burn Old John's ranch to the ground. In the face of that rumor, Jacoby and Boyce had sent another partisan, John Roady, to Payson, the nearest seat of law, to try and raise a posse there. Meantime, the execution of the burning order on the Fewkes ranch house was said to be set for daylight of September 2nd, now only hours away.

Frank cursed and stood up. "It's a trap to pull you out of the brush and down to the cabin," he snarled. "Don't you play to it, Jim."

"We ain't got no choice," said the half-breed, dead-voiced. "We're goin' down."

"If they catch you in them cabins," said Frank, his voice as flat as Jim's, "you're dead and done. You not only ain't got a choice, you ain't got a chance." He paused, rasping it: "But I have, by God."

"Such as?" queried Ed Fewkes.

"Garth Graden," breathed Frank. "I'm goin' after him." Then, voice dropping swiftly: "If I can't get to him, Jim, I'll see you at the lower cabin before sunup." He wheeled on the newcomers. "Which one of your horses do I take, boys?"

"Take the bay," said Jacoby unhesitatingly. "I pulled his shoes yesterday. He goes real quiet in the dust."

"He'll need to," growled the dour Ed, "to get Rachel up to Garth through forty other Gradens."

Frank did not hear him. He was already gone.

Frank lay half the night, belly-flat, on the ridge above the Graden Ranch. The light in the main cabin burned late and mounted men continued to come into the place until long past midnight. In the whole of the time he caught no glimpse of any stranger who might pass for a brother of Judd's or Tom's. With the 4:00 a.m. dawn beginning to streak the east and the ground-sleeping men around the cabin beginning to stir and saddle up, he knew he was not going to get his shot.

Still, he stayed. Thinking, now, not of Ed or Jim or John, or of any of their women and young ones, but thinking only of a twisted juniper and a silent pile of granite boulders waiting high and lonely above the deserted sweep of Apache Bench. At 4:15 the Gradens came out of the cabin. Judd first, followed by Tom. And then he came. He was tall, taller than Tom by half a head. And big, hard big like Old Man Stanton had said. He moved quickly and lightly, coming to his saddled horse and easing up on him in a way that told a man he didn't have to look to the low hang of the cross-belted Colts to know he had his hands full with this one.

He found the broad back in the rear sight, cheeking the Winchester hard and close. He held a long three seconds, then cursed viciously. The stock slid away from his cheek. He waited another moment, then pushed himself back and down from the skyline. He swung up on the bay, guiding him quickly along the base of the ridge and out through the backing timber of the flats below it. Again the curse came, hard and bitter.

In the end a man always came squarely up against himself. Against the warped code by which he had lived and would no doubt die. And against the gall-bitter, senseless pride of that code that had time without memory made him ride with the pot when he could have cleaned the table with one sandbag bet. In the end, he could no more shoot Garth Graden in the back than he could have any man on the long dark list before him.

XXI

As Frank drove the unshod bay across Cherry Creek, the coming sun was just tipping the ancient, barren shoulders of the Mazatzals. By-passing Young John's place, he cut through the timber straight for the elder Fewkes's main cabin. Minutes later, he was inside the cook shack with Jim, his warning rapping out tersely.

"They're comin', pardner. Tom, Judd, Garth, the lot of them.

At least forty of them, all told. You ready here?"

"Will be," replied the other, "soon as John gets back." There was no excitement in the statement. "Him and Jacoby went up to his place with Billy Beshar. The kid wanted his hosses brung down."

"Jesus, Jim! Why'd you leave him go?"

"You ever try to stop John?"

"There's a first time for everything," grunted Frank. He was moving for his horse.

"Hold up, Rachel! You can't go up there now!"

"Ever try to stop Frank?" The big rider mimicked him acidly, stared him down a minute, swung up on the bay. He was gone across the meadow before Jim could answer.

Breaking around the brush clump that hid the upper cabin from the lower, he saw it all in the same instant.

Jacoby, Beshar, and John Fewkes were just clearing the cabin, hazing the latter's horses ahead of them. Across the meadow, cutting between him and them, galloped Anse Canaday, Clint Bivins, and a dozen Parker's Store cattlemen. In the same moment John and his companions saw him and spurred toward him, their Winchesters hammering into the front of the advancing cattlemen. Frank levered his saddle gun, the shots so close they could not be counted. The cattlemen split in the face of the wild fire, half of them veering north of John's cabin, the other half following Anse into the timber, southward, toward the main cabin. Frank and his companions drove their racing horses in the same direction. They had no other.

Anse executed his hasty ambush with calculated viciousness. He held his men up in the border pines, letting Frank and his followers break clear of the trees and forty yards into the meadow. Then he gave it to them where he liked to put it—in the back. Billy Beshar spun off his horse, knocked free of the falling animal by a bullet through the shoulder. He lit on his feet, ran crouching for the pines. Frank, riding last, saw the dust puffs spring from Jacoby's spine, knew from the oat-sack slump of his body that he was dead. John was twice missed by shots that ripped through his shirt before the final slug tore off the back of his head. He slid into the clearing dirt not ten feet from the stumble and fall of Jacoby's horse.

Frank leaped his bay over the struggling animal and drove on, still unharmed, for the cabin. He hit the ground, running doubled over, dived through the door, rolled to his feet, ran for the north window. There he was in time to see the most brutal killing he had ever witnessed. Jim Fewkes, joining him, saw it, too.

Billy Beshar had made the cover of a corded stack of logs where Old Man Fewkes had been cutting stove wood among the fringe pines. The splitting block, cross-buck saw, and double-bit axe lay where the old man had dropped them the night before. The wounded man's attackers now worked swiftly toward this refuge on foot, spreading through the sheltering timber in a closing, three-sided net.

As they watched, the cornered fighter's ammunition ran out. They saw him snap the empty guns, drop behind the woodpile, cursing. The next instant he had slipped around the pile and was running for the cabin. He wasn't ten feet from the chopping block before he had been hit half a dozen times. He lurched drunkenly back toward the woodpile, fell over and behind it again. He was stumbling out from behind the pile then, still miraculously alive. But the first of his tormentors was behind him like a cat, sweeping up the axe as he sped past the chopping block. The sickening swing of the double-bitted weapon caught the wounded man between the shoulders, driving him soddenly to the ground. The axe-man hit him twice more, crunching, bludgeon blows aimed at the slack head. Even across the quarter mile of the meadow, the crazy, woman-high laugh carried jarringly. In early light like this, with the black powder smoke drifting heavily and his own nerves standing on edge, a man's eyes might fool him. His ears never would. That had been Anse Canaday with the axe.

For the next five hours and until the sun stood noon high overhead, the besiegers kept the little cabin under ordered constant fire. They had plenty of time, plenty of ammunition. They were in a position if need be to spend a week of one and a wagonload of the other. That the need would never arise was as clear to the men trapped in the cabin as it was to those waiting outside it. With nightfall and using the cook shack and hog pen as approaching cover, resolute men could easily get to the main cabin and fire it. 1:00 p.m. dragged slowly toward 2:00, and the sun blaze of the meadow's heat mounted intolerably. Within the cabin the desperate men cursed and shifted continually from window to window. Outside, Graden's men lay among the rocks of the south ridge and waited. With 2:00 sweated under and the heat and the fly drone and the choking stifle of the gunsmoke in the cabin thickening by the minute, it happened.

XXII

The bodies of John Fewkes and Bill Jacoby lay in full view of the cabin's occupants, midway between that shelter and the meadow's edge, and directly under the attackers' guns. At 2:20—they remembered the time because Old Man Fewkes had just pulled out his pewter watch to check the hours until sunset—Mary Fewkes spoke in sudden horror from the north window.

"My God, Jim! Here come the hogs!"

"The sow has spotted them." The slow words were Jim's, their simple statement framing the dread fear growing in the minds of all of them as they crowded to the tiny window.

Seconds later the fear became grisly fact.

"Jesus, it ain't possible they'd stand by and see them hogs eat John and Bill. . . ." Ed Fewkes trailed it off, white-faced.

"Maybe it ain't." It was Frank acidly. "But they're standin' and them hogs is eatin'."

"Get away from the window!" Jim turned as his order went to the blank-faced Mary. She did not move and he took her arm, forcing her roughly. "I said get away from that window, woman!" He hissed the words. "And keep the kids away from it, too! Frank"—he wheeled on the big rider—"cover me. I'm goin' out there."

"You won't need to, Jim." Frank's quiet words swung all their eyes toward the open cabin door. "Mary's beat you to it."

Already halfway to the cook shack, young John's wife continued her slow walk. Behind her in the cabin, the Fewkes men waited in wordless, bitter shame. On the ridge beyond the cabin other men watched and waited, their guns forgotten, their eyes tight, their thoughts their own.

Mary was coming from the cook shack now, moving head up across the meadow, a rusted shovel, stark and rigid, in her right hand. Even the brute hogs seemed to sense the cold courage of the moment, the whole herd backing away from the bodies in tusk-chopping, surly defiance.

Mary Fewkes buried the two men in a common, shallow grave, heaping the clods of the meadow turf over them. When she had finished, she dropped the shovel across the mute pile, walked slowly toward the cabin. The moment she disappeared within, the cattlemen resumed firing.

An hour later, with the sun dropping swiftly behind the Mazatzals, Tom Graden readied his final move.

"Garth!" The tall gunman lounged forward in response to his brother's summons. "You take the bunch that will move up with dark and fire the place."

Garth nodded, moving for his horse. He said nothing, being of the kind to whom words were largely a waste and simple action was the mother tongue. Anse Canaday was of a different breed. He moved forward, confronting him noisily.

"Hold up, Graden. I reckon your brother has got his names a little mixed. I'm takin' that bunch."

Garth nodded. "Somebody's a little mixed up." He had a flat, dry voice, strangely foreign to his towering size. "Likely it's not Tom."

"Don't call me, Graden. Get outta my way."

"I never call your kind," said the tall man softly.

Garth stepped into him, driving his knee upward into his groin. The balled fist smashed into his jaw. Anse spun half around, slid to the ground, stayed there.

The big gunman put his boot into the unconscious form, shoved it over contemptuously, removed the Colts from their holsters, passed them silently to Tom.

"Like I said." He nodded quietly. "I never call your kind."

"Jake Bivins!" Tom stepped toward the fallen man's half-brother. "You haul Anse back to the picket line. When he comes around, put him on his hoss and head him out of the basin. I told him if he ever put off on me again, he was through."

"Haul him back yourself." Jake backed off, as Simm stepped forward to side him. "I ain't touchin' him."

Jake and Simm were both watching him when Garth eased forward. Still, they did not follow the slight motion of the wrists that brought the Colts out and up.

"Pull out," the tall man said quietly. "I got a cabin to burn." They watched him a moment longer, then the bull-like Simm nodded sullenly, swung Anse's limp form over his shoulder.

Jake, turning to follow him, paused long enough to snarl at Garth: "We'll be back! The whole three of us!"

Garth nodded, easing his guns into their leathers. "If you

should feel called to," he drawled slowly, "be sure and tell your brother to bring his little axe." He paused, letting it come between his teeth: "The dirty murdering bastard!"

With the western shadows running long and black across the meadow, the firing from the Graden men suddenly and unaccountably slacked off. Within seconds their entire line had fallen silent. And the cause of the cease-fire was apparent to the men in the cabin: a solitary horseman jogging into the meadow from the east.

"It's a trick," growled Ed, lining his rifle and laying his sights. The barrel steadied and held, and in the last moment Jim's eyes widened.

"Hold off, Ed! It's Jack Maddows from Payson!"

"Yeah, it's Jack, all right. I hope to God he's got a posse along!"

"It's a beautiful thought." It was Frank coming up behind them with the caustic agreement. "Let us dwell upon it."

The Payson justice of the peace pulled his horse up in front of the cabin, keeping him well clear, where he could be seen from the ridge. "Hello, the house!" His deep voice carried echoingly in the clearing stillness. "Who's inside and what's the trouble?"

Jim nodded to Frank and the latter slid the door open just far enough to let his answers out. Tersely he named the cabin's living occupants and called the brief roll of the meadow dead. In all, he used less than twenty words, the quiet-faced officer less than ten.

"All right, you folks, set tight. I'll be back."

They watched him as he loped his horse toward the ridge and halted him at its base. His slow voice carried clearly to the topmost of the silent rocks.

"You boys all know me, so don't waste my time. I've got a

posse fifteen minutes behind me. Any man left within rifle range of this meadow in five will be indicted for the murders of John Fewkes, William Jacoby, and Billy Beshar." There were no answers from the rocks and Maddows nodded.

"All right, boys, you play it any way you want. I'll be holdin' a coroner's inquest out past that hog pen in exactly one hour. Any one of you wants to attend and speak his piece is cordially invited." He paused, letting the silence soak it into them, then turned his horse with the final nod. "You got five minutes. Use them any way you want."

It was one thing to trap and kill enemies who were as far beyond the law as yourselves—quite another to buck Jack Maddows and a Yavapai County posse. The cattlemen's withdrawal was sullen, but notably swift.

Ten minutes after the last word of the called-out ultimatum had fallen, the ridge and the surrounding meadow edges stood in full and vacant silence.

The moon had not yet risen and the guttering flare of the coal-oil lamp provided the sole candle for the dead Mass that night spoken over the shallow graves of John Fewkes and William Jacoby. The inquest was mercifully short. Jacoby had been shot three times in the small of the back, each bullet shattering the spine. John Fewkes had been hit only once, the slug entering the base of the neck, ranging upward and disintegrating the back of the skull. The forepart of the head appeared to have been smashed with a rock, but whether this wound was the result of his fall from his horse or of a brutality unseen in the excitement of Frank's arrival at the cabin was not established. The body of Billy Beshar could not be located and Maddows refused to include his killing in the findings of his hard-eyed coroner's jury.

With the lantern-lit inquest concluded, the men of the posse quickly deepened the graves, digging them narrowly side-by-side. The bodies were rolled back in, unwrapped, and the wordless group filed away, leaving the dead alone in the meadow, separated from their God and His eternity by two feet of loosely shoveled, boot-stomped dirt.

Maddows and his posse left the basin that same night. No warrants were ever drawn or served against the murderers of John Fewkes and William Jacoby.

XXIII

The return to the Cherry Creek hide-out was made in the early morning hours of September 3rd. Joe Boyce, joining them on the ride, accompanied them a short way, then left to scout Parker's Store to pick up what news he could of Anse Canaday—Jim's having sworn to kill the Texas renegade for his part in the meadow murders. Boyce returned to the hide-out before dawn, his news bringing a dark smile to the half-breed's face.

Tom Graden had ordered Anse out of the valley, and Simm and Jake had gone with him, apparently bound for Holbrook. Clint, not having been involved in the argument and being a particular crony of Judd's, was still at the Graden ranch. It was enough for Jim. He and Ed left at once, heading for the north rim and Holbrook.

Before leaving Frank, Boyce dropped one last piece of information. A drunken JT hand had boasted, in reply to another Graden hand's statement, that he had heard Frank Rachel was looking for Garth, that "by God, Garth got the hoss! Now you watch him get the man!"

For a moment Frank's heart leaped. Then as quickly subsided. Even if Garth had been in on the original theft of Red Boy, it was a certainty he had not brought the horse back into the basin. Not unless he had him stalled up in secret on the Graden place. And even if by some crazy, long-shot chance he did have him there, it could have no bearing on what Frank had to do now.

All the following day, and the next, for forty-eight catnapping hours, he lay on the ridge above the Graden Ranch, waiting for Garth to return, his mind far from Red Boy and the big stallion's possible fate. But the cabin remained dark, its chimney cold. The stock in the corrals bawled ceaselessly, complaining against their hunger. No one appeared to feed them. Not a solitary rider passed up the Payson trail north of the meadow.

Frank knew then that the Gradens had somehow sensed his surveillance, were deliberately staying clear of the place. The birds were gone. He was watching an empty nest.

Back at the hide-out, he found no sign that Ed and Jim had been there. But an hour after his return, they slipped into camp through the downstream brush. In twenty seconds of Indian-short grunts they had made their report. Perry Odens, long-haired, fancy buckskin-dressing sheriff of Apache County had single-handedly killed Anse and Simm Bivins, a young nephew of theirs with them at the time, and seriously wounded Jake, all in the cool and due process of serving a Texas murder warrant on Anse.

"All by his lonesome," concluded Jim abruptly, "and carryin' only his saddle gun."

"Well," said Frank slowly, his mind reaching beyond the fate of Anse Canaday and his half-brothers, "hats off to Sheriff Perry Odens of Apache County. And amen to Anse. Now, how about us?"

Jim looked across the rush and bubble of Cherry Creek a long time before he answered. "Us," he said at last, "we stay in the brush and in the basin until the last Graden is dead or the last Fewkes buried."

"Amen again," said Frank. "Let's get to it."

But Garth's hired gunmen were back in the field on a twenty-four-hour schedule. Frank and his slant-eyed fellow outlaws were pinned to the Cherry Creek brush, not daring to move. Twice within the first three days, mounted search parties passed so close they could hear the blowing of the horses.

The fourth day of their hiding came and was ridden under by the tireless mounts of Garth's prowling gun hounds. Frank and the brothers lay close in their perilous cover, thinking little, saying less, their tired, trapped minds unable to progress beyond the blind terminal of tomorrow. And from where they lay and from what they could see and hear, tomorrow was going to be like yesterday and the day before: nerve-strung and endless and without hope. Their trouble was one of human limitations. They simply could not hear or see far enough.

On the 4th of September, Justice of the Peace Jack Maddows reached Payson. On the 5th he wired Sheriff Billy Mulvehey at Prescott. On the 6th Mulvehey was exchanging wires with District Attorney John G. Harnden. On the 7th both Mulvehey and Harnden were meeting with Territorial Governor C.M. Zellick in Maricopa County. At the end of this conference, the chief executive ordered Mulvehey to raise a posse large enough to invade the basin and arrest every man of either side encountered. Billy Mulvehey's gun blood was boiling over. He had been duly elected to keep the peace in Yavapai County, and he was now officially ordained to do so to the extent of killing as many "honest citizens" as might choose to get in his angry way. On the 9th he wired Deputy Sheriff Jules French at Flagstaff to meet him in Payson with all the men he could deputize from his area. On the 10th he left Prescott with his own famed deputies: George Brisling, E.M. Tucker, and Ed "Shanghai" Sullivan.

The following day he was in Payson meeting with Jack Maddows. The two officers went at once about the grim business of raising and equipping the biggest peacetime fighting force of law officers in the territory's history. It was a task that took precious time—and time for the Gradens and the Fewkes was not something to kill, but something *with which* to kill.

Mulvehey waited and cursed and struggled with his marching order, and the Fourth Horseman struck again in Peaceful Basin.

The second week drew to its close. The three men trapped in their tiny camp were near the breaking point. That raw nerve edge that is never far from the surface in cornered fighting men was already frayed to its last shred when Joe Boyce rode up the creek in the early evening of the 17th. His news snapped the end thread for Frank Rachel.

Garth Graden had just been seen leaving the Graden Ranch for Parker's Store, riding alone. There was no one at the store save its proprietor, Charley Parker. Against Jim's vehement objections that he might be seen in turn, and trailed back to the hide-out, Frank mounted. An hour later he was loping down on the crossroads.

But a quarter of a mile uptrail of the store, he was throwing his horse into the brush and sliding off of him quickly and quietly. Maybe Boyce had been right to begin with, but right now that damned store was a blaze of lamplight and no less than eight saddled horses stood, head-drooped, at its hitching rail. Frank tailed off his curses, turned his pony away.

When he went for Garth, he had to know it was no worse than fifty-fifty, with the fastest fifty cashing in the chips. And more. Garth had to know *who* he was bucking. And *what* was in the pot. He had to have time to look around the table and remember the third, forgotten player in the game. The one whose last raise had been high enough to lead Frank Rachel to bet his life on it. He had to remember Libby Fewkes.

The fading *clip-clop* of Frank's pony was still audible when the two other horsemen pulled out of the pines a hundred yards downtrail toward the store. The taller of the two nodded quickly to his companion.

"Harry, you get on down to the store. Tell Garth his gamble paid off."

"Yeah, it sure did. Which one of them you suppose it was? Ed or Jim?"

"Neither," his companion replied. "Too big in the saddle. That was Frank Rachel. Get goin'!"

The other nodded, wheeled his pony for the store. His companion watched him go, then turned his own pony uptrail, after Frank. He passed quickly out of the pine shadows and into the open starlight. It was Joe Ellensburg, the cowboy who had seen Jim Fewkes fleeing the scene of Billy Graden's murder.

Jim Fewkes came up on one elbow, the disturbed chatter of the sleepy mountain blue jay dying away as he did. The next instant his guarded whisper was going to his companions: "Ed! Frank! You awake . . . ?"

"I ain't slept for six weeks," growled Ed, reaching for his Winchester. "That was a jay, wasn't it?"

"It was. Frank?"

"Yeah? What the hell's the matter with you god damn' Injuns now? Can't you let a white man sleep?"

"We heard a jay chattering downstream. Roll out. Something's moving down there."

Frank was still in his blankets, reaching for his rifle, when the first of the looming horsemen crashed into the camp. He fired from the ground, into the horses, Ed and John diving free of the tiny clearing and into the brush, their own Winchesters roaring.

The yells and curses of the attackers rode in over the smashing hoofs of their mounts and the blinding explosions of their guns. The whole wild mêlée was cleared in a matter of seconds, the uncontrollable horses of the cattlemen careening on through the camp and into the upstream timber.

After an endless minute Jim moved, gliding around through the trees toward Frank. Ed's shadow joined his and together the half-breed brothers slipped behind the boulder where the big rider lay.

"Follow me," was all Jim said. It was more than enough. The three shadows melted away from the clearing, moved quickly up the granite outcrop backing their camp, bellied down in the rocks atop it, guns trained upstream.

With only the starlight for illumination, they could make out little more than the blur of the mounted group gathered along the near side of the creek, two hundred yards upstream. But in the minds of the three, there was no room for doubt. They were trapped. The cattlemen had only to wait for daylight. The feud was over—or so they thought.

Ten minutes after the opening assault, the cattlemen forded Cherry Creek above the fugitives' camp, struck the open trail of the Parker's Store road on the far side, turned quickly south. And in the brief moment of the retreat's crossing, the watching eyes above had seen its reason: two led horses, their riders sack-limp and motionless across the swaying saddles. They were Joe Ellensburg and Harry Mattson, a sometime Hash Knife cowboy. The former was to survive his wounds crippled for life, and to leave the basin. The latter was to die two days later and be buried alongside Billy Graden at the home ranch: the eleventh known man to die in the Peaceful Basin War. The cattlemen had found the enemy—and found him deadly. Even in the dark!

XXIV

Three days later, in the evening, Frank, with Ed and Jim Fewkes, appeared at Joe Boyce's cabin in answer to a cryptic message sent by the latter: *A man at my place wants to see you.* The man proved to be Jim Hook, Sheriff Perry Odens's deputy. They faced him now across the cabin's one room, Winchesters in hand, alert for anything. Hook spoke rapidly.

"The war's over, boys. Billy Mulvehey is hid out up at Haggler's ranch with Jules French, Jack Maddows, and forty men. Billy sent me to call you in on that deal he made with you, Jim."

"Go on," the half-breed said.

"Billy's goin' to pull the Gradens in first thing tomorrow. You're to have your whole bunch at your old man's place by sundown. It's the deal, Billy said."

Frank watched him closely. "That all Billy said?" he asked quietly.

Jim Hook eyed Frank back. "Not quite. He said . . . 'Take it or leave it.' "

"It's big talk," said Frank.

"It's a big posse." Hook shrugged. "What'll it be, Jim? Take it, or leave it?"

The half-breed hesitated, trapped by his own word to the Yavapai sheriff. As he did, the big man at his side spoke softly.

"You do it, Jim." Frank Rachel had been thinking. The big rider knew the end of a trail when he saw it. He moved closer now, putting his hand on his friend's narrow shoulder. "It's the only chance you got to leave the basin alive, pardner. You take it now, you hear me, Jim?"

The half-breed stood a moment more, then turned to the waiting Hook, head down.

"We'll take it," he said dully. "We'll be there."

Hook nodded, his eyes holding on Frank. "The deal includes you, Rachel. Don't stall me. I only got an hour."

Frank moved into him, pale eyes narrowing. "I make my own deals, friend. And not with deputies." He stepped back, fingers flexing. "Hop your hoss, little man."

"Now hold up, Rachel . . . !"

"Hop it!" grated Frank, dropping his hands. "Your hour's done run out!"

Mulvehey moved on Parker's Store at midnight. His plans had been made with the utmost secrecy and he was satisfied no word of his coming had reached the basin ahead of him. Every chance rider encountered since the posse had left Payson had been taken into custody. The choice of the deathtrap was a murderous one.

The Peaceful Basin store had been built in the 1870s for use as a fort against the Apaches. Its walls were a foot thick, its windows narrow-cased and so set as to insure a field of fire in any direction. The breast-high stone foundation across the road from the store, where he himself would wait with a part of the posse, was heavy enough to flatten a six-pound shot. By 4:00 a.m. both groups were in place, those in the store under deputy Jules French. The main springs of Mulvehey's trap were cocked. The Yavapai sheriff was ready to plant his poisoned bait.

He called Deputy Sheriff Joe McKimson of Apache County to him and the two officers talked quickly. Shortly the Apache deputy and his five men mounted and rode off toward the southern foothills.

Crouched in the 4:00 a.m. blackness atop the ridge overlooking Graden's meadow and the Parker's Store crossroads, Frank blew the chill from his fingers, flexed them carefully, re-gripped the Winchester. He cursed the darkness and the wind and the cold. He cursed Jim Hook and Billy Mulvehey and the whole bad way the thing was winding up.

With the Yavapai sheriff in the basin and due to jump the Graden place at daylight, he might never get his chance at Garth. All he could do was what he was doing: staking out on that damned ridge and hoping and praying for just one clear sight of Garth before Mulvehey and the posse showed up.

Suddenly he tensed. Was that a man moving down there in those cabin shadows? Yes, by God, it was. It was Tom Graden.

He watched the JT owner mount and guide his horse out of the corral and across the meadow toward the store. Then he was watching something else—and so was Tom Graden. From the rail in front of Parker's Store, six shadowy horsemen swung away, starting south down the Cherry Creek road. Tom let them pass the meadow, then sent his own mount after them, keeping well back, clearly trailing them.

At 5:30 Frank made ready to leave the ridge, sure he had missed and that Tom had been alone in the cabin. He had not moved a foot, when he froze. He watched the approaching horsemen coming north up the Cherry Creek road, knowing from their number and direction they were the same six who had ridden away earlier. He recognized the leading rider as Joe McKimson, a deputy from Apache County. At the store the horsemen tied their mounts and went in.

Nothing happened. There was no movement from the Graden cabin in response to the small posse's appearance. Frank swung his glance across the store road to the cabin of Al Ross, one of Tom Graden's chief lieutenants, belatedly thinking the rest of the Gradens might have holed up there. Nothing moved at the Ross cabin.

But McKimson's posse was coming out again, the same five men—but, no, the sixth man, swinging up on the Apache deputy's horse, was not McKimson. He was Jules French, Mulvehey's right-hand gun. Frank's eyes narrowed. A man could chew that up and spit it out any way he wanted. It came out in the same-size chunks. Billy Mulvehey and his Payson posse were holed up at Parker's Store!

What followed came so fast he could only watch it, forgetting his own man and his own gun in the blazing suddenness of it. The small posse headed north, pushing its horses up the creek road with obvious urgency. Mulvehey's twice-tainted bait now paid off. The posse was still in sight when Frank saw the two smoke puffs break from Al Ross's cabin. A second later the flat reports of the rifle shots reached him, and were replied to by three answering shots from the cabin below him. There were Graden men in both cabins! He cheeked the Winchester, snapping its sights onto the Graden cabin door. He let Judd pass out, and then Clint Bivins, knowing the next man had to be him!

But no third man came out. He had only time to curse and then his eyes and thoughts were forced to follow Clint and Judd. The two men rode slowly to the store, circled it cautiously, pulled their horses up in the road south of the building, talking briefly. Frank saw Clint gesture toward the stone foundation across the road from the store. Judd nodded and both kneed their mounts forward. Five seconds after that they were looking over the rock wall and into the double-barreled face of death.

Frank saw them raise in their stirrups to look over the foundation, saw the quick haul back of both horses, and the simultaneous appearance, around the corner of the breastworks, of Billy Mulvehey.

"Throw them up!"

The heavy bark of the Yavapai sheriff's command carried clearly to the ridge. The next sounds, and the last ones, were the blending roars of the black-powder replies and counter-replies.

Clint drew first. His Colt had just cleared its holster when the twelve-gauge buck slugs tore his belly out. He was dying the instant his horse reared, and dead before his body struck the ground. Judd, half a second slower, never got his pistols clear.

109

The second barrel of Mulvehey's shotgun missed him, smashed into the head and neck of his mount. The animal reared and fell backward, Judd getting away from it and landing on his feet. He twisted toward the wall, still clawing for his guns. The belch of the posse's rifle fire rolled once across the foundation and after that there was nothing save the echoing stillness of death occupying the Parker's Store crossroads.

Judd lived long enough to ask for a drink of water. And for Mulvehey to tell him he was sorry, that he had missed his second shot deliberately, shooting for the horse rather than the man, hoping till the last that Judd would surrender. Whether the second Graden brother heard or understood was never known. He died with the first taste of the water unswallowed in his slack mouth.

Frank, watching the huddle of peace officers around the dying man, broke his eyes suddenly back to the Graden cabin. He could not have looked away for more than ten seconds, but with a man like Garth Graden that was nine and a half too many. Frank saw the horse flash out of the apparently abandoned and hoarded-up box stall behind the main cabin, race across the meadow, and disappear into the lodgepole pines beyond. That was all. One second you were wondering how in God's name Garth had gotten out of the cabin and onto that horse so fast, and the next second he had a hundred yards of timber between you and your half-swung Winchester. But even in that half moment of time, it wasn't anything about the man or his speed that stopped you. It was the horse!

The mount Garth had ridden since his return to the basin was a raw-boned buckskin. The flash of that horse's rump just vanished into the pines was not buckskin. Nor anything close to buckskin. It was bay! Bright, blood-red bay! Frank still couldn't believe it, much less understand it. But the mare had not been foaled or serviced that could carry the twin of that crazy-running bay Garth was riding. Horse ghost, hope mirage, name him any way you would. That was Red Boy running yonder! He saw the stud break out of the pines half a mile up the meadow, skirt the low hills flanking it, come racing out on the Payson trail to the north.

He shook himself, the fierce joy of seeing the stallion putting the ache of sudden memory, hard and tight, in his throat. Then he was forcing his eyes back to the crossroads and the store, knowing his next move had to be guided from there. He saw the main body of the posse gather, waited only long enough to see it start for the Graden cabin below him. He was sliding back off the ridge then, going for his horse.

Mulvehey and that posse were coming after Tom—they thought. The quick grin hardened Frank's mouth as he drove the bay into the pines. They would have to close on that cabin mighty tightly to squeeze Tom Graden out of it.

Breaking free of the foothills and coming out on the Payson trail, Frank threw a quick glance at the climbing sun, nodded his quick satisfaction, rode quickly on. It was a day and hour patiently waited for. And long to be remembered.

XXV

It was perfect trailing weather. The ground was still damp from a mountain shower, the breeze strong and steady from the Mogollons. Where there was soil, it held Red Boy's familiar, twisted prints in clean relief, letting Frank read them from the saddle while holding his own mount on a high lope. Where there was sand or dusted silt, the wind blew it away and broke it up as quickly as a horse might raise it, keeping the man ahead from seeing that he was being closely trailed. And there was need for close trailing. Either he caught up with Garth before he reached the open basin beyond Diamond Butte and the south slope of Apache Bench, or he would lose him, for there was no question who had the top horse in this race. Red Boy was a racer, bred and trained; his own bay plug was a worn-out cutting horse that should have been pasture-pensioned long ago.

Ahead now, the trail went up and over Antelope Saddle, and from the summit of the saddle he would have his last opportunity to see how far Garth had him headed, and he could weigh his chances of getting up to him short of Payson or Prescott—or maybe any place in Arizona. He held up on the summit, the curse coming as his squinted eyes adjusted to the dance of the sun on the bare granite below. In this clear air the size of that mounted dot just disappearing into the boulder field at the base of Diamond Butte meant your man was a solid five miles up on you. And it also meant that another mile would take him free.

Frank's mouth twisted. His only hope had been that Garth would hold Red Boy down, figuring he had gotten away from the ranch without being seen, and saving the stud for the long pull out of the territory. But Garth's breed had never flourished on *figuring*. His kind had to *know* a thing. He had pushed the big stallion all the way, had not only headed his slower-mounted pursuer but had opened up that heading by four full miles since leaving the meadow. The realization of the fact tightened the twist of Frank's mouth, and, even as it did, the hard-eyed gods of chance reversed themselves, smiled briefly upon him. Abbreviated and wry as the grimace was, it put the sudden hope of his hatred hammering within him. The distant horseman had not appeared *beyond* the far boulders that marked the edge of the basin's open floor. And he did not! As Frank watched, unable in the first moment to absorb the full extent of his luck, Garth appeared *west* of the boulders. West of them, and forcing Red Boy up and across the lower spur of Apache Bench. He disappeared again now, beyond the spur and still climbing, and suddenly Frank knew what it meant. Garth Graden had done the one thing, above all others, he should not have done. He had left the open safety of the Payson trail. And he had picked, instead, the trail for the last place in Arizona Territory he should have chosen—Frank Rachel's Apache Bench ranch.

Either Garth had been with Anse Canaday and the bunch that had run off Red Boy, or he had talked to them enough to know the Diamond Butte trail. There was grass and water at the abandoned ranch, and a five-mile view of the country a man had left behind him. A man could rest there, graze and water his horse, have time to roll a smoke, boil coffee, make out if anybody was on his back trail. Then, either way, there was that good trail up and across the wall behind the ranch, leading out past Camp Verde and north safely west of Flagstaff. Yes, Garth Graden knew where he was going. And so did Frank Rachel. The only difference was that Frank knew a better way to get there. He was remembering Jim's long-ago words now, as he turned his horse to take that better way. *I got a cute way up to that Apache burn out,* Jim had said. *There'll be times you'll want to remember it.* The half-breed had been right and this was the time. It was a cute way, all right. Its name was Dry Cañon.

The Dry Cañon trail was shorter by ten miles, but the last three of those were up a granite goat track as steep as the pitch of a snow-country roof—and Red Boy's blazing speed might possibly have outmatched Frank's memory of the half-breed's short cut. The thought grew swiftly in the big rider's mind as he forced the failing bay up the final precipitous mile.

Before the mile was out, the torment of the suspicion had built into a foreboding certainty. He halted the laboring pony in the rock jumble that clogged the cañon's exit, then he was peering across the bench, lean face darkening. There was harsh memory enough in the first glance to bring the scowl: the lonely set of the empty corrals, the staring ruin of the burned cabin, the high drift of the cotton clouds above the brooding silence of

Libby's look-out. Yes, in these and a hundred other things that rushed unbidden to a man's mind there was memory enough to bring the scowl. But these were the things you saw with your heart, and they were the things that could kill you only slowly. It was what you saw with your eyes that could kill you in the next five minutes. And what you saw was Red Boy standing, cinch-loosened, in his own corral!

Quickly then, Frank saw the rest of it. Garth was hunched over a tiny coffee fire at the corner of the stud's corral. From his position he could see the bench from north to south, and he *was* seeing it. The shifting, nervous swing of his glance—from the fire to the silent hay sheds to the open grass of the bench— was never still. And between him and Frank was a solid mile of that open grass! Garth would have time to mount up and roll a smoke before he could hope to gallop within long rifle range of him.

Frank cursed. Right about now a man wished he had Jim Fewkes with him. The half-breed would know how to come up on that wary white bastard out there, and without him knowing there was another human within sixty miles of him. He would do it like the damned Indian he was—naked-footed and bellying back of every grama clump, outcrop rock, or piece of juniper scrub big enough to hide a runt grass rat. The thought of Jim's savage ancestry was swiftly broken by a following thought, the first grim father to the second. Jim had always said he should have been an Indian! Frank's scowl dropped away under the sudden flash of the old grin. Seconds later he was in the grass.

Behind him the silent rocks of the cañon's throat stood guard over a little pile of personals that would have gladdened Jim Fewkes's half-red heart: a pair of run-over Texas boots, an 1873 Winchester, a sun-faded black Stetson, a set of twin holsters. The right-hand holster was empty. . . .

Frank knew how long it took to boil a can of coffee. And to

blow a tired horse. He had no more than fifteen minutes to get up back of the stud's box stall and make his play. The open-grass part was the easiest. Garth could not know of the Dry Cañon trail, would likely keep his watch pretty well to the south part of the bench. Frank gambled on that, and in five minutes was raking in the first half of the pot. He was in the pines under the wall and Garth had not moved from the fire.

In three minutes more he was behind the first hay shed and getting his last look at his enemy before he would lose him for those final seconds beyond the intervening bulk of the box stall. He hesitated in those last moments, his hand dropping to the curved handle of the Colt. Then he was shaking his head, pulling the hand away.

It was a long seventy-five yards, and no matter how Bill Hickok and the other old-timers lied about it, you didn't open up with a belt gun at anything over twenty-five—and preferably not over ten! If you meant to call a fast man and then hit him in the belly with six slugs where you could cover the spread of them with one hand, you got in close enough to powder-burn his shirt.

Past the corner of the box stall, he would see Red Boy moving nervously in the stud corral. He scowled, testing the wind with a wetted finger. The scowl deepened. The wind was wrong, carrying from him and toward the stallion. If the big bay should wind him on his way in. . . .

His stockinged feet made no sound in the deep dust of the yard. Red Boy did not even grunt. He was behind the box stall then, wanting to gasp for breath and not daring to. He slid to the corner of the building, crouched there to let the passing seconds slow his breathing and steady his hand.

In the corral beyond the box, Red Boy suddenly threw up his head, nostrils belling with the memory stir of a forgotten man-smell. The neigh was high and sharp—fierce with the sudden joy of remembering.

Frank was leaping into the open with its first echo. But Garth Graden was ahead of the echo. His first shot hit Frank high in the right lung, spinning him back and around. He fell, twisting for the cover of the box stall corner, and Garth's second shot shredded the butted logs as he did. Ricocheting wickedly, it tore through Frank's thigh. In the second following the two gun bursts, he heard the slam of the stall door, and knew that Garth had leaped inside the fortress of Red Boy's box.

He lay against the bottom logs of the west wall, writhing with the pain of his wounds, his mind racing. He had had his chance and it was gone. His right arm and side were useless, his left thigh too badly hit to bear his weight. Garth was in the box with two guns and a full belt of shells. There were no windows in the stall and the front door was a full one. The only way into the box now was the half-door separating it from Red Boy and the stud corral. All Garth had to do was watch that half-door and wait.

The continued harsh neighing of the bay stud rode in over Frank's dimming thoughts. Again the stallion blasted his whistling challenge. And then again. The angry grating sound forced its way into Frank's mind. It was crazy, he thought. It would never work. Garth had had the stud a long time. Still— and yet if he had not worked at gentling him. If he had used him as roughly as that Spanish spade bit he had on him suggested. If the big nasty-tempered horse was remembering him, Frank, as strongly as that wild neighing sounded like he was. If the gunshots and the smell of the blood had him crazy enough. There had been a time when no man dared touch the stud when Frank was near him. He could be handled by a hard horseman, but not when Frank was in sight or close by. Libby had been the only one who had ever done that. Even Jim, a top hand with any horse, had known better than to lay a hand on

Red Boy when Frank was around. Maybe, by God—just maybe

Somehow he reached the closed front door, dropped the heavy stove bolt through the hasp that locked it from the outside. Then he was dragging himself back along the west wall, hunching foot by foot on his braced left arm. It took him five minutes to round its corner and cover the fifteen feet of the south wall. It was the long way around, but the half-door latched on the south side, making that the side he had to work from.

At the south corner, he writhed under the bottom poles of the corral, lay panting and listening against the east wall, six feet from the half-door. There was no sound from within the box. But Red Boy was wild with excitement now, racing the corral fence, dashing up to him, rearing over him, racing away again, wheeling and neighing crazily. He waved him desperately away, not daring to call out to him or to take his eyes from the open top of the half-door. But the silence in the box held.

He braced himself up along the wall, shoved the Colt barrel under the stove bolt, popped it free of the hasp. Garth's shot smashed through the planking, whining away across the bench. But in the same instant Frank's foot was in the sagging crack of the door, shoving it and kicking it wide open, and Garth's second and third shots went wild into the dust of the corral. Frank lurched back against the wall, free of the opening, his shrill whistle going to the lathered stallion. The stud wheeled, threw up his head, thundered toward the box stall.

"Inside, you red bastard! *Inside!*"

Frank screamed it at him, breathing a prayer behind it as the stud came racing across the corral in answer to the remembered command. The big horse was past him then, ears back, eyewhites rolling, lunging into the familiar gloom of his box. Frank heard the wild curse, the double blast of the ricocheting shots, the stallion's continual, high, piercing neigh, and after these sounds there were only those of the log-jarring smashes of the great rump against the inner walls and the angry, sodden, lashing drives of the steel-shod forehoofs. He closed his eyes then, leaning weakly back against the wall. He felt the weakness grow sickeningly, coming up from the pit of his stomach in thick, slow-pulsing waves.

He called haltingly to the stud in the box. "Easy, boy, easy! It's all right now. . . ." With the words his head slumped. His body remained braced against the logs for a moment, then pitched and slid soundlessly forward into the corral dirt.

Presently the stallion came out of the box. He nuzzled the still form, whickering eagerly. He put his slim nose under the slack arm, nudging it in the old game. It flopped limply and fell away. Red Boy backed off, cleared his nostrils of the blood smell, whickered, and stomped demandingly. There was no reply from the man.

Twice more he came back to nose at the still form. Once, he started back into the stall, shied back out and away from it, snorting loudly. He went away then, to the far end of the corral. Stretching his neck over the top rail, he watched the silent ruin where the house had stood—and where *she* had always waited with the sugar and the dried apples. Repeatedly he whickered.

There was no answer.

The flies in the corral droned on. The noon shade crept out from the east wall of the box stall. Its shadow lengthened, and lengthened again. The crumpled body of the man did not move.

XXVI

He first heard the whistle of the stallion, wild and faint and far away. Then it was loud, close, insistent, the demanding shrill of a studhorse calling to mares. His eyes opened and he lay for a long minute, not knowing where he was. He got his left elbow under him, then the hand, pushing himself up, his mind clearing now. Red Boy was at the far end of the corral, arching his neck over the south top rail, whistling fiercely down the bench. Through the fence poles Frank saw the mares coming, cautiously at first, moving up through the junipers to the south, ears pricked, nostrils flaring in uncertain puzzlement. He recognized the lead mare first—Libby's favorite little dun, a red-bay weanling colt at her flank. Then, swiftly, the others—the roan, the three blacks, the chestnut with the nose snip, the steeldust with the white front stockings, the little gray—his mares. His and Libby's and Red Boy's—all that was left of them.

They came on now, beginning to remember the bay stud's call, whickering and grunting in eager answer to its imperious summons. Frank tried his arm then, and couldn't move it. Hunching himself up the stable wall, he tested the leg gingerly. It took the weight. Stiffly and with searing pain at first, but it took it. The blood had stopped, he saw, thick and fly-crusted on his thigh and chest. His strength grew a little as he rested against the wall.

Moving along it after a moment, he turned the jamb of the open half-door. He peered into the gloom of the box stall a long time, the twist of his wide mouth not pleasant to see. He did not go inside. There was no need.

He rested against the wall again. His glance moved across the corral, and across the grasslands of the bench beyond it. His eyes, pale-slitted now, traveled upward along the granite wall towering behind the bench. They rested on the gnarled juniper halfway up its sheer face.

"It's done now, Lib," he whispered. "And there's more than mud on his boots."

Breaking his glance from the juniper, he hobbled slowly across the corral. He was a full minute hoisting himself to the top rail of the fence. The stud watched him curiously but did not come to him. When he was ready, he called him softly.

"Coo-eee, boy. Red Boy. Easy, son, easy. . . ."

The big horse came up the fence, gentle and easy as a weanling filly, crested neck arching to the toss of the fine head. Frank let him come. When he was alongside, he knotted his good hand in the long mane, forced his injured leg out and across the sleek back. He sat him a full minute, closing his eyes and gritting his teeth against the pain and the weakness. His head cleared then, and he turned the big horse quickly away.

At the cañon's head, he slid off of the stud. The bay stallion followed him a few steps, then stopped, and looked back toward the mares that had trotted curiously behind them all the way. Presently Frank came back out of the rocks, leading the old brown gelding. He looked more like himself in the high boots and dirty black hat. Red Boy whickered gladly, trotted mincingly toward him.

Frank let him come up to him, then circled the proud neck with his uninjured arm. The stud nuzzled him, bunting eagerly at the arm. It was the game. Remember the game? It had been a long time but the stud was remembering it now. He bared his yellowed teeth, nipping playfully at the silent man. Frank cursed him softly, swallowed hard, tightened the circle of his arm around the arching neck. One of the mares, watching anxiously, whinnied and moved forward from the group. Another followed her, curious-eared. A third edged forward to join them.

Seeing them, Frank nodded. Quickly he unhooked the cinch buckle of Garth's saddle, gently slipped the cruel roller of the dead gunman's Spanish bit. He dumped both saddle and bridle among the nearby rocks, then hobbled back toward the stud. The tall bay stepped away, swinging his satin rump, sidling it playfully toward the approaching man.

"Hee-yahh!" Frank yelled suddenly, and swung the big black hat with the yell. Red Boy jumped away, eyeing him uncertainly, still not quite remembering that part of the game.

"Hee-yahh!" Frank yelled again. "Get outta here, you big red bastard!"

This time he threw the hat with the yell, and suddenly the bay stud remembered. Remembered and understood. It was the rest of it, the other part of the old game! The signal to run with the mares, free in the pasture, racing through the junipers!

He reared, lashing out with his forehoofs, whinnying in mock fury at the man. Then he was gone, galloping across the bench, herding and driving the squealing mares before him. He was free now and with his mares. And at long, long last, home again!

Frank watched him go.

He stood a long time, until the last mare had passed the ranch, until the whole herd was small with distance and lost, finally, in the sunset shadows of the wall beneath Libby's look-out.

"He was always your hoss, girl," he said at last. "Feed him good. . . ."

The rising wind whipped the muttered words away and across the lonely bench. The big rider turned to go. He came to the old bay, climbed stiffly aboard him. The piled rocks of Dry Cañon closed quickly behind them. Frank Rachel did not look back. Thus passed the last horseman from Apache Bench.

And, passing from the bench, he went down and through the cañon's gorge, to the nightfall gloom of the basin floor. And eastward across the floor, through the thickening shadows toward Cherry Creek. And beyond the creek, south-turning at last, toward Jim's cabin and Mulvehey's waiting men.

The big rider's thoughts were his own. They were not turning on horsemen. He would not have known the last horseman from the first. Nor the second from the third. He had never heard of the Four Horsemen. And had he done so, he could not have known that he was one of them—and the last one of them.

Old Jim Stanton, though—he could have told him. From the

moment of his first uneasy look into those pale, lion-still eyes. Even then he could have told him. For Peaceful Basin, and for all of those so long since and silently departed from it, Frank Rachel *was* the Fourth Horseman. . . .

He passed John's cabin, hunching his shoulders to the building chill of the night wind. The empty windows stared at him, black and lifeless. The wind whimpered keeningly around the sag of the open, swinging door, whirled across the deserted dust flats of the corral, drummed along the rusted iron belly of the empty water tank, fled away to die, thinly lisping, in the pines.

Frank shivered, feeling sick again now. Feeling the cold flow of the weakness and the pain. Knowing one moment the rage and ache of the fever. And the next, the shake and sweat of the chills.

He rode on, hurrying the old horse. The lamplight, once, in those other years so warm and dear, fell wan and foreign now from the cabin windows ahead of him. The oaks stood black and gaunt against the lesser darkness of the night, their broad trunks backing the uncertain shadows of the many saddled ponies standing in the yard.

The plank door opened and he recognized the thin ramrod of the silhouette—Mulvehey. He stopped the tired bay, letting him stand facing the converging shadows of the dismounted posse men. He heard Mulvehey's low command—"Hold up, boys."— and then his soft query: "Rachel?"

"One name's as good as another. . . ." His own voice sounded strange to him. Strange and far away. Like it wasn't he it was coming out of.

Mulvehey was standing by the bay horse then, peering up at him, his deep voice softening as his eyes narrowed. "You all right, Frank? We thought you wasn't comin' in. We was just about to ride without you."

Frank swayed, caught at the horn. Straightening in the saddle, he fought back the blackness and the cold that roared in his ears now.

"We made a deal," he said. "I'm here."

Mulvehey caught him as he fell.

★ ★ ★ ★ ★

Santa Fé Passage

★ ★ ★ ★ ★

I

Coming slowly out of the main current to nose gingerly among the clot of mongrel craft tied up along the levee, the trim packet flashed her stern paddles disdainfully. Choose as she might, she could do no better than a narrow berth between a pig-stinking Ohio hog barge and a broad-beamed old slut of a Natchez cotton steamer. Accordingly the *Prairie Belle* backed haughtily, chuffed an irritated cloud of blue wood smoke from her twin stacks, and prepared to slide daintily in through the opening.

Leaning on the rail of her Texas deck, just forward of the glassed-in holiness of the pilot's house, Kirby Randolph thought he knew how the *Belle* felt. And looking past the swarming levee at the sprawling huddle of log hostelries, canvas saloons, and clay huts that was St. Louis in 1839, the mountain man allowed he shared her feelings. *Town's sure enough a sinful ugly old devil,* he mused, turning from the rail. *Funny how a feller cain't hardly wait to get his arms around her.*

Going below, he threaded his way through the welter of material and humanity littering the boiler deck. He stepped past shaggy bales of buffalo robes, neat bundles of beaver skins, ragged cords of dried buffalo beef, and immense rolls of Indian-tanned doeskins. Prowling what free deck space remained, the chaperons of this polyglot lading matched their merchandise in outlandish character. Forcing his way through the sweating crowd, Kirby wondered if the *Belle* hadn't made a mistake. Perhaps she should have gone gallantly to the bottom somewhere up around the mouth of the Cannonball, taking the whole smelly crew with her.

A quick look at the Ohio pig boat coming alongside convinced him that, for all her elegant airs, the *Prairie Belle* was trafficking in the same trade. The only difference was that the pigs on this boat had two legs. Otherwise there was the same amount of squealing and milling around.

"Plank's down!" the cry of the rope man in the bow of the *Prairie Belle* announced her tie-up, interrupting the mountain man's thoughts. He let himself be carried along the deck and down the plank in the rush of the men to be off the boat.

He swung up Walnut Street to the Square, walking with the loose, bent-kneed stride that stamped his breed wherever it might go. From the shoulder-length black hair, unwashed since the summer before, to the beaded toes of the Arapaho hunting moccasins, he was the picture of the professional frontiersman: dirty, wild-haired, hard-eyed, lean, long-muscled, deceptively slow in motion.

Going around the Square toward Carondelet, the old town called Vide Poche after the traditionally empty pockets of its French inhabitants, he marveled at the way the town had boomed. It struck him that now there were more than twenty thousand people camping in St. Louis the year around. Anywhere a man might want to look there were people. And the noise of them! They were making more racket than a flock of magpies ripping the boudins out of a live buffalo. The young trapper was glad to get off the main street and into the quiet of the old town.

Vide Poche hadn't changed much. Kirby felt more at home the minute he passed into its narrow, spicy thoroughfares. His reaching stride increased as he came into the familiar, crooked lane of the Ruelle des Femmes.

He was nearly there now and he kept his head down, not

wanting to look before he was actually to it. And then, at last, there it was before him, the door and number so well remembered. Twenty-six Ruelle des Femmes, haunter of a hundred dreams on lonely beds of snow and mud and sweet prairie grass. Twenty-six Ruelle des Femmes, beacon over uncounted waves of restless plain, guide sign through unnumbered mountain passes, a whispered memory in the close caresses of forgotten teepee darknesses. Would Nella remember him? Would she be glad he had remembered her?

There it was below the number, her name—*Mlle. Nella Tourneau.* His hand closed on the bell cord and the sudden jangle of the bell seemed to signal a halt in the noisy life of the street.

Within the house there was no answering sound and Kirby, conscious of the growing silence around him, began to wonder if his long, downriver dreams were to prove formless, then he heard the sudden, sharp *click* of the latch. He was looking away when the throaty whisper came, sweeping away the whole street scene as cleanly as a thrusting river would undercut and cave a sandbank.

"Kirby! Oh, Kirby . . . !"

He stood a delicious moment, his broad back to her, feeling the low words fall over his shoulder like soft arms. Then he turned, letting his head settle forward and his eyes go to drinking of her like a tall horse that had been long without water.

"Hello, Nella. By damn, ye look good to this son." Kirby didn't know he had spoken; the words just came out of him while his eyes kept drinking.

"Come in, Kirby." Low, that voice, like spring water over moss rocks. "Come on in, honey."

She stood aside and he went in, still not knowing he moved, his eyes never leaving her. As he brushed past her, the warmth of her came to him clean through his buckskins, as though he were naked. He came around, turning, bent-kneed, his nostrils all at once full of the heated, fresh-bathed smell of her. Their eyes caught and held, hers sloe-dark with longing, his frost-gray with long suppressed hunger. He had her then, she as full of longing as he, yet pushing back the way a woman will. Their bodies surged against the heavy door, the panels giving and swinging closed as the thick latch dropped, chocking shut.

"Kirby, Kirby! Not here, boy. Not here. . . ."

II

Kirby lay back in the hot tub, luxuriating in the feel of the steaming water against his body. By cripes, this was something. Though his shanks might be doubled up to get in down at the bottom of the thing and his spreading shoulders a mite cramped against its head, a man knew fully well there weren't many tubs like this in St. Louis' corner of the world. Cussed thing must be five feet long and tarred-in so slick that it wouldn't leak a pint in twenty minutes! By cripes, Nella had for sure come up in the world.

Half an hour later, lying naked on Nella's bed, the spring sun sneaking in through the lace curtains to go all over his body like warm oil, Kirby let his thoughts drift to what had brought him downriver from the beaver camps. And now that he was back and had seen Nella, he was worried.

For a long spell he had thought he'd been off-centered by wanting to see her, but now he knew it wasn't Nella who had taken him away from the sets. He had quit and come down the river to find himself a good woman. That's what old Sam Beekman, his upriver trapping partner, had told him in the first place. And old Sam was smart. Like an aged buck beaver with his trap foot chewed off. Get married up to a decent woman of his own color and have some young ones, that's what Sam had said. Make a pile of plunder, find the right girl. . . . But where was a man to begin when he set about searching out a *good* woman? And how would he know her when he saw her? It was enough to sweat a man. Especially one crowding twenty-six.

When Nella Tourneau came into the room, Kirby was asleep. She stood a long time looking with eyes that were far away at the man who was so nearby. What the octoroon girl saw was not the long, flat-bellied body of him. Not the clean jaw, or hawk-fierce nose, or Indian-high cheek bones. Not even the thick, jet hair with its blazing-strange forestreak of grown-in silver where the Absorokas had scalp-marked him four springs back. These things others would see in Kirby Randolph. Nella Tourneau saw something different.

Somehow Kirby had always been different. When she had first seen him, an awkward, shy boy out from the Virginia settlements, he had been that way. But even then, at eighteen, wild and long-haired as a broomtail colt, he had been quiet and wise. Quiet in the right way, too. Sometimes a man was quiet because he was mean. Sometimes because he was in trouble. Sometimes because he was afraid. Or ignorant. Or just dead serious. But other times a man was quiet because he was smart. Smart to learn everything he could and afraid he might miss something while listening to himself. That kind of a quiet one kept his voice down and his mouth loose, could grin or snarl fast as light, either way. That kind of a quiet one had a weather eye: warm when the wind blew right and the words were light, cold as a block of river ice when the chips were down and all hands frozen to the blanket. That kind of a quiet one had worn his eye corners crowfooted from squinting into sun and snow all his life—and from grinning more than he growled when the river didn't wash his way. This boy, Kirby, was that kind of a quiet one.

Kirby went out of the Ruelle feeling as empty as any pocket in Vide Poche. For him Carondelet couldn't get behind quickly enough. Well, one thing, sure, he wouldn't be needing a woman for a spell. No, sir, by damn, not for a considerable spell. But as the mountain man thought about his problems, the Fates were busy making his decisions for him. Shambling along under the flaring torchlights of the Square, head down and scowling, Kirby failed to see the flashy brougham until it was on top of him. The shoulder of the off-wheel horse clipped him in the backside, sent his lank body sprawling gutterward.

Kirby lay quietly in the mud, speculating on his immediate past and direct future. What in tarnal hell was six feet of grown mountain man to do about getting his behind knocked into a muddy Missouri gutter by five feet of red-haired girl? Of course, a man couldn't be too sure about the girl from just one gutter-flying look, but if she wasn't a willow stick of a filly about sixteen, with a bright chestnut forelock and teeth that flashed cleaner than fresh snow, he'd eat his buckskins.

He eased his gutter companion, a very much *rigor*ed and *mortis*ed alley cat, away from his dripping chin, and reared up on one elbow. Best forget the whole thing likely. After all, the mud wasn't any more stinking than plenty he'd slept whole nights in up on the plains, and probably the girl hadn't swung the team into him on purpose at all. A man was always too quick to make out that accidents were insults.

The almost Christian philosophy was shortly dispelled by one Ephraim Beckwith, torch-post-lounging eyewitness to the accident, an old mountain crony of Kirby's. "She done it a-purpose if thet's whut ye're ponderin', Kirby boy," the older man said, nodding. "I stood right hyar and seen her steer them bays squar into ye."

"The hell," growled the young mountain man, parting slow and painful company with the fluid soil of old Missouri. "Did ye mark who it was?"

"I allow I did," the old man observed dryly. "As would

anybody whut hadn't spent his last three years squeezin' caster outen beaver sacs. Thet kid's the one thet's supposed to be old Marcelin Saint Vrain's niece."

"Whut ye mean, *supposed* to be?" demanded Kirby suspiciously.

"Jest that. Boys over to fur headquarters at the Rocky Mountain House say she's really his daughter, sired outen some red squaw out thar to Fort Saint Vrain in the territory. Ye realize them's the Saint Vrains as makes up half of the top-dog Santy Fé tradin' outfit of Bent and Saint Vrain."

Kirby whistled under his breath. "Wal, old salt, appears I've stepped myse'f into mighty fast company."

"Faster'n, ye know, likely," the old trapper said, grinning. "The boys say this gal's a real fuzztail. Wilder than a greenbroke colt. Old Marcelin had her brung into Saint Louis from out thar to the fort so's he could put her in a convent and cool her off somewhut. From whut I hear, it ain't worked. I allow all them half-breeds are alike, jest crazy wild underneath. It's the red blood does it."

"Wal, I aim to find fer myse'f whet color she is, old hoss." The tall youngster was grinning again now, his weather eye warming to its memory of the girl's flashing looks. "White or half-white, I owe thet chit somethin', and happens right now is as good a time as any to give it to her."

The eight-foot split-log stockade around the St. Vrain mansion gave Kirby a pause—a pause long enough for him to ease up to it, pull himself to the top, and swing-vault to the opposite side. He hadn't more than landed when he saw the lantern flash down by the carriage gate and heard the *crunch* of wheels on the gravel drive. He went into cover like a coyote running the length of the tree-lined drive ahead of the approaching horses. Inside the carriage house, he stepped behind a parked landau, pressed back into the shadows, and waited noiselessly. The beam of the brougham lamps, entering the building, flicked across him to light up a face-splitting grin.

The girl brought up the bays, wrapped the lines expertly, stepped down off the driving box and out into the lamplight almost before Kirby's grin died away. There were still traces of it lifting the corners of his mouth when he stepped up behind her.

" 'Evenin', ma'am," he murmured, his left arm sliding around her neck with the greeting. The girl's gasp was cut off in its infancy as the crotch of the lean arm tightened on her throat. At the same time a rough buckskin gag whipped across her mouth and cinched down on her struggling tongue. Finding a convenient bundle of hay, the mountain man set dutifully about what he had come to do—turning the spoiled St. Vrain brat over his bony knee and whaling the tar out of her.

Applying his outsize hand to the bobbing target beneath it, Kirby's pleasures were not entirely derived from objective feelings of poetic justice. By cripes, that little nubbin bottom of hers wasn't so little and nubbiny, after all. And it wasn't just her bottom that missed being puny, either. The mountain man felt another pair of firm bobbles where her squirming front lay across his knee. Still, the trapper didn't let his gift for quick physical assay alleviate the force of his primary object. She strained and twisted in his grasp, perfect slim fury, but the hand that could neck-down an eight-hundred-pound Indian pony wasn't too tired. What terminated the spanking was the coming bob of a lantern from down the drive.

Of course! The Negro who had let her in down at the gate would be coming along to the carriage house to see to the horses. He'd have to let up on her, or else he wouldn't have time to give her a good look at him before he had to make his tracks. Easing up off the hay bundle, he straightened, spinning the girl around to face him.

"Take a good look, honey," he said, his voice purring through his wide grin, "so's next time ye run over this son ye'll know him!" As the words got out of him, Kirby began to see what she was looking at. The grin fell open and became a gape.

The girl's eyes flared at him, green as a trapped she-wolf's, her nostrils spread thin and wide, whistling with the breath in them. Her hair, becoming red in the smoky lamplight, spilled, thick and wild, to her shoulders, a heavy forelock of it shadowing the dark face and high-flushed cheeks. From the corner of the wide, full-lipped mouth, a thin trickle of blood showed bright under the twisted gag.

"Lord Almighty, ma'am . . . !" The mountain man breathed the phrase, his own gray eyes fired with the beauty of her, and the movement of his belt knife flicking up to sever the cruel buckskin was no quicker than the one that followed. His arm went behind the girl's head, his body stepping into hers before she could move. The next instant his lips, more cruel than any gag, were driven into her bleeding mouth. Kirby tasted the fire of that kiss long after the blood of it had ceased to salt his lips.

The girl shot him low down in the left side, the little pistol ball plowing up and across the last four ribs. He hadn't felt her pull the gun, had no idea where she had found it. He just knew that he felt it ease into his belly, and that his wild twist, sideways, timed with the hammer fall, was pure reflex. Reflex, too, was the snake-fast strike his left hand made for her right wrist. But the backhand slash of his right hand across her face was deliberate. The blow set her back across the piled hay, limp as a broken doll, leaving Kirby towering over her, the silver-mounted pistol smoking in his left hand, his face black with the distortion of pain and anger.

"Ye half-breed vixen!" The snarl came out of him twice as bitter for its choking softness. Her eyes were open, staring up at him blankly. He saw them widen before he heard her strange warning cry: *"A-ah!"* The sound sprang from her with startling force. Kirby, struck by its foreign sound in that time and place, nevertheless responded to its message without question or delay.

A-ah! It was the Dakota Sioux warning word. *A-ah!* Beware! Sudden danger! Look out! As the mountain man spun around, he snapped his long body over into a doubled-up crouch. The dull flash of the thrown knife hissed past his bent shoulder.

The figure following the knife was the tallest redskin the trapper had ever seen. Dressed in the plain shirt and leggings of a Sioux hunter, the Indian loomed over Kirby like a mountain over a foothill. And Kirby stood six three with nothing between him and the bare ground but the thickness of an elk-hide moccasin sole.

The white man hung in his crouch until the giant Indian was right above him, then drove his right fist up into the snarling red face, snapping his body straight up behind the blow. It was a lucky shot, taking the Indian's chin flushly, dropping the reaching figure to its knees.

Ducking around the dazed Indian, Kirby looked for the girl. *"Ha-ho,"* he said in Sioux, "Thank you." Then quickly: *"Niye osni tana leci?* How many winters are you here? How old are you?"

"Wicsemna sokawin," she responded, wide-eyed and unmoving. "Seventeen."

"Woyuanihan!" Kirby bowed toward her, touching his left fingertips to his forehead. "I respect you!"

With that he was gone, racing down the graded drive, his tall figure fading, quick and light as a shadow. Behind him lanterns were already blooming around the main house and excited voices called back and forth across the darkness. In the carriage house Aurelie St. Vrain remained motionless across the piled hay, her slant green eyes staring after the departed mountain man long after his lithe-swinging form had melted into the black of the driveway trees.

Going over the St. Vrain stockade, Kirby grinned. For some reason he felt better than he had in four years. He had done a mile before he remembered the wild-eyed girl had shot him with the little pistol, and he recalled it then only because he suddenly realized he still had the fancy little gun in his left hand. The young trapper threw back his head and sucked in a big lungful of the balmy night air. The war whoop that came with the air when he spat it back out would have curled the hair on a wooden Indian. But the hard-bitten citizens of Mudville by the Mississippi didn't miss a snore. Drunk or crazy or up to their armpits in love, mountain men were no novelty in St. Louis.

When Kirby reached the Rocky Mountain House, after a pause at a handy horse trough to sponge off his wound, he found that bad news was still a high-stepping traveler. His bearded and buckskinned cronies knew all he did about the ruckus at the St. Vrain place—and then some!

First off, the giant Indian he had clobbered turned out to be not a buck at all, but an immense Sioux squaw called Ptewaquin, The Packing Buffalo, who was the St. Vrain girl's nurse, watchdog, and armed guard rolled into one. Secondly, Old Marcelin St. Vrain was red-hot as a rutting elk, swearing by God and by Joseph that no louse-head mountain man was going to get by with assaulting his little niece and knocking her Indian maid's jawbone slanchwise. He was preparing a warrant for Kirby's immediate arrest. Thirdly, Old Marcelin had heard about the girl's knocking some innocent foot walker into the gutter up on Courthouse Square and was allowing he'd had his belly full of her shenanigans, too. So he was packing her up and shipping her down to his brother's folks in Santa Fé, somewhat sooner than instanter—namely, tomorrow morning, on the *Prai-*

rie Belle, bound for Westport Landing and the head of the Santa Fé Trail.

"Whut's the gal say to thet?" was Kirby's first question to his chief informant, Ephraim Beckwith. The oldster watched him slyly as he answered.

"Why, she's all fer it, boy. Says Saint Louie is dead and jest ain't covered up yet. Claims she ain't see'd but one proper man since she left Fort Saint Vrain, and thet was the mountain son thet tanned her bottom."

Kirby felt the thrill of the old man's words, and his next question lifted cheerfully in response to them. "Whut ye allow I should do now, Eph?"

"Put yer plunder aboard a quick-bought horse and skeedaddle."

"Happens ye're right," said Kirby, nodding soberly. "Say, Eph"—trying here to sound nonchalant, and naturally failing—"most of them trains takin' out fer Santy Fee nowadays are takin' up in Westport, ain't they?"

"I reckon the gal will start from that," said the old trapper acidly. "Mebbe ye kin wave her farewell as her wagon goes past Injun Crick. Thet is, happen Old Marcelin don't ketch ye, meantime."

"How fur is Santy Fee, Eph? From Westport?"

"Oh, seven, eight hundred mile. Why fer? Ye ain't thinkin' of goin', are ye?"

"Naw. Jest thet I ain't never bin thar."

"It's a hell of a place," said the old mountain man with a grimace.

"Allus figgered I'd like to see it."

"Yep." Ephraim Beckwith nodded knowingly. "I calculate thet 'allus' of yers took a holt of ye rather sudden. Like mebbeso about five minutes ago!"

III

Kirby, figuring he had plenty of it, took an easy week's time riding down to Westport. Once on the wagon grounds west of town he found out the errors in his frontier arithmetic. The St. Vrain girl had arrived just in time to miss the last train Bent and St. Vrain were putting down the spring trail. But the train's wagon captain, a young Spaniard named Armijo who was rumored to be a nephew of the governor of Santa Fé, had ridden back to Westport from Council Grove to look for a wagon scout to replace one who had just come out second-best in a knife fight. He hadn't found his scout, but he had picked up the St. Vrain girl and her bear-size Sioux squaw and ridden back to Council Grove with them in tow. And, though a man could easily be wrong about such things, from the looks of the way the slick-handsome Spaniard son and St. Vrain's top-cream half-breed girl were grinning and chinning when they rode out through the wagon camp, they appeared to be considerably better met than just old friends.

Kirby's source of information, a grizzled Missouri muleskinner, was quick enough to give the young mountain man the only other piece of intelligence he required. "Fust camp's Round Grove, young 'un. Twenty-five miles due west. All ye got to do is stay in the wagon ruts, boy, and don't let the Kaws take yer pony away."

The first leg of the Santa Fé Trail was the hundred and forty-five miles to Council Grove, and Kirby pounded Old Brown every mile of it. He had himself a girl to catch and the trail between him and that green-eyed objective wasn't of much importance. He made three sleeps, the first at Wakarusa Point, the second at Hundred-and-Ten-Mile Creek, and the third at Big John Spring. Of this first part of his projected trip to New Mexico, the young mountain man made dubious summation: *Kansas Territory has the muddiest mud and the dirtiest Indians* ever. Further summation: the Kaws could have it.

But Council Grove was something else! The morning he left Big John Spring came up as blue as a snow-water lake, and twice as clear. He had only a short two-mile trot to Council Grove, and, when he topped the last rise, he saw he had to pull up Old Brown and give himself a long look. Council Grove proper was better than a quarter section in size, and, if ever a man saw more fine old hardwood trees, he would have a time remembering where. It didn't take a wagon boss to figure why Council Grove was the main outfitting place for the traffic down the South Road. Why, in that stand of timber a good hand with an axe could cut himself all the spare tongues, axle trees, wheel spokes, and oxbows he would be apt to need for six trips to Santa Fé. The Bent and St. Vrain wagons were spanned out in a neat square, tongues out, on the west fringe of Council Grove. As the young trapper rode in, he made passing note of several things: the wagon mules were tight-bunched not far off, the Conestogas were loaded and lashed, a meeting of the train crew was in progress about the main campfire, and *not a woman was in sight, anywhere.*

As Kirby came up to the group by the fire, the men, after the manner of old prairie hands on the approach of a stranger, held up their talk, waiting, hard-eyed, for him to make his play. Even before he spoke, his ranging eye picked out the lean figure on the far side of the fire and he knew he had met his man before he opened his mouth to ask for him.

"Howdy. I'm lookin' fer Bent and Saint Vrain's wagon boss."

"Yuh're lookin' at him, mistuh. Whut do yuh want of Laredo Parkuh?" There was no return of the "howdy" in the smooth Texas drawl, no invitation to get down.

"Wal, Laredo, I heered Mister Armijo was lookin' fer a wagon scout." Kirby kept his words carefully respectful. He had heard in Westport that this Laredo Parker was all he-coon, and he allowed quickly that he had heard right.

"What's that got to do with yuh-all, mistuh?"

"I'm allowin' I'll scout fer ye," said Kirby, letting his voice harden as his eye ran around the circle of listening muleskinners, "unless thar's a better man fer the job."

Laredo Parker laughed. It was a soft laugh, like his voice. "Hell's fire, mistuh. Yuh-all couldn't scout foh me if all I had was two Dearborns and a buckboard."

"Happens I don't agree with ye," said Kirby evenly.

"Now haul yore freight, mistuh." The swart Texan was on his feet, his narrow black eyes sizing the gaunt mountain man. "We got. . . ."

"Hold on, Mister Parker. What is the difficulty?" None of the men had noticed the speaker's arrival. Turning in his saddle, Kirby saw the tall, elegantly attired young Spaniard lounging gracefully against the nearest wagon wheel. He didn't need Laredo's greeting to let him know this was *Don* Pedro Armijo.

"Oh, howdy, Mistah Armijo. This ovuhgrowed son was allowin' he was goin' to scout foh yuh and I was allowin' he wasn't."

"My name is Armijo." The Spaniard addressed Kirby, ignoring Laredo, a dark flash of a smile breaking across his face quick as summer lightning. "Do I understand you are looking for a job?"

"Mine's Randolph," Kirby answered. "And I *was* lookin' fer a job. But. . . ."

"You're a mountain man, aren't you, Mister Randolph?" The Spaniard's interruption was quick, for all its satiny ease.

Kirby looked at the young *don* with new interest. "Somewhut. Why?"

"Have you ever been down the trail?"

For a Spaniard, Kirby thought, this young cockerel spoke mighty smart English. He looked at a man straight, too. It might do to hear what he had to say. "Nope. Way I see it, a trail's a trail. I bin known to foller one when the light's just so."

Young Armijo nodded, his voice still soft and pleasant. "Well, Mister Randolph, I like your attitude. We'll get along."

"And jest wheah does that leave us, Mistah Armijo?" Laredo's break-in was brittle as scum ice around a water hole.

"With a new wagon scout, Mister Parker." The Spaniard straightened, chopping his instructions like a man who had given plenty of them. "Sign Mister Randolph on and count him in on your elections. We're late now, Mister Parker. I want to see wagon dust in thirty minutes."

IV

In Armijo's half hour Kirby got his head full of the way a hard man ran a hard business. Laredo wasted no time showing him.

"This heah's a company train, twenty wagons, all ten-mule-hooked," the Texan began, his slow voice loud in the silence that fell as he spoke. "I aim to roll it thataway. Most of yuh have drove foh me befoh, and them as hasn't can speak out if they heah somethin' they don't cotton to. Pay is thirty-three dolluhs a month and found, foh 'skinnuhs. Found is fifty pounds flour, fifty bacon, ten coffee, twenty sugah. Any questions?"

A wiry little Mexican who Kirby subsequently learned was Popo Dominguez, the mule-herd wrangler, smiled deprecatingly, his patient voice barely audible. *"Pues, señor,* we are told *Don* Pedro has along the *Señorita* Saint Vrain. A woman like that on the trail, *señor.* . . ." The little wrangler ended the statement with an eloquent flourish of upraised palms.

Kirby straightened his back along with his hearing, listening with his heart as well as his ears. Aurelie, by damn! He had it worse than he'd thought.

"That's right, Popo, *Señorita* Saint Vrain." The wagon boss' voice dumped some of its usual purr. Apparently even Laredo

Parker liked the smiling Latin. "What's yuh got in mind, *hombre?*"

"*Pues*, who am I to say?" Popo shrugged apologetically. "But if the Indians come to hear of it. *¡Madre!* What a ransom, *señor!*"

"Now, who'n hell put yuh in mind that the red buzzards would try foh the gal?" Nobody met Laredo's black-eyed challenge, and the wagon boss finished off abruptly. "Seattuh out and ketch up. And see that yuh jump it. Yonduh comes Armijo now."

Turning with Laredo's back-handed thumb wave, Kirby didn't see the half dozen coffee-hued *arrieros* who were urging along the *don's* personal pack train. He didn't see *Don* Pedro Armijo, jauntily cantering his sleek black stud ahead of them, or the towering form of the Sioux giantess, Ptewaquin, stick straight on her plodding mule. All he could see was the figure sitting the flashy bay-and-white pinto filly at the black horse's side. And the figure sitting that filly, red-gold hair flying freely in the morning sunshine, green eyes and white teeth flashing brilliantly in the dusky face, hard young figure tight in a near-white set of fringed Cheyenne buckskins, was Aurelie St. Vrain!

V

Riding up the line of westward-rumbling Conestogas, Bent and St. Vrain's new scout sought out the wagon boss. "Wheah the hell yuh-all bin?" Laredo greeted him. "Yuh're supposed to be leadin' this train, not pushin' it."

"Thet's whut I'm aimin' to ask ye," answered Kirby. "Jest whut am I supposed to be doin'? This trail's as broad as a buffalo's bottom and jest as easy to see."

"All right, now listen." Laredo's voice went flat. "Scoutin' this trail don't mean a thing till we hit along about Cottonwood Creek crossin'. That's five days on. Once we hit Cottonwood, we pick up Pawnees."

"These hyar Pawnees bad Injuns?" Kirby spoke to the wagon boss as one professional frontiersman to another.

"Yeah. They ain't rightly killers like the Kioways and Comanches, but they'll gut yuh quick enough if they figger it's needed to get what they're aftuh. And what they're always aftuh is yore hoss and mule stock."

"Happens thar might be trouble at Cottonwood crossin', then?"

"I always figger so."

"What ye want I should do?"

"Ride ahead. Scout out the track up to Cottonwood and twenty-five miles beyond. If yuh spot any sign, drift back *pronto*. Otherwise camp in at Cottonwood and we'll pick yuh up theah."

"I got ye," Kirby said, glad to be going on, keeping clear of Aurelie and Ptewaquin. "Reckon I'll drift."

"See that yuh don't drift too far," grunted the Texan. "Me. I got it in mind that all yuh no'thun trappuhs is more or less skin lovers." The wagon boss paused, narrow black stare drilling Kirby, his final words dropping softly into the chert-hard silence. "And I ain't meanin' *white* skin, neithuh, mistuh. . . ."

That day Kirby rode through a country as desolate as the far side of the moon. There wasn't a tree big enough for a short dog to bother stopping at between him and the endless sweep of the southwestern horizon. One after another, he rode into and passed the famous wagon campgrounds: Diamond Spring, Mud Creek, and Lost Spring. Along the whole, too-quiet way, he didn't see one solitary unshod pony track. About 4:00 p.m. he came to Cottonwood Creek, which crawled in out of the prairie to snake across the trail, and found the same story—no Indian sign fresher than a long ten days. The place was lonelier than a curlew talking the sun down back of the Big Horns, making even Old Brown nervous, and Kirby, beginning to be disturbed by the continued quiet, quickly rode on.

Sundown caught him five miles short of Turkey Creek, and in a country so flat and short-grassed that a man and a horse stuck out on it worse than a tumblebug crossing a cow pie. His instincts, whittled war-axe sharp by seven years of keeping his hair on straight among the Dakota Sioux, were beginning to tighten Kirby's spine now, and on a sudden hunch he swung Old Brown toward a slight rise in the prairie to his left. Leaving the gelding in the shallow depression behind the rise, the mountain man topped the little undulation, belly-flopping from sheer force of habit.

When he poked his head over, peering squint-eyed into the setting sun, he had reason to be well content with that particular habit. Two miles out, straight across the prairie, heading in toward the trail, black as dominoes against the dust-red sun, came a single file of mounted warriors. There were upward of a hundred, Kirby figured, coming at an easy shuffle-walk—with not a squaw or a travois in sight.

This was a war party.

VI

Four days later, nerve-edgy with its new scout's Pawnee report, the train pulled into Cottonwood Creek. Hunkered over the coals of Laredo's cook fire, Kirby and the wagon boss discussed their trade's finer points, the Texan's easy drawl leading the forum.

"Allowin' yuh was a Pawnee, Randolph, and was layin' out theah in the dark figgerin' how to run off our stock without a shootin' scrape, how would yuh aim to do it?"

Kirby sucked his pipe, thinking of the lay of the camp and the country around it. Finally he spoke: "I'd figger thet the new grass was almighty short and thet last winter's hay, still standin' all around us hyar, was almighty thick and close together. And plumb dry."

"How would yuh figger the breeze?" Laredo eyed his new scout carefully, his early, short opinion of him beginning to stretch a little with respect.

"About right," said the mountain man. "She's a south wind blowin' right into us, and tolerable fresh."

"Uhn-huh. Now, if yuh was a Pawnee and countin' on havin' yorese'f a mule roast, wheah would yuh strike yore flint?"

"About a mile down south thar. Ye figger they'll try it, Laredo?"

"Mebbeso a little closuh than a mile," said the wagon boss, ignoring Kirby's closing question. "So's not to give us time to get anything back acrost the crick."

"Ye figger they will?" Kirby repeated the question, pinning the Texan down.

"Comes about two in the mornin' and yuh see them cloud bellies down south, theah, glowin' sore-red as a blistered heel"— the lean wagon boss eased back in his blankets, yawning—"and yuh wake up with yore nostrile snotted-up with grass smoke, yuh'll have yore answer."

After an hour Kirby gave up trying sleep and drifted out to the grazing mule herd. *"¿Quién es?"* The sibilant Spanish hissed at him out of the darkness.

"It's all right, *hombre*," Kirby called back. "It's me. Randolph. The scout."

"Dispenseme usted, señor." Kirby recognized Popo's voice now. "One gets nervous. You will understand, *señor*. With the wind just so, and the grass so tall. . . ."

"Nervous is the word," said Kirby, grinning. "Tell me, *anciano*, have ye heered anything?"

"Nada, señor, nothing. It is too quiet."

Kirby nodded shortly. "Listen, Popo. I want ye to drift the

herd around the other side of the wagon corral, close to the spot whar Laredo left thet one Conestogie out of place. *¿Sabe?*"

"*Sí, señor.*"

"Good. Now. First sign of a flicker down south, thar, ye drive them jacks through thet open space and into the corral. I don't give a hoot if ye trample every one of them *gringo* 'skinners into their blankets. *¿Comprende?*"

"*Sí. Hasta la vista, señor.*"

"*Vaya con Dios,*" responded Kirby, hoping he and his halting Spanish had said the right thing.

"*Mil gracias, patrón,*" the soft answer floated back, letting him know he had.

For hours only the ordinary sounds came in off the prairie. Then, with the slice-thin moon dipping back down under the earth, it started. A mile out east of the wagons, a coyote yipped dolorously. Its mate caught up the lament well down to the south. Over westward, a rival joined the chorus. Too perfect, those cries. Too close together. Too well timed. Kirby, lying atop a low hummock a hundred yards out from camp, leaped to his feet and went for the wagons as fast as he could leg it. "*¡Hacerlo! ¡Hacerlo!* Put them in. Popo! Put them in!" The mules were already moving behind him, frantically hazed by Popo's yelling Mexican herders, as Kirby got into the wagon corral, his voice bellowing the alarm: "Roll out! Roll out! The red sons have fired the grass! On yer feet!"

So far the mountain man had not looked behind him to see if he was right or not. He had come to lean so strongly on his ability to *feel* Indians that it never occurred to him he might miss a snap guess. And, in this case, he hadn't. Even as the startled muleskinners came stumbling and cursing to their feet, the night clouds, south, east, and west, had their bellies bouncing to the ugly glow of Laredo Parker's "sore-red as a blistered heel."

As the mules came bombarding into the corral, Laredo ran the square of prairie inside the boxed Conestogas, roaring his orders. "Back-fire, boys! Dammit, we got to back-fire! Get out theah past the wagons and start her goin'. And foh Gawd's sake don't let her start eatin' back on yuh!" The men were running for the grass beyond the wagons now, grabbing grain sacks and saddle blankets as they went. A few seized smoldering firewood brands from the banked campfires.

For twenty minutes every muleskinner in the train was on the fire line, the leaders plunging their flaming brands into the dry grass, the others beating with sacks and blankets at the fires that backlashed toward the wagons. By necessity, the work was carried forward among the growing flames of the back-fire. Hair, eyebrows, beards, and mustaches were charred off to the raw skin. On exposed hands and feet the skin itself blistered and shriveled in a matter of seconds. But in ten minutes a three-quarter circle of fire was growing steadily outward from the wagons. And, in less than fifteen, the rolling sheet of fire lit by the Pawnees flared across the mile of open prairie, its belching front roaring flames forty and fifty feet high. Quick as Laredo's men had been, their back-fire hit the oncoming blaze a scant seventy feet from the wagon corral. As the hideous glare of the coming holocaust bore down on the back-fire, Laredo shouted furiously: "Scatter back! Get back and get down before she hits! On yer bellies and hold yer wind!"

One firefighter, off to Kirby's right, hesitated, still flailing at a small back flame.

"Get back, ye infernal idjut!" Kirby's roar matched Laredo's. "Get on back!"

The fighter turned, confused, the rolling fore wall of smoke fronting the coming flames engulfing him even as Kirby yelled his warning. Throwing his blanket over his head, the scout dived into the black cloud. He got the still figure up on his shoulder, then stumbled and fell clear of the blind inferno with his last strength. Seconds after he had scooped up the unconscious form, the living flame of the Indian fire vomited in over the spot where the man had lain.

Kirby remembered staggering a dozen lurching steps, tripping and falling with his burden face forward into the hot ash of the back-fire, then the fumbling, hazy effort of pulling the sodden horse blanket over their uncovered heads, and that was all. After that, for a long time, there was just empty, pleasant blackness.

VII

Kirby awoke to a funereal dawn. Smoke, gray and greasy as an old blanket, lay in slow-drifting banks among the shrouded tops of the Conestogas. A fine fall of silver ash piled in sifting drifts against the wagon wheels and mounded the huddled forms of the men who lay where injury or exhaustion had dropped them. Through palled smoke and suspended ash, the morning sun filtered, sick and red as an abscess.

Kirby found Laredo and half a dozen muleskinners hunkered over a chip fire chewing cold fat back and gulping hot coffee. As he drifted up, the wagon boss looked at him and waved him to a seat. To the mountain man's surprise, the scowling Texan poured and handed him a tin of coffee. "Thanks, Laredo," Kirby said, finding that the words cost him a grimace of pain as they escaped from his cracked and blistered face. "I allow it won't injure me none."

Nobody answered him. They all sat staring into the smoke, or their coffee, or the smolder of the chips. They were like men hit by more than they could properly handle, Kirby thought.

"We got to move," said Laredo, talking to his coffee cup.

"I reckon." Kirby answered him only when it was clear the others weren't going to say anything. "How many able to drive?"

"Most. All but one. Young Clint Cooper got his fatal bad. Lung burn. He must've breathed just when the flame rolled over. We'll bury him befoh the day's out."

"How's the gal?" Kirby asked the question without thinking about it, and was shaken out of his lingering half shock by Laredo's short answer.

"Yuh're the one ought to know. Yuh drug her in."

The scout's gray eyes widened as Laredo's words got into his stumbling mind. "Ye mean to tell me thet leetle cuss I snaked outen the smoke was . . . ?"

"Miss Saint Vrain," grunted Laredo shortly, not giving him time to finish. "Who'd yuh think it was? *Don* Pedro?"

Kirby, not knowing what else to do with it, let it go. "Ye figger the Pawnees have gone on, Laredo?"

"Like as not."

"Like as not." The scout paused, the hoarse bray of a suffering mule breaking into his agreement. "Ye aimin' to roll now?"

"Yeah. Yuh're all right, ain't yuh? Yuh kin ride?"

"Sure. I was lucky. Though I allow I owe somebody fer draggin' me in last night. Who was it anyhow?"

"Wal, get ridin' then." Laredo ignored his question. "Mebbe them Pawnees is still hangin' around. Wagons'll be along in half an hour."

"All right, Laredo, but ye ain't answered me. Who drug me in last night?"

"I said get ridin'," growled the dark-faced Texan. "Everybody was gettin' drug in by somebody. It don't make no difference. Hit yore hoss, Randolph."

Kirby rode all that day and the next, the wagons following close up, in double rows of ten each, the loose herd of replacement mules stepping between the wheel tracks. There was no sign and no Indians.

At sundown of the first day they took Clint Cooper out of

the bed of the cook wagon. Laredo asked Kirby if he would read over the boy and the mountain man said: "Sure, Laredo, I'll say the words."

Shallow the grave was, and lonely as Kansas. The muleskinners stood, head-hung and wordless, the Mexican *arrieros* restless and muttering and crossing themselves continuously. Armijo stood by the gravehead, the girl and the giant squaw beside him. Across the darkening prairie the coyotes were beginning to yip, and somewhere off against the red ball of the sun a loafer wolf howled dismally.

"The Lord is my shepherd," said Kirby, "I shall not want. He leads me into green pastures and He makes me to lay down by still waters. The Lord He gives and the Lord He takes away. Clint was a man growed and the Lord He saw fit and tooken him away. Amen."

"Come on, Uncle Thorpe." Laredo's soft voice, strangely kind, broke the heavy stillness, going to Thorpe Springer, a gnarled Missouri teamster and uncle of the dead boy. "Lay offen yore holt of the blanket. We got to covuh him up now."

The rain began as they put the first wagon into Turkey Creek the following afternoon. By the time the last Conestoga was over, it had built into a steady downpour and the creek was running bank full. Men and mules had had enough. Laredo ordered a span-out and a rest camp set up. "We stay right heah," he announced, "till the stock is grazed back into shape and the lousy damn' rain lets up."

Kirby had been in some wet camps but never a one to touch the slop of that one at Turkey Creek. There wasn't a stick of wood within twenty miles, and what buffalo chips they were able to gather were so wet they had to be wrung out before they would even make smoke. The muleskinners had sheeted in their wagon wheels, tight and fast, and crawled under the bed to weather the blow.

Withal, slop or no slop, a guard was run, Kirby standing the first quarter, Uncle Thorpe taking the second. The younger man had no more than pinned the sheets of their Conestoga and skinned out of his wet buckskins after the oldster's departure, when the muleskinner was back, scratching for admission. "Hold on, Thorpe," Kirby said, laughing. "Keep yer old bottom puckered, ye won't be drowned!"

In a second he had the bone lacing needles pulled and the canvas flap held back. The figure that squeezed in out of the storm was a shade smaller and shapelier than old Thorpe. "It's some wet out, mister!" The white teeth flashed under the raindrops coursing the dusky skin. "Thanks for asking me in."

"Gosh, ma'am," Kirby stammered. "I didn't have no idea it was ye. I'm sorry I called out so rough."

"It wasn't rough enough to worry about, and besides . . ."— the voice, a low, throaty one, struck Kirby as being powder-soft, and the long green eyes would have looked smoky anywhere—"a man's got more than rough talk to be careful of in front of ladies."

Following her direct gaze, Kirby looked down at himself, gasped, clutched at the gaping blanket, scrambled for his hat, jammed it over his ears. "Well, now that you're dressed"—the quick candlelight of her smile lit her face again as she gestured to the crammed-on hat—"don't you ever ask visitors to take off their things and sit down?"

"*Uh*, sure. Yes, ma'am." Kirby's natural ease with women was swimming to the top of his first flood of embarrassment. The girl nodded, pinned the flap behind her, took off her hat to reveal the bright hair piled beneath it, slipped the dripping poncho off over her head, crawled over by the smoking whale-oil lamp, and set down across from him.

"Have you got another dry blanket, Mister Randolph? My

leggings are soaked through. And, just in case you haven't heard, my name is Aurelie Saint Vrain."

"Sure," said Kirby, taking a blanket from the pile on Thorpe's war chest. "Pleased to meet ye, ma'am. Anything else?"

"Turn your back and count ten," she told him, taking the blanket.

When he finished his count and turned to the girl again, his eyes widened. She had draped over the Conestoga's rear axle not only the leggings, but the fringed Cheyenne skirt as well. The blanket was wrapped carelessly around what had been covered by the leggings and the skirt. When she spoke, the dark rose of her cheeks dimpled in another curtsy to the curving smile beneath them. "I came over to thank you for saving my life in the fire, Mister Randolph."

"It wasn't nothin'." Kirby shrugged, easing back away front the light of the lamp as he noticed the girl beginning to look at him with a curious frown. "In a tight like thet, everybody works."

"Where have I seen you before?" asked the girl quickly, ignoring his answer. "You know the first time I saw you in Council Grove I thought I'd known you somewhere. Now I'm sure of it. Where was it?" She hesitated, then added: "I never forget a face. That's the Indian in me."

Kirby took note of the emphasis on the last phrase but was too interested in covering his identity to go to worrying afresh about the girl's pedigree. "It's a funny thing how people will get the idea they seen other people before, when they ain't," he said slowly.

"I've heard that voice before, too," said the girl, ignoring his answer again.

"Ma'am, ye'd best go. This ain't no place fer ye to be."

"My place in this train is any place I am. My father and uncle own these wagons."

"Wal, ma'am, *Don* Pedro then. He wouldn't. . . ."

153

"*Don* Pedro is nobody to me but a distant cousin. He hasn't any more to say about me than you have. And that's nothing, mister."

Kirby felt his back getting up. A man didn't take to having his haunches spurred like that by any kid of a girl. He must have been out of his mind to figure her a woman grown.

"Wal, that Injun Ox Woman then, dammit! I don't want to have to lambaste her again. . . ." He snapped his teeth down on the statement, but he was too late to more than cut off the tail of it.

"Let's have that hat off, mister!" The words came snapping with the hand that shot out and knocked the hat sailing. The guttering light of the lamp was not so bad but what the broad white lock through the scout's dark curls stood out clearly as a streak of silver across a cut-mine face.

The girl recovered first, rebellion starting with a flash in the green eyes, ending in a snarl of the snowy teeth. "If I had a gun, I'd shoot you again. I'd . . . I'd. . . ."

Kirby, for all his recovery was slower, made a better job of it. "Ma'am, I've got jest the thing fer ye. Bin totin' it along fer jest sech a celebration. Hyar . . . ketch!" The little pistol flashed dully as he tossed it toward her. Her hands caught the gun, then, fumbling, dropped it into the deep pile of the buffalo robe beneath her. She snatched it up, holding it on the man across the lamp. "If I could just be positive it was you!"

Watching her, Kirby's eyes narrowed, his breath surging. In catching the gun, the girl had twisted and partly opened the blanket around her. A bare leg, slim and graceful as a doe's, rose-pink as a prairie rambler, curved wickedly from beneath the rough cover. It glowed, satin-naked, to the point where swelling roundness of the thigh molded into the sculptured upturn of the soft belly curve.

He was over her then, brown-muscled shoulder bared as his

arm supported his crouching weight. "Ye shot me once when I kissed ye, ma'am." The arm came slowly behind her neck. "Let's see if ye'll do it again." The arm tightened, leaping and crushing inward like a sprung trap, the wide, hard mouth seeking and finding the soft, full one. He felt the fragrant heat of her as she came into him, felt its racing flame spread like fire beneath him, felt the steel go out of the arching back, the sudden pressure of the bared arm sliding behind his dark head tensing in blind spasm to return the fury of his kiss.

He didn't see the gun fall from the nerveless fingers or the fire burst of the green eyes as she tore her lips from his to bury her white teeth frantically in his cupping shoulder. As he recoiled from the sharp pain of the bite, the quick-hardened edges of his craggy features were smoothed by the flicking grin that preceded his slow drawl.

"Wal, anyhow, ma'am, ye didn't shoot me this time. Happens we're makin' a leetle progress, Miss Aurelie."

The girl didn't answer, cowering, arm-braced, where he had forced her back, long fingers touching the bruised lips, green eyes watching him in wide open wonder. "Ye'd best go now, ma'am." Kirby's voice had the old, quiet sound, the passion gone from it. "I'll turn my back fer ye to get yer outfit on." Again there was no answer, but when he turned once more toward her, she was at the entrance flap, the cold cling of the wet buckskins molding the bold curves of her crouching body.

The scout's eyes, running over the poised, wild beauty of her, carried his mind to the almost identical memory of her half-defiant, half-worshipful regard of him that other time back in the St. Louis carriage barn, reminding him of his bitter words on that occasion. His low voice grew softer still under the clear caress of her gaze. "Before ye go, ma'am, I want ye to know thet I'm sorry I called ye what I did back thar in Saint Louie. I reckon I know, now, thet ye ain't no half-breed. Ye jest couldn't

155

be, Miss Aurelie."

He saw, without understanding it, the hard stab of pain that narrowed her widened eyes—heard, without realizing its cause, the sharp intake of breath that accompanied the stricken look. *"Oh, wasicun! Wasicun . . . !"* was all she said before the entrance flap and the driving rain closed behind her. But the hard sob beneath the fierce words drove into Kirby, searing and deep as a war arrow. And deep as the sob had driven the shaft, the Sioux meaning of the words drove it deeper still.

Long after she had gone, Kirby sat motionlessly under the candle's guttering glance, the dark litany of the blood-admission in her passionate outcry reading itself over and over into his sinking thoughts: *Oh, wasicun! Wasicun . . . ! Oh, white man! White man . . . !*

VIII

The rain held three days, leaving the trail ahead a sea of slop-glue mud, hock-deep to a tall mule. Nevertheless, they pulled into the Big Bend of the Grand Arkansas on the fifth day, the spirits of the company rising under the drying rays of the fat sun that put in a belated appearance on the last afternoon.

An hour after span-out time, with the prairie dark shut in around the camp closer than the walls of a twelve-foot teepee, Kirby rode in from the west. He brought information that undid the sun's hard work in something less than the twenty seconds it took to tell the news. Ahead, at Walnut Creek, they had color-ful company. Red colorful. Big red colorful. Not even Kirby guessed how big and how red that company was until Laredo topped off the scout's terse description of its wolf-lean young leader with an ominous name—Young Satank.

Kirby waited at Laredo's fire while the wagon boss went to tell *Don* Pedro that the train was up against two hundred hostile Kiowas under the white-hatingest chief on the trail. The Texan was back soon enough, hearing Armijo's order to Kirby to come at once. The mountain man grunted his acknowledgment of the message, and slid off through the dark to comply with its directions. Sometimes a man wished he didn't walk like a cat—and see like one, too!

The two figures stood close-bound as pages in a book, *Don* Pedro muttering a thick Spanish oath and stepping back quickly as Kirby came up. Aurelie swung around, lips still half-parted with the temper of the interrupted kiss.

"Beg pardon, ma'am." The young mountain man's words were as hushed as his approaching footfalls. "I didn't see ye-all."

"I . . . I was just. . . ." The girl's voice faltered in mid-sentence, letting Kirby imagine the bite of the white teeth on the full lower lip.

"Miss Saint Vrain was just going," *Don* Pedro finished the sentence for her, his way as easy as though he and Old Marcelin's niece had been sharing a tin of coffee instead of each other's lips. Kirby, turning his shoulder on the girl's shadow, heard her quick-caught breath behind him, then running footsteps dying away.

"Now then, Randolph"—the scout didn't miss the omission of the usual "Mister" as the *don*'s velvety voice stiffened— "Mister Parker tells me you've scouted two hundred Kiowa hostiles at Walnut Creek. Under that young killer, Satank. Do you confirm that?"

"One or two of them, might have been off in the brush," said Kirby, nodding sourly, "but I allow two hundred is within ten of bein' right."

"And you agree with Mister Parker, Randolph, that they will probably leave us alone?"

"No." Kirby's statement was flat as the whack of a rifle bullet. "If they're as hot fer runnin' off mules as Laredo says, I allow they'll have a prime chance right sudden."

"How do you mean that, Mister Randolph?" There was that "Mister" back in again.

"Buffler," was Kirby's clipped reply. "I seen big sign up ahead today. Gnat swarms and miles of fresh chips. Happens the Kiowa savvy buffler hazin' the same as the Sioux. They kin part us from our loose herd without half tryin'."

"Well, Mister Randolph"—Kirby sensed the sardonic smile in the words and relaxed a little—"we'll worry about your *buffler* when we see them. Meantime, I called you up about another matter."

"Such as?" Kirby demanded bluntly.

"A reward, my friend, but of course! For your excellent work in saving the mules at Cottonwood crossing. No, no! Don't interrupt, *señor*. It is truly such a little thing. Only a horse. *¡Por supuesto!* I have seen that crowbait you ride, and I have seen you looking at the tall blue *yegua* that runs with my Diablo. No?"

The Spanish son had indeed seen him looking at that leggy, blue-roan mare with her dished Arab face and short back. Any man that ever sat any kind of a horse wouldn't miss that high-bred one. The mountain man had the true Plains Indian's love of fine horseflesh, and now he felt his Sioux tastes in such matters overtaking his dislike of the tall Spaniard. "So?" he grunted, trying to make it sound casual.

"So, I am giving you that mare, *hombre!* Her name? *Dispénseme, señor. Mil perdones.* Jacinta Salvaje. Wild Bluebell. She will go all day and all night, takes only a breaking hackamore, sits soft as a cloud, travels easy as the wind. Her bad habits, *señor?* Absolutely none. She reins true or will go by the knees alone. She is afraid of nothing and always watches where she puts her feet. Her temper? Good! *¡Excelente!* Tough as a bitch lobo, tender as a ripe breast, sweet as a maiden's inner thigh. She is yours. Take her."

Damn! He hadn't been ready for that. This Spaniard was an odd stray. Got a man off balance with his dark smiles and easy, quirky ways. Didn't let a son set his mind to hating him or liking him, he was that turnabout. Well, one thing, a man didn't have to think twice about that mare! "I'll take her," Kirby muttered awkwardly. "And I allow I'm right beholden to ye."

"*De nada* . . . it is nothing," said the Spaniard, sniffing. "And, *señor,* here is something else. You saw tonight how it is with Miss Saint Vrain and me. I have seen it in your looks that it is the same with you. We are then in conflict, of course. But I wish to say this, *señor.* I will not count you my enemy until you declare it."

"What makes ye think I'd go to makin' any declarations?" Kirby, forgetting everything but that clinging picture of the two of them, was suddenly angry.

"Your kind always does, Mister Randolph . . . fortunately."

"How come fortunately?" The mountain man's voice was still thick.

"Because it allows lesser men to beat you. It is a quirk in the *gringo* mind, some Anglo-Saxon vanity. You Americans enjoy a good killing as much as any son of old Castile. Yet you must forever be crying the intent before the deed, as though death were something to be hawked abroad before being handed out. It is a bad habit, Mister Randolph. I suspect it will kill you one day."

Kirby, squatting in the darkness, knew that he'd been right as calf bait in a wolf trap with his hunch that this tall young *caballero* was a plenty dangerous *hombre.* "I got a notion ye're crazy as hell," he said suddenly. "Ever hear of *Don* Quixote?"

"*¡Caray!* But of course."

"Wal, I reckon ye've bin warnin' me, too, Mister Armijo."

The *don* laughed delightedly. It was a boyish laugh, sounding genuine to Kirby, and Kirby was a man who had always found it tough to hate a man who could laugh right out and mean it. "Why, dammit, Randolph! You've got the makings of a gentleman!"

"Wal, I'll go along, Mister Armijo." Kirby grunted the statement, deliberately ignoring the momentary friendliness in the Spaniard's voice. "We're in fer Injun trouble tomorry, I'm thinkin', and a leetle sleep won't bother none of us."

"*Buenas noches*," said *Don* Pedro, nodding. Then he called softly after the disappearing Kirby: "You've had your warning, Randolph. You won't get another!"

Kirby stood a moment, looking back through the darkness. "Thanks," he growled. "Now I'll give ye a tip. Don't expect no Anglo-Saxon vanities from me. Ye've got a mite to learn about mountain men, Mister Armijo."

"*¡Hasta la vista!*" cried the Spaniard, laughing.

"Go to hell," echoed Kirby.

The moon, fatter now by eight days than it had been when the Pawnees fired the grass at Cottonwood Creek, loafed around until 2:00 in the morning before it gave up and slithered wanly down over the rim of the prairie. When it went, the dark clotted in behind it blacker that the unopened paunch of a grizzly. Hunched against the off wheel of the lead Conestoga, blanket-wrapped and chilled with the cold of the ground mists snaking up from the creek bottom, Kirby nodded.

The day's drive had taken the watchful train from Big Bend on up to Walnut Creek. Through the entire, nerve-strung trip, the outriding Kirby had not seen so much as a lance tassel of his big band of Kiowas. A pin-careful search of the campsite at the Walnut ford crossing had revealed their cold cook fire ashes, and that was all. Satank and his two hundred hostiles had evaporated into the clear prairie air.

Now, six silent hours of moon-bright prairie scanning and

ear-cupped listening had failed to add a single Indian sign. In spite of his intention to sit the night out, the weary scout drowsed.

The next thing he knew was a sharp pressure just over the right kidney, the point of a skinning knife held firmly against his back.

"*A-ah, heyoka!* Look out, fool!" The powdery voice was at his ear, the soft lips so close the warmth of their breath slid along his cheek. With the warning jump of the low Sioux gutturals, the pressure of the blade eased away from his back.

"Damn ye." Kirby's snarled whisper held all the honest venom of a grown man who has been made a fool by a wet-nose kid—and for the second time since he'd had his bottom knocked into that St. Louis gutter. "I ought by right to slap yer silly. . . ."

"You ought by rights to stay awake!" The caustic jolt came laced around with a laugh low and female enough to wilt the whiskers of any man's indignation. "Where's your hand, Kirby!"

Holding forth his hand, he felt the knife haft, warm from her grasp, come into his open palm, and from the feel of it recognized his own knife. "All right," he said, the ruffles of his dignity still well starched, "now ye've made an idjut outen me, whut do ye want?"

"I want to talk to you, Kirby. You've been acting so strange since last. . . ."

"We got nothin' to talk about," interrupted the scout. "Get on back to yer blankets. Daylight's comin' on."

"Kirby, you saw me with *Don* Pedro last night."

No answer.

"It wasn't the way you thought, *wasicun.*"

Still no answer.

"I wasn't kissing him."

There are limits to the endurance of any young man feeling

161

the way Kirby did. "The hell ye wasn't!" His exclamation was short and ugly.

"The hell I was!" The denial came as quickly as the charge, but it came like a caress for all its sharpness.

"I don't give a damn if ye was or if ye wasn't. I reckon it's true what I heerd about ye in Saint Louie, that's all."

"Whut did you hear about me in Saint Louis, Kirby?" Again the caress in the voice and with it, now, the soft hand stealing through the darkness to find his. At the touch of the slender fingers, Kirby's hand trembled, the tremble spreading up his arm, racing around his heart coming to rest in the core of his belly. Damn! How was it some women could do more with a fingertip than others could manage with their whole bare bodies? Nella Tourneau had been like that, and another one, a thirteen-year-old gold skin girl from far back in the plantation memories of boyhood Virginia. And now this one. This dusk-colored, green-eyed chit with the dawn-red hair and snow-bright teeth. They had all done it to him, each of them in the same way. A look. A whisper. A touch. And a man's guts were as gone as a drawn chicken's.

"Kirby, what did you hear in Saint Louis?"

It shamed a man to be that way about color-blood. All three of the girls who had taken his pride and his strength out of him had had color in them, all three of them sisters in that one, stark way. A way that turned his heart hard and his stomach cold even as he felt the glow of her pressing hand and heard her voice softly questioning him for the third time.

"They said ye was a 'breed." His voice sounded coarse and loud, strange even to his own ears. The words came and they were his words, but he wasn't proud of them. "They said thet Old Marcelin, he ain't yer uncle, he's yer father. And thet yer mother was a Injun squaw." He went on, plunging harshly ahead, getting out what was in him that had to come out. "I didn't believe whut they said, figgered they was dirty trapper's lies, I reckon. Seein' ye with Armijo, after the way ye kissed me and the way I thought ye felt, I done changed my mind. Happens ye kin allus tell color in a woman when she bodies up to every white son thet eyes her. Color-blood flows thetaway. It's why a man wants a *wasicun* woman when he starts to lookin' fer keeps."

Across camp, the sleep-thick voices of tired men muttered briefly, the 2:00 a.m. guard shift changing over.

"Marcelin Saint Vrain *is* my father." The words were so low that any stillness less than that of the predawn prairie would have lost them. "And my mother is a chief's daughter." Her shadow grew noiselessly taller as she slipped away along the wagon's side. Then she paused, her low-voiced call drifting back to the head-hung scout: "And I wasn't kissing *him*, Kirby. *He* was kissing me."

By the time the rattled mountain man got the meaning of that puzzle it was too late to call after her. He hunched back against the wagon wheel, miserable now from far more than the chill of the creek fog or the belly frost of thinking about two hundred Kiowas.

What he needed now was old Sam, his beaver-camp adviser and frontier foster father. Sam had been the one to tell him what was wrong with him in the first place. Had told him to get shut of Three Forks and the Yellowstone and the whole passel of white plew hunters and rag-tag Indian women. To get on back to the settlements and find himself a marryin' kind of a white woman. Well, hell. He had found her. He had found her and she wasn't anywheres near white. Maybe old Sam had the answer for that, too. And there certain sure had to be an answer to it, somewhere. But where in tarnal hell was that answer and who in tunket had it? Well, one thing was mountain water clear, anyway. Kirby Randolph didn't.

IX

Laredo Parker, heading the train, the late afternoon sun slashing into his squinted gaze, anxiously searched the prairie ahead. That cussed scout should be back. He had been gone the best part of the morning and now it was the long shank of the afternoon. A man wouldn't dast take the wagons up to Ash Creek without that scout got back to give him an all clear for it. The object of Laredo's concern cantered up out of a swale in the road ahead a short ten minutes later. His report was as abrupt as his appearance. There was a tremendous herd of buffalo in front of them, drifting south along the trail and away from the Arkansas River. They weren't grazing much and not bedding any. It was hard to be sure from the distance, but it appeared they were being driven.

"How come yuh to figger they're bein' hazed?" Laredo's question was short and uneasy.

Kirby looked ahead, scanning the rise of the prairie beyond the trail. "Drift a big herd two days without water, then sundown of the second day they get upwind of Ash Crick. They're smellin' water and the only thing betwixt them and a good guzzle is twenty-five wagons and four hundred mules. Ye figger it from thar."

Laredo was silent for several seconds, his dark beard following the thought twists of his thin mouth. "It ain't hard," he said finally. "I jest hope yuh're wrong about them buffler bein' drove, Randolph."

The following day they made the rest of the nineteen miles to Ash Creek, their flanks, point, and drag covered the entire way by shoal after shoal of nervously drifting buffalo. Since early morning they had been winding through one immense herd of the surly brutes. It was a tricky, touchy business, requiring the utmost in care and knowledge to avoid a stampede that could flatten every wagon and human in the train in a handful of bellowing minutes. Kirby savvied the black-horned devils as few men did, knew a buffalo had a built-in dislike of being headed, would go far to avoid crossing the trail behind the wagons. Instead, he would press on ahead of the lead wagons, increasing his speed accordingly. During this maneuver he would pick up the speed of the whole herd; the bulls in the rear would begin to run to catch up, pushing their fellows ahead to greater speed. In short order, if the wagon boss were green or his caravan inexperienced, the prairie would see the seasoned plainsman's favorite nightmare—a full-out buffalo stampede.

By mid-afternoon their progress had slowed to a practical standstill and all doubt as to the origin of the great herd's movement had been dispelled. Laredo joined Kirby at the head of the stalled train. "How do yuh see her now, Randolph?" The Texan's narrowed eyes swept the vast brown tide lapping in on them from every point of the compass.

"Them bulls have bin walkin' into the wind all day," grunted Kirby, his eyes, with Laredo's, staying on the herd.

"Yeah, they're bein' drove, all right. Damn them lousy Kiowas."

"Uhn-huh." Kirby's grunt was absent-thoughted, his scowling gray eyes still studying the surge of the great stream passing on their left. Yonder was the tree-dark strip of Ash Creek. They had to go through here, somewhere. And they had to go quickly. "Laredo," said Kirby, his voice cracking with tension, "I'm goin' to swing the wagons right hyar. Either them bulls is played out enough to split and let us through, peaceable, or they'll start runnin' on us. We ain't got no choice. We could drift from hyar to the Rockies before the black buzzards opened up and *let* us out."

With the words, the wagon scout turned, giving the backward hand wave that would turn the train left and south into the very belly of the rumbling herd. As the wagons swung in obedience to Kirby's signal, the shaggy horde, seized by one of the unpredictable impulses common to wild cattle, parted as meekly as so many muley cows to let the train rumble through, offering not so much as a tail lift or a dust pawing in challenge.

At the stream, Kirby ordered the wagons parked in an unorthodox, open V, the point aimed toward the outer prairie, the open end backing on the creek. He then ran a reinforced picket line across the open base of the wagon triangle and the best mules, full-hitched in ten-head tandems, snubbed to the flimsy rope by their leaders. It was a crazy, dangerous picket, but clearly their best hope to hold onto some of the mules. The two hundred spare wagon mules were tight-bunched in the grass pocket behind the wagon V. Checking the finished layout, Kirby shook his head grimly, then turned to the last touch.

Everyone worked now, Aurelie and Ptewaquin included. By the time darkness stopped them, they had dug a string of twelve crude rifle pits across the neck of land in front of the wagon V and had set a dry-chip fire, to be tended by the two women, between each pair of rifle posts.

An hour after dark the herd began to come in to the water, and with each passing hour the sounds of strife among the huge annuals grew. The milling, pawing, lowing, and challenging was incessant, the dust pall thrown into the air by the chanting animals so thick that a man saw things as through a driving rain.

For a while the ring of fires served to steer the vanguard of the herd around the campsite, but by midnight it had become necessary to shout into them and split the water-wild buffalo off and away from the wagons. Kirby and Laredo roamed the V behind the pit riflemen, wary to spot the first glint of polished horn or beady black eye that would warn that the brutes had ignored the fires. Each of these individuals was a potential leader for invading thousands, and, as they showed up, froth-mouthed, their heads tossing, Kirby and Laredo shot them, both firing at the same animal, making sure he went down where he was, quick and quiet.

About 3:30 there seemed to come a lessening of the advance. "By damn, Laredo, I think we've done it!" Kirby, feeling the lift of his second trail victory, was jubilant.

"Buffler is like Injuns," said the Texan sharply. "They're theah when they ain't."

"Like hell, Laredo. We've turned them!"

Even as Kirby spoke his piece, the first of the little chip fires began winking out. Half of them were gone by the time Aurelie came panting up to report, and the other half went as she talked. "We're out of chips, mister. No more fires tonight."

She had been mistering him ever since he had cut her with the color line the night before, and, looking now at the high-flushed beauty of her, the young scout figured he had best begin to get his wedge back in. "Don't worry about it, Miss Saint Vrain, honey." He grinned. "We got them wupt anyhow. The next sound ye hear will be Mister Parker's charming voice hollerin' . . . 'Roll out!' "

As a matter of fact, the next sound Aurelie heard was neither Mr. Parker's charming voice nor the cheerful call of "Roll out!" It was the screaming of an Indian stampede screech. And the Indian screaming it was Satank, war chief of the Arkansas Valley Kiowas.

"The next sound *you* hear," hissed Aurelie's acid voice, "will be my little feet pattering for the wagons."

"Not a bad ideah, ma'am!" Laredo moved to the girl's side. "Mind if I join yuh-all?"

As Aurelie, escorted by the wagon boss, sprinted for the Conestogas, Kirby's mind threw off the shock of Satank's first scream and faced up to the problem. *God Almighty! Those bulls are running!*

Wheeling, Kirby raced along behind the resting riflemen, now alerted by the Indian yells and building buffalo noise. "Stampede! Stampede! Hit fer the wagons! Roll out! Scatter back!" Delaying his own retreat until the last man had jumped and run, Kirby made it into wagons a short three pony lengths ahead of the first bull to come crashing into the parked Conestogas.

Half a dozen teamsters had sprung to the wagon seats along the point of the V and these now reinforced by Laredo, Kirby, Ptewaquin, and *Don* Pedro sent a hot stream of fire into the first ranks of the shaggy invaders. By the time the main front of the herd hit, the pointblank marksmanship of the defenders had piled up more than thirty dead bulls around the point of the V, and in the end it was this barrier of dead and downed buffalo that saved the wagon spread. The pushing herd, its original momentum slowing perceptibly, could no longer surmount that shambles of mushy carcasses. More and more they began to split around its pulpy abattoir, and ten minutes after the first head-long rush they were streaming by both flanks of the V, shunting off north and south to plunge in twin cascades of heaving, hoarsely lowing black torrents over the steep banks of Ash Creek.

The choked mass of them in the narrow streambed soon became impassable, and the following thousands were forced into a still wider split. Twenty minutes later the danger was really and finally past.

The dazed, shock-stupid men climbed down off the wagons, threw their guns into the dirt of the wagon yard, followed them with their own weary, unnerved bodies. They were only beginning to recover when Satank, pushing rapidly in on the heels of the herd he had stampeded, broke his Kiowas in a sudden two-pronged, war-whooping rush around both sides of the wagon V, driving pell-mell past its flanks and down on the loose mule herd behind it.

The screaming hostiles went so close past the wagons that even in the dark and twister-thick dust, Laredo called out several of the subchiefs for the dazed Kirby: Yellow Fox, Bad Liver, High-Hump-Dog; there they went, the red sons; there they went and there wasn't one damned thing a man could do to stop them. Kirby ground his teeth, whimpering his helpless rage as he went stumbling aimlessly across the wagon yard to fire after them. But the hour for shooting was past. Satank had out-marched them.

By the time the exhausted men could get themselves off the ground, scramble for their guns, get up on the end wagons of the V to fire over the heads of their picketed mules, it was all over. The Kiowas just hit the loose herd and kept on going—taking most of it with them. The terrified *arrieros* managed to hang onto their serapes and forty head of their braying charges, but for all practical purposes the caravan was out of the spare-mule business.

X

The hundred miles from Ash Creek to the ford of the Arkansas would have taken the sap clean out of a fresh-sawed stump. Sitting over the coals of the ninth fire he had made since losing the mules to the Kiowas, and the last he would make short of the main crossing, Kirby stirred up the embers, threw on a handful of damp chips, humped his lean belly up to the stink and the smoke, and settled down to some mean worrying. And he wasn't fretting about busted wagons or trail-muck rains, or anything else but five feet of slant-eyed, copper-haired half-breed female.

Not an hour gone, he had sent Laredo over to Aurelie's fire with a message to Ptewaquin—if her small *shacun* (redskin) charge would behave herself, the tall *wasicun* scout would hold words with her. Ptewaquin's answer had been equally brief.

Sorry. But the little *shacun* had that very evening given her promise to the Spanish *don*. She was going, now, to live in the great lodge of the Spaniard's uncle in Santa Fé. *Nohetto*, there you were! Hadn't the tall scout himself told the Little One he would not marry a half-breed?

Hearing that Aurelie was going to marry *Don* Pedro had been more than enough for Kirby. Damn her and everyone like her that carried color. They were all alike. Quick to twist into a man's body, slow to go away from his mind. Once they had you, they held onto you. Like this cussed Aurelie was holding onto him now. Pulling his eyes back to the peach curve of that dusky cheek, the heat lightning of that flash smile, bringing to his ears the memory of those passion-parted lips, burning moist on his cheek, and the throaty, panting words of them—*Oh, wasicun! Wasicun!*

Toward twilight of the next day the axle-squealing Conestogas pulled the long, climbing cross ride that let them look down on the halfway point of their journey—the Arkansas crossing at last! They made their own camp on the flat, close up to the stream. As Laredo and Kirby boiled their coffee and fried their salt side meat, they received an unexpected caller. *Don* Pedro made known his errand without wasteful flourish.

"Boys"—this familiarity was a mild shock in itself—"I've had a double stroke of luck. That Mexican army camp across the river, there, is commanded by my old friend, Colonel Juan Jimenez. And"—the jubilant *don*'s face showed excitement for the first time in Kirby's experience—"I've been given the marriage promise of *Señorita* Saint Vrain."

Much as he wanted to kill the handsome Spaniard, Kirby knew the *don*'s visit wasn't inspired by the chance to gloat. *Don* Pedro Armijo was elegant and overbearing. He kept his nails clean, shaved every day, brushed his teeth with grit and ashes, prayed seven days a week, and wore a silver cross around his neck. Still, when you got through faulting him, you knew you weren't horsing anybody but yourself. This black-headed son was all *hombre.*

"Wal?" Kirby tried to make it sound like a simple question and not like he was calling the *don* a dirty descendant of a female *perro.*

"Congratulations, comin' and goin'," said Laredo, covering for Kirby's bluntness. "We'll miss the gal, though. I allow we've all taken quite a fancy to Miss Aurelie."

Don Pedro laughed, his white teeth flashing in the gloom. "I'm sure we all agree on that, Mister Parker," he said, staring flatly at Kirby.

"Whut ye want, *Don* Pedro?" Kirby's return glance was equally flat. "We're plumb tuckered out and aimin' to get some shut-eye."

Ignoring the sullen address, the Spaniard bowed easily, his voice showing the patient restraint of a proud man speaking under studied control. "Colonel Jiminez is giving a party this evening to celebrate my engagement," he said, directing his smooth words to Kirby, "and I am asking you and Mister Parker to be our guests. The *señorita* joins me in the invitation."

"I ain't goin'," said Kirby, angry at himself for letting the girl upset him, wanting, really, to attend the Mexican celebration.

"Señor,"—the velvet voice stiffened—*"por favor,* I have asked you like a gentleman."

Laredo, eager to lap up the wine of old Spain, threw in his lean weight. "Come along on, Randolph. God Almighty, I should think yuh. . . ."

"I said I ain't goin'." The words were as sharp as the snap of a broken bowstring. "Now ye vamoose, *Don* Pedro. I don't want to turn ugly about it."

"As you will." The young Spaniard laid the phrase down with great care not to fracture the thin ice of its composition. "A courtesy refused is an insult offered. *Buenas noches,* Mister Randolph. Come along, Mister Parker. You shall taste such wines as you never dreamed could grow in a grape."

Long after they had gone, Kirby watched the flamelets in the fire, trying to get them to show him what Aurelie might look like there at the cross-river fandango. He knew she had fancy clothes. He had seen those rawhide trunks in the number three wagon. She was a rich girl and there would be no end to the foofaraw she had brought out from St. Louis. But what would it be tonight? Silks? Crinolines? Laces? Velvets?

"Kirby. . . ."

Whoa, hold up, boy. That voice of hers, calling his name out of the fire just then, had been a little too real. Made a man wonder if he hadn't been on the prairie too long, spent too many nights talking to shadows and looking into fire faces.

"Kirby! Answer me!"

He looked up, then, startled. Closing his eyes, he waited. When he opened them again, she was still standing there. *"Hau, wasicun."* The powdery voice shivered the tall scout clean to his moccasin soles. He came to his feet, not answering her, just standing and staring back.

The fire had been all wrong about the clothes she would be wearing. Kirby had seen a thousand Indian girls on a hundred May nights dressed just the way Aurelie St. Vrain was dressed. She had nothing between her and the warm breath of the river air but her moccasins and a simple Sioux camp dress. *"Hau,"* he answered, at last his deep voice matching hers for softness. *"Hohahe,* welcome to my tent."

She slid around the fire and past him, into the shadow of the wagon behind them. He was after her in three long steps, asking no questions, expecting none. She was waiting for him there in the blackness, no gloom deep enough to hide the lambent green eyes, the copper glow of the flushed cheeks. Her arms came reaching for him as he bent to take her in his own, the coiled longing of them weaving around his corded neck with a melting warmth that turned his kiss into a fury.

They clung thus, trembling and moving blindly while the earth floated beneath them and the stars swam crazily above. After a dozen sobbing breaths, she broke her mouth from his, buried her face in his cupping shoulder, and wept softly. He held her, stroking her hair and crooning strange Sioux gutturals until the wrack of her sobs slowed to the quiet rhythm of easy breathing.

"Kirby. . . ." Her voice, small and weak, seemed to be calling from afar.

"Yes, *wastewin?*"

"I walked out in the dusk tonight. Found a little stream. Above the crossing. . . ."

"Yeah, honey, I mark the place. Seen it from the rise comin' into camp this afternoon."

"I've got to talk to you, Kirby. Meet me there in half an hour. We can't go together."

"Reckon not, Aurelie gal. I'll be thar."

She looked up at him, lips parted. Standing quickly on tiptoe, she kissed him on the mouth, the words rushing with the lips to caress him: "Kirby, Kirby! Oh, *wasicun,* I love you so!"

Watching her fade noiselessly away, Kirby muttered half aloud: "By cripes, if I have to spend the rest of my life gruntin' Sioux and strappin' cradleboards to thet plumb beautiful back of yers, I'm goin' to have ye fer my squaw. God help me, I mean it, Aurelie . . . and color be damned!"

Kirby turned up the creekbank, ears tuned, eyes searching. Ahead lay a high cutbank sheltered by crowding willows. At its base lay a tiny white beach, closed in by the bending foliage. She was waiting for him there, standing centered on the little spit of sand, her braided hair glowing ash-silver in the moonlight.

He came up to her, not touching her, just standing and looking at her in the moonlight. She returned the look and, after a worshipful minute, began to talk.

"Something's happened, Kirby. I'm not going through with my promise to *Don* Pedro."

"I don't foller ye. Guess I'm jest plain dumb. Whut happened?"

"When he came to me tonight and told me about the celebration across the river, the first thing I did was ask him if you were going to be there."

"Yeah, I kin foller thet."

"He was angry," Aurelie went on, passing Kirby's muttered statement. "Stomped away proud as only a Spaniard can be. Then he changed, the way he does. Smiled and bowed and said he would go personally to invite you. When he came back and said you had refused to go, I told him I wasn't going, either. He was furious but Laredo was with him and he never let on at all. He's a devil, Kirby. He scares me."

"He scares me, too," said the mountain man simply. "But ye ain't refusin' to marry him on account ye're scairt of him."

"No, that's not it."

"Wal?"

"Kirby, when I spoke right out about you to *Don* Pedro, I knew I had to quit lying to myself. I knew that no matter how you might feel about a half-breed girl, I couldn't do anything about the way a half-breed girl feels about you."

"It don't make no difference about thet breed part of it no more," the scout replied. "Ye know thet now, don't ye?"

"I think so, Kirby."

"I don't know much about love, Aurelie, but I allow it ain't give to many to feel like we do about one another. I got nothin' but a hard life to offer ye, but if ye'll have me, I'll go down the trail with ye till we cain't neither of us see to foller it no more."

"Kirby, oh, Kirby! I'll ride any trail with you!"

They stood silent then, a long time, his great hand patting her shoulder, stroking her bowed head, playing with the thick braids of her hair. When Aurelie looked up, she was dry-eyed, and the quick smile that was such poison to Kirby's backbone played around the corners of her mouth.

"Kirby, can you swim?"

"Thet's a hell of a question."

"Want to? Now, I mean?"

"Sure, if that's whar the meetin's come."

"Well, that's where it's come, *wasicun!*" The words and the girlish laugh that interlaced them were muffled by the upsweep of the doeskin dress as it went off over her head. Kirby gasped as the white blaze of the moon struck the girl's body. From the full, high-pointing breasts to the slim insteps of the dainty feet, she stood stark naked. "Does it look different in the moonlight than under a whale-oil wagon lamp, Mister Randolph? I declare, I never saw a man's mouth so open."

Her laugh closed his gaping mouth. "Don't rightly know, ma'am." Kirby was shucking his leggings, skinning out of his shirt. "Wait'll I peel this buckskin and I'll give it another look!"

"I allow you won't. . . ." The girl's words slowed and stopped as Kirby tossed his shirt away to stand as the Lord had made him, in front of her. It was Aurelie's turn to stare. And six-feet-three of skin-naked, trail-hard Kirby Randolph was something to stare at. Maybe when the Old Boy above had got around to the face, He had finished the job a little rough, but on that body God had taken His royal time.

"Kirby, man, you're beautiful!" Aurelie St. Vrain was one of the rarest of Nature's works, a purely natural woman; there was nothing of sensuousness in her look. "You're just plain beautiful," she finished, her long eyes continuing to sweep the moon-carved symmetry of him. He felt the quick pride of her looking at him like that, and talking like that. It set his blood to hammering like a scalp-dance drum, started him moving, narrow-eyed, toward her. Ducking inside the reaching arms, she flashed away, diving, clean and flat, into the silver water. Under the moon's white light, the train of swirling bubbles behind her boiled and glittered with phosphorescent life. Watching her smooth body play, now over, now under the moon-shot surface, Kirby found himself thinking that God had all along cut him to size for an Indian girl. He just hadn't been brainy enough to see it. Likely they would make it down the trail pretty fair, him and Aurelie St. Vrain.

She climbed out presently, joining him on the clean sand of the spit. Fascinated. he watched her body, animal in its every sinuous motion, as she came, flushed and smiling, toward him. She took his hand, sinking gracefully down onto the body-warm sands. He remained awkwardly standing for a moment, his hand still clutching hers. Impulsively she pulled him down toward her, and this time when his lean arm came sliding behind her and his clean teeth to nipping at her neck and ear, there was no girlish wriggling away, nothing held back, no laughing.

XI

Aurelie, her head cradled in the warm laxness of Kirby's arm, stretched languorously, feeling the goodness of the long relief ease slowly down her arching back, flood deliciously through her thighs, disappear in the outflung slenderness of her legs. Kirby, one knee up, the other angled carelessly into Aurelie's soft side, pressed idly with his back against the warm sand, reassuring himself that he was still lying on firm ground. The moon, slanting low over the cross-river sand hills, was in his eyes. And a little of it was in his heart.

"Kirby . . . ?"

"Yeah, honey?"

"Kirby, I wonder if you'll ever tie your pony in front of my teepee?" The High Plains brave makes his wedding announcement by staking his favorite war horse before the entrance flap of his beloved's lodge, and the girl's question echoed a wistfulness that wasn't lost on the Indian-wise mountain man.

"I figger to, little *shacun*. When the time comes. Right now, ye'd best get yer things on. I allow we'd do well to drift before *Don* Pedro breaks off his shindig yonder."

Kirby had no more than rolled into his blankets when Laredo came cat-footing it up through the dark to tell him that his idea about beating *Don* Pedro back to the wagons had soured up on him. The Spaniard had caught the girl sneaking in from her upstream rendezvous with Kirby, had lit into her something fierce. And she hadn't been lit into worth a damn. She had up and told the *don* just the way it was with her and the wagon scout. She'd said that the Governor's mansion in Santa Fé would have to struggle along without her.

"Whut ye reckon Armijo will do?" Kirby, out of his blankets and on his feet the minute the wagon boss sprung the news, was thinking now, his words low and tight. "I allow he ain't the stud to leave somebody steal his queen mare offen him."

"He sure ain't. The average *hombre* would give up once yuh had beat him to the bedstead. But not that Spanish son. He'll come aftuh yuh, Randolph." The wagon boss had scarcely spoken his opinion when both men caught a sudden darkening of the light of the fire's outer fringe. There was no mistaking the easy-swinging grace of that tall figure.

"Watch him close, man." Laredo's side-mouthed warning went to Kirby. "I'll back yuh!"

"Thanks, old hoss." The mountain man nodded easily as he stepped toward the fire to meet the Spaniard. "I allow we kin handle him atwixt us."

Armijo came to the fire's far edge, bowed slightly, addressed Kirby with his gentlest smile. *"Buenas noches, señor."*

"Whut do ye want?" Kirby took one step forward, muttering his blunt challenge deep in his throat. The young mountain man was one who never looked for a trouble, but when a trouble came looking for him, that trouble better come walking up mighty softly and with its eyes wide open. *Don* Pedro neither heard nor cared for Kirby's growl. But he was walking softly and keeping his eyes open.

"I want you, *señor.*" The smile didn't vary the least mocking curve.

"All right." The animal sound deepened in Kirby's purr. "Hyar I come." With the words, the mountain man made to step around the fire, found himself looking into the twin muzzles of *Don* Pedro's double-barreled Spanish pistol.

Kirby stopped, his moccasins almost in the blaze. Behind him, he sensed Laredo moving up quietly. "Ye aim to use thet thing?" The mountain man's query meant just what it asked. There was nothing of fear in it, just the straight out request of the gambler asking the price of the game before buying into it.

"I do, Mister Randolph. Tonight you violated a life that had been given to me. *¿Comprende usted?*" Kirby crouched wordless, without motion, every nerve its him keyed to the next second. "Very well," the *don* said, the thin smile still on his lips, but gone from the slant black eyes. "The first barrel in the loincloth, *señor.* That is for Aurelie Saint Vrain. The second in the pit of the gut. That is for *Don* Pedro Armijo. I shall make a count of three, *señor,* just to let you remember that I gave you fair warning long ago about coming between this girl and me. One. Two. Thr. . . ." The *don*'s final count was begun, and no more than begun, when Laredo made his move. The square toe of the stiff cowhide boot drove into the banked fire, sending a flaring splatter of live coals and choking ash up into the young Spaniard's swarthy face. *Don* Pedro fired twice, fast and blind. But the shots, triggered into where Kirby had stood when Laredo's fire kick broke up the meeting, missed by several feet.

The twin echoes were still hanging around the wagon camp when Kirby's knee drove into the pit of the *don*'s groin, jack-knifing him forward to bring his chin smashing into the mountain man's right fist. It was a slicing, cross-swinging blow that nearly tore off the Spaniard's jaw, but it didn't finish him. Clutching his groin, face dead-fish gray with pained sickness, *Don* Pedro struggled to rise.

Kirby let him get to his knees before he kicked him. When it came, the huge foot whistled with the throw of a hundred and ninety pounds behind it, crunching viciously into the soft ends of the ribs, directly over the heart. The young *don*'s breath exploded in a piercing burst, his head, arms, and shoulders all seeming to sag and melt aimlessly. He pitched straight forward into the kicked-out ruck of the fire, not even the gentle motion of breathing marring the stone stillness with which he lay.

"By God, I think yuh've killed him," muttered Laredo.

"No, I ain't," said Kirby, the old Virginia softness pouring back into his voice. "I ain't kilt him, Laredo, but I wisht I had."

Laredo shrugged, nodded to the unconscious *don*. "Yuh-all bettah turn in, Randolph. I'll lug this *hombre* over to his tent."

When Kirby awoke, it was lead-gray in the east and the towering form of Ptewaquin, Aurelie's Sioux shadow, was bending over him. "*Ha ye'tu mani,*" said the Indian woman, "I have been walking in the night."

"*Woyuinihau.*" The mountain man nodded, sitting up. "I respect your eyes. *Kas'i s'ui?* What appeared in your sight?"

Quickly the squaw told him. When the Spaniard had wakened from his beating, he had sent for his servant, Chavez, the

179

Comanchero, the little brown man who had been here at the crossing awaiting his master's arrival from the east. The two had talked and Ptewaquin had heard the mention of a name that had a bad sound to Indian ears. An-gyh P'ih, Heavy Foot Track, the Comanche.

"Big Foot!" The name burst from Kirby's clamped lips. A bad sound, indeed. There wasn't a red son on the prairie with the Comanche's reputation in his nasty profession—ransom-grabbing white victims out of the Texas settlements and the Santa Fé Trail traffic.

Aye, the squaw nodded, Big Foot. Well, the little brown one had departed very suddenly. And he had departed, *south*. Across the Jornada, the desert crossing. Toward the Cimarrón. Toward the land of the Comanches. Toward Big Foot. That was all Ptewaquin had thought the *wasicun* scout should know.

As the slit-eyed giantess turned to go, Kirby quickly reached out to place his hand on her shoulder. *"Ta ye' e' ca' no ue,"* he murmured earnestly. "You have done well, mother."

"Ha ho, I thank you," growled the squaw, and was gone.

An hour after the next night's cook fires had burned down, Ptewaquin came again to Kirby's wagon. *Hau,* Ptewaquin gave greeting. And would the *wasicun* scout go now to see the Spaniard? Chavez, the Comanchero, had returned from the Jornada, his eyes very big with excitement, and the Spaniard wanted to see the wagon scout.

At *Don* Pedro's tent Kirby noted that the young Spaniard moved with difficulty, placing his feet gingerly and hunching his body carefully, as a man might who had been gut-kicked something fierce and recent. Beyond that physical reminder, there was no reference to last night's affair. *Don* Pedro said what he had to say, direct and level as usual, his first words shooting Ptewaquin's story about Chavez and Big Foot dead-center, leaving Kirby without any support for his suspicions except his own dislike of *Don* Pedro.

"Randolph, we're in trouble. My man, Chavez, who has a brother among Big Foot's band of Comanches, met us here at the crossing with a story he'd heard from some Comanchero traders at Bent's Fort. The story was that Big Foot was waiting at Lower Cimarrón Spring beyond the Jornada to ambush our train and abduct Miss Saint Vrain. Last night I sent Chavez to visit his brother. Tonight he has returned. The story is true. The Comanches are waiting for us across the Jornada."

Kirby's racing mind returned at full gallop to the day when he rode into the Bent and St. Vrain camp at Council Grove, and heard these same dark fears expressed by little Popo Dominguez, the *arriero*. The mountain man thought Popo was talking idly then, and he didn't think the *don* was now. "Go on," he grunted, noncommittally, "I'm listenin'."

"My plan is a simple one," said the *don*, nodding. "If you can better it, I am ready to listen, of course."

"Go on," Kirby said again, flatly.

Don Pedro would take the St. Vrain girl with her Sioux guardian and all of the Mexican *arrieros*, and leave tonight, riding hard up the Arkansas for Bent's Fort. There he would take on additional Mexican guards and bring Aurelie over Raton Pass and down the mountain route of the Santa Fé, meeting up with Kirby and the wagons at Mora River crossing, where the mountain and desert branches of the trail came back together. Kirby and Laredo would, of course, stay with the train, taking it across the Jornada by the regular route. Forewarned as they were, they should be able to repulse any Comanche attack. *Don* Pedro respectfully suggested that it would be well for Kirby to leave early, scouting the way for the wagons, riding well ahead of them. *Así nomás*, it was that simple. Did *Señor* Randolph see it any more clearly?

It developed that *Señor* Randolph did not. After a brief discussion of details, the mountain man arose to depart, saying he had best mosey over and say his good byes to the girl.

"*Por supuesto*, but of course!" The young Spaniard was his complete smiling self again. "Are not such enforced separations the very headiest wines for the further heating of true young love?"

"I'll be damned if I know," grunted Kirby. "I ain't the true young type."

Kirby sent Blue Bell splashing across the Arkansas at 4:00 in the morning. Across stream, he paused to survey the crowding blackness of the sand hills ahead, then swung the mare on around the base of the first of them.

Minutes after he disappeared, another rider drew rein at the same spot, a short, squat rider, sitting a big Spanish mule. He waited until the sand hills swallowed the soft *cloppings* of Blue Bell's passage, then put the mule hard left, cutting into the hills on a side trail. A late moon ray, wanly lingering along the deserted track, took a second from its passing to light the rider's face. It was a wide flat face, vacant under its immobile toothy grin—Chavez, the Comanchero. . . .

It was late afternoon, almost dusk, when Kirby, coming off the pure hell of the Jornada desert crossing, topped the last of the cherty hills beginning to front him and saw what Blue Bell had caught wind of the hour before: a tumble of weird, white stone hummocks littered with bright-hued pebbles shouldering in along the course of a dry riverbed and buttressing the finest sight a dry mountain man ever saw—the spreading, cat-tail marsh that rimmed the green-scum pond that was Lower Cimarrón Spring. Even as the exhausted mare went in a stumbling trot toward the water hole, Kirby was down off her, flinging himself on his belly to suck feverishly at the brackish sludge.

Two minutes later, when he raised his eyes from the fetid pool to take his first good look around, he got them full of the biggest Indian he had ever seen.

"*Hohahe,*" said Big Foot, grinning, speaking Sioux with a commendable accent. "Welcome to my teepee."

Kirby didn't move off his belly, lay flat and still while his chin dripped scum water and his eye traveled stride for stride with his careening thoughts. He could see eight of them, and his working knowledge of the red brother's tactical mind told him he would have five times that number out of eye-tail range behind him. That was nice. Nothing between him and getting back to the wagons but forty or fifty Canadian River Comanches.

The mountain man's grin measured the Comanche's, hard line for hard line. "*Wonunicun,* excuse me. *Mini ya, hin yanka,* I am thirsty, you will have to wait." He drank slowly, having no fear Big Foot would not be there when he was through.

So that was An-gyh P'ih sitting across the rushes there on that skewbald stud horse. That was the evil-famous Heavy Foot Track, eh? Sitting there with a mouth big enough to slide a watermelon in sideways, with a nose you could kennel a small dog in, and still have room for a litter of pups, with a jaw as long and muscle-lumpy as a jack mule's. Well, let him sit. As long as a man was taking his last suck, he might as well make it a good lengthy one.

When he did look up, the scout was surprised to see that the Comanches had not unslung their bows, were slouching on their ponies, loose and easy, waiting for him to finish.

Damn it, there was something wrong here. Happens a bunch of hostiles caught a *wasicun* scout at a desert water hole, with no horse under him and his rifle hanging on his saddle horn, they had ought to feather up his bottom in a hurry. These red sons were just sitting there, slack-tailed and stupid. Why?

He got his answer a moment later when he stood up, spat his last mouthful of water disdainfully toward the waiting redmen in front of him, turned slowly to count the Indians that should have been crowding the hillside behind him. The flinty hillock was deserted save for one memorably squat and ugly figure.

"*Buenos días, señor.*" Chavez's grin had not flickered a muscle since Kirby had last seen it at the wagon camp the night before. "*¿Que paso?*"

"*Que paso* my behind!" growled Kirby. "Ye know whut passes, ye greasy frog. And so do I, now."

"*¿Como se dice?*" Chavez's question was deprecatorily apologetic.

"I say it's real cute," answered Kirby bitterly. "I ride out ahead of my train and disappear. Then the Comanches ambush my wagons and my boys see me ridin' like a brother amongst them. I'm a stunk skunk on the frontier and *Don* Pedro gets the gal. Cripes, I ought to blow my own brains out and save ye jaspers the bother."

Chavez stretched his grin one more tooth. "You are pretty smart, *señor,* but not so smart as *El Patrón.* It is true that you will ride with us like a brother, *but not after the wagons, señor!*"

Kirby took that in his teeth and chewed it. When he spat it out, the taste was bitter as bear gall. Aurelie, by damn! *Don* Pedro meant to have her grabbed by the Comanches and to have him seen helping them. "Why, the God. . . ."

"Slowly, *señor,* slowly." Chavez's mocking leer interrupted the scout's white-lipped snarl. "The best part is yet to come. After you lead us in the capture of the *señorita,* Big Foot has still more plans for you."

Kirby's eyes flicked to the hostile chief; the towering Comanche looked down at him, thick lips smeared with the brush of pure pleasure. "Hear me, White Stripe," the Comanche leader said, naming Kirby for the white streak in his black hair.

He pointed an arm the length and heft of a fence post at one of his followers. "Do you mark this chief?"

Kirby started to deny any recognition, but the trail miles of memory suddenly rolled back, back to the heaving buffalo horde at Ash Creek. Sure, he knew this one, all right. The wonder was that he had needed more than one look to remember him. "Ta-dl Ka-dei," he answered evenly. "Bad Liver, the Kiowa."

"You may say his name with your bowels loosening," said Big Foot, grinning, "for when I have done the Spanish chief's bidding with you, Ta-dl Ka-dei will take you back to my friend, Satank. There seems to be some small matter of your cheating him out of two hundred wagon mules at Ash Creek."

Chavez edged his mule forward, interrupting the chief's loose-lipped oration. It was evident from the string of short-barked Comanche and the flourish of High Plains hand language that Chavez thought the speech making had gone far enough. Apparently the chief agreed, for he turned on his men, lashing them with sudden, bursting phrases of the bickering Comanche dialect. The result of this exchange was that Kirby found himself astride Blue Bell with his feet lashed securely under her belly, and a stout lead rope tying the mare to Chavez's big mule. With these preparations completed, Big Foot reined his pony alongside Blue Bell.

"*Hopo!*" He grunted the Sioux go word at Kirby. "*Hookahey,* let's get out of here."

"*Waste,* good!" The scout deliberately made his voice inveigling, hoping to charm some further information out of the Comanche. "White Stripe is eager to ride with his Comanche friends. Eager to hear how savagely and with what great cunning An-gyh P'ih plans to seize the red-haired *wasicun* squaw. . . ."

Big Foot's answering smile was the spirit of warm appreciation. Kirby saw the great arm coming, couldn't, for all his trained speed, move in time to avoid it. The blow was like one from a giant-swung wagon tongue, nearly tearing his head off his shoulders. The scout was still conscious as the following smash came crunching in—saw the clubbed fist whistling down on him, big as a bean pot, felt the searing, instant pain of it explode across his ear and the side of his reeling head, remembered nothing more.

Looking at the bloody-headed figure flopping across the withers of the startled Blue Bell, Big Foot turned his paint stud away, summed up his whole Comanche viewpoint of the situation in a single, back-flung English phrase to the waiting Chavez.

"Damn, him talk too much, quiet now!"

XII

That ten-day march with the Canadian River Comanches, dogging the main track of the Santa Fé Trail south and west, up the Cimarrón, across to the Canadian, and down to Point of Rocks, was one for any mountain man to remember—and Kirby never forgot it. It began with a two-day brush with six trappers from Bent's Fort, caught out in the prairie flats west of Middle Spring of the Cimarrón, continued with a full day's stopover at Big Foot's home-base camp at Willow Bar on the same river, and a hair-raising all-night buffalo barbecue among the nomad *Ciboleros*, the wandering Mexican buffalo hunters, far south along the Rabbit Ear River, concluded with a murderous attack on four white herders from Santa Fé and a five-hundred-head herd of top-grade horses.

This last fracas, resulting in the running off of the entire white horse herd, ended the recreational aspects of the Comanche outing. A man with any kind of an Indian nose could smell that the slit-mouth sons were getting down to cases now.

With night coming on, the savages left the main Santa Fé Trail at the jagged landmark spot of Point of Rocks, pushing the stolen herd due west across a trackless and rapidly climbing country. Inquiring of Chavez, whose empty-headed company he was learning to enjoy, Kirby discovered that the hostiles had two mighty sound reasons for the detour. Firstly, the trail reached the main crossing of the Canadian just a few miles south of Point of Rocks, and here were stationed the Mexican Customs Guards who met and taxed the westbound wagon outfits. Secondly, the westward course of the stream they were following, Ocate Creek, led into the Bent's Fort Road to Santa Fé. Chavez thought the *señor* would recall that this was the road down which *Don* Pedro would bring the flame-haired *señorita*.

¡Caray! That brought a spark, eh? *Por Dios,* one should think so. Once on that road, all the Comanches had to do was follow it north to a place called Vermejo Creek. Remember that name, *señor,* Vermejo Creek. That was the place where Big Foot was to meet *Don* Pedro and steal the *señorita.* Aha, another spark, *señor? Por supuesta,* but of course. What was that? Oh, the distance? Not much, *señor.* Thirty miles, maybe. There was plenty of time. Big Foot never rushed things. Always a careful one, that chief. A real big planner. *¡Hijo!*

Forty-eight hours later, Kirby had his chance to see how big and how real. That night on Vermejo Creek was a faithful tracing of the previous ones on the long trail from Lower Cimarrón Spring. Kirby spent it laced cozily to Chavez by an old-fashioned Spanish leg iron, the two of them surrounded by the heavy snores of Big Foot's ugly bevy of sleeping braves.

The following morning he was awakened by a now familiar prodding in the rear. *"Arriba,"* said Chavez, nodding. "An-gyh wants to see us."

They found the chief squatted on a rock spur jutting high over the tumbling creek and giving unlimited view of the rolling country to the north. With him were Ta-dl Ka-dei and two wolf-grinning subchiefs, Horsehead and Crazy Legs. Big Foot and company were in good spirits.

Splitting his face with the third grin Kirby had seen there since meeting him, Big Foot waved the captive scout to a seat in the chosen circle. Followed then, through the usual conglomerate of hand signs, broken Sioux, and butchered English, the full story of *Don* Pedro's perfidy, which left the white scout groping for some place to set a solid thought in the quagmire of its belly-queasing revelations.

Hau, listen to this, *wasicun,* and learn what it took to make a name as lofty as Big Foot's in a career as touchy as ransom captures. Yes, the young Spaniard, whose uncle was the Great Father in Santa Fé, had offered a price in gold for the abduction of the girl, whose father was no less a one than the main St. Vrain chief. To make things look good, the Spaniard was to be captured, too. Then, to make them look even better, he was to escape, return to Bent's Fort, and conduct the successful ransom bargaining. To make sure the white scout was put completely out of the running with the girl, he would be seen by *Don* Pedro's surviving Mexicans as leading the attack. White Stripe was to understand he had heard only the young Spaniard's part of the bargain. Now came Big Foot's part, which, had the Comanche thought of it sooner than this morning, would have spared White Stripe a long ride. It was a simple idea, too—just a small change in the original agreement. Now, when Big Foot captured the girl and *Don* Pedro, there would be no escape for the young Spaniard. That was all. No more than that. But, *wagh!* Did not White Stripe see the master's touch there?

The dumbfounded mountain man did, indeed. The slippery devils were planning to hold *Don* Pedro for ransom, too. Aurelie would be worth her weight in gold, but the young Spaniard could be hefted in the same golden coin—and he weighed a hell of a lot more than the cat-slim St. Vrain girl! *Wayuonihan!* Touch the fingertips in Big Foot's direction, he was a real chief and a blue-chip trader to boot.

Chavez had finally arrived at the same dry water hole of thought, his tongue clacking with the fear dust of the discovery. "What of me, cousin?" The Comanchero's words stumbled uncertainly, his empty smile capped by the frown lines cupping the sweat-beaded paste of his forehead. "What of your old friend, Chavez? The companion of your campfires? The half-blood of your brothers? The. . . ."

Picking his battered musket from the rock beside him, Big Foot skyed the piece, sighting casually along its rusted barrel, his easy words interrupting the Comanchero. "Oh, him? Faithful Chavez? He is only a little problem"—the musket dropped with the words, centering squarely below the glistening frown lines—"like a sick dog that is no good any more." With the pleasant-faced shrug that accompanied the phrase, Big Foot shot the Comanchero between the eyes.

Chavez had been sitting close to the edge of the jutting council perch. The heavy lead ball splattered his nose like a metal fist, driving his head back, toppling his slack body over the rock ledge. Kirby could not see the fall, but before his next breath the dull splash came up from below, putting its harsh period to the sentence of silence following the Comanche's shot.

"I never liked him," apologized Big Foot. "Too greasy and sweating and smiling the whole time."

XIII

An hour after Chavez's death, with the stone pipe starting its fourth round of the silent group on the sunlit ledge above Vermejo Creek, the aquamarine sky behind Raton Peak broke into a climbing bloom of cottony smoke blossoms. Instantly the pipe stopped passing, the four sets of Indian eyes squinting into the distance. "There is Black Dog talking with the smoke. We shall know how soon the Spaniard comes." Big Foot's grunt brought a wash of silent nods from his slant-eyed companions. Seconds later the distant smoke series broke off as cleanly as it had started and Big Foot turned triumphantly to Bad Liver. "*Aii- eee,* did you read that, brother?"

The Kiowa was his usual taciturn self. "Black Dog is an artist with the blanket. Very clean work. So the Spaniard and the girl come tonight. This means you will attack in the morning, eh, cousin?"

"In the morning. Very early."

"With this new plan of yours there is no need for White Stripe. Is my tongue straight?"

"As a wagon track. You want to start back with him now?"

"*Hau.* I will take White Stripe and go. It is a long way. Satank will be wondering already."

Hearing his Comanche name, Kirby watched the hand signs going between the Kiowa and Big Foot. What he picked up in the next seconds put the short hairs along his spine to standing straight on end.

"Yes," Big Foot said. "You take White Stripe and go, old friend. Tell Satank he is welcome to this *wasicun.* Tell him I caught one Saint Vrain and one Armijo cub, and sold them back for more gold than any Kiowa ever heard of. You tell the young wet-nose that. White Stripe is yours now. Go on. Go."

"I will need help," said Bad Liver, shrugging. "I cannot keep these two eyes open all the way to the Arkansas."

"By all means. Horsehead and Crazy Legs will go with you. You hear that, you two? You go with Ta-dl Ka-dei. Now."

"*Hopo,*" gestured the first brave indifferently, "I am ready."

"*Hookahey,*" said the second, "let's get out of here."

They set out in a northeasterly direction, Bad Liver leading the way. Kirby spent the first part of the ride looking over the cut of the opposition. Ta-dl Ka-dei was past forty, of middle height, lean as a piñon. He was a light-colored, sullen Indian, totally lacking the ready humor common to his race. His blank, cut-rock face looked dumb as a stone, fronted a mind as honed as an old axe blade. Looking at him, Kirby figured you didn't make more than one mistake with Bad Liver. Horsehead was a big buzzard and homely as blue sin. His long, pony-nosed, slack-jawed face was set atop a body as muscular and heavy as a bear's. A man might hope to get around him—providing he did his getting fast. But happens he got those grizzly paws on you, you were done. The third hostile was a barrel-chested little Comanche with a prune of a head that looked like it had been parboiled in salt-water and sun-shrunk to half size. Crazy Legs, with his bloated body, shriveled head, and ricket-twisted legs looked like a first-rate Comanche clown—and was about as funny as a kick in the groin. Kirby read real danger in the bird-quick shift of the little man's eyes.

Having toted up the enemy, the captive scout concluded that all a man in his saddle could do was wait for the time and the trail to bring him his chance. Six hours of monotonous, sun-drowsy jogging and a sudden, blind turn in the climbing rock track gave Kirby his opening.

Facing them, as Bad Liver signaled the halt, was a fifty-foot rock slide. Beyond its top Kirby could see nothing but sky, he judged from that that the trail topped out above, most likely dropping sharply on the far side. Bad Liver grunted a short word to the two Comanches, turned, and put his pony up the sealy talus. Scare-footed and wary as a cat, the wiry Indian cayuse negotiated the slide, disappeared over its top rise. Horsehead, nodding to Kirby, waved at the slide, proudly unveiled his secret command of the scout's mother tongue: "Him big damn' hill you climb same fast Bad Liver!"

Blue Bell took the slide nimbly, coming out above on a sight that stole Kirby's wind. There was a level rock bench up here and then there was nothing but one of the biggest holes in the ground Kirby had ever looked over. That cañon, hidden back of the rock slide climb, was at least eight hundred feet deep. Evidently the trail continued down its nearly vertical face from the spot where Bad Liver sat his pony at the far edge of the bench. The captive scout didn't wait to see.

Ten feet from Bad Liver, Kirby heard the Kiowa's sudden growl. "That's enough. Hold that pony. It's a bad trail over here where we go down."

"Whar ye go down, ye slant-eyed son!" Kirby dug his heels into the startled Blue Bell, leaping her into Bad Liver's standing mount with his soft-cursed answer.

There was a belly-wrenching moment, and Kirby wondered if Blue Bell would take him over the edge as well. Then, with the tiny, twisting images of the Kiowa and his mount five hundred feet below and still falling, he felt a shift in balance as the clawing mare moved back over the safe edge of the cliff. If there was any time left now, it was all-fired short. Wheeling Blue Bell, he hurled her back across the rock bench.

Horsehead, coming up over the lip of the slide, had hardly got his eyes open when Blue Bell crashed, fully breast on, into his pony. This time Kirby could not hold the mare on the bench; the two of them cascaded down the slide behind the falling Comanche and his pony.

Fifty feet below, Crazy Legs saw Horsehead and his pony in time to get his own mount almost clear of the avalanching rocks. Almost but not quite. A knee-high wave of rotten granite knocked his mare's legs out from under her, sending Crazy Legs sprawling. It went a little harder with Horsehead. The big Comanche bounced onto the hardpan of the lower trail with force enough to stun a range bull, but had enough dumb strength to struggle halfway to his knees before his own horse landed squarely atop him. Kirby heard the crunch and splinter of the bones and knew they weren't horse bones popping like that. A second later Blue Bell, still upright, hit the hardpan and leaped clear of the moving slide.

Kneeing the stumbling Blue Bell around toward Crazy Legs, Kirby knew he was playing in more luck than even a mountain man dast count on, thought sure his string was due to snap. And Crazy Legs nearly snapped it for him, too. With the blue Spanish mare booming down on him, the little Comanche snake-rolled halfway to his feet, nocking and letting drive an arrow all in the same motion. The shaft took Kirby low in the left side, hit a rib, and glanced outward. The next instant Blue Bell's stabbing forehoofs smashed into the red bowman's shoulder and Crazy Legs lay, thrashing and twisting in the trail like a run-over rattler. The collision gave Kirby enough time to pivot the mare, lean far down on the return pass, and scoop the Comanche's steel war axe off the ground three feet ahead of its owner's frantic reach.

After that, it took Kirby only a moment to slash the razored blade across the rawhides that bound his feet under Blue Bell, leap off the mare, and go cat-crouching back toward the crawling Comanche. Crazy Legs died quickly and easily, the axe blade parting his skull from pate to jawbone in one clean, professional slice.

Kirby sagged to the trail where he was, vomited hard, lay face down and resting for ten minutes. Then he sat up, forcing his weary mind to work. At this point a man had best do some figuring, happens he wanted to beat Big Foot to Aurelie St. Vrain.

XIV

Through the lingering upland twilight and on into the black night hours, Kirby pounded his way westward, riding Crazy

Legs's spotted mare and leading Blue Bell. At midnight he was on the Bent's Fort Road above Vermejo Creek.

Two hours later, with Crazy Legs's pony run clean into the ground, he spied his target—the star-hard jut of the landmark spur overhanging Vermejo Creek. Now the Mexican camp of *Don* Pedro Armijo was only onto a mile ahead. So far, so good.

Next, he did something he had to do—unsheathed Horsehead's borrowed skinning knife and ripped it clean across the little Indian mare's jugular. The mare shuddered a mite, staggered two steps, went to her knees. The scout grimaced, spat disgustedly. A man hated a thing like that, but you couldn't leave a Comanche pony wandering night free within winding and wickering distance of her friends in Big Foot's horse herd.

Don Pedro's camp was in an open meadow on Kirby's side of Vermejo Creek, the hard starlight letting him see the whole layout, good and clear. He had no trouble spotting the *don's* tent and, right next to it, the familiar white cone of Aurelie's teepee. With the shift of the stars now showing about 3:00 and the Comanche attack set for first light at 4:00, a man didn't have any time to be standing around scratching his seat. Tethering the nose-wrapped Blue Bell in a piñon clump, he unsheathed Horsehead's knife and started moving in.

There was no trouble. Inside Armijo's tent the mountain man lay on his belly to locate the breathing. It came steady and regular. And it came alone.

After that, it was something any wet-nose cub would find simple. You took the loaded haft of the knife and smashed it back of the ear—once for certain—twice to make sure. Then you were mighty careful how you tied the hands and feet with your buckskin shirt laces and how you stuffed the mouth with a torn-off wad of the *don's* fancy nightshirt. When you got through, you figured maybe the Spanish son would strangle, but he would stay where you left him—and stay mortally quiet.

Bellying out of Armijo's tent, Kirby crawled into his first hitch. Silhouetted against the ground line in front of Aurelie's tent squatted a figure no man could miss. Snaking to within twenty feet of the nodding Sioux giantess, Kirby wet his lips. The sleepy bull bat twitter wobbled a little but it did the work. Ptewaquin's head swung in his direction.

"*Tahunsa, Ptewaquin.*" The scout's whisper rode softly. "*Kola.* It is your friend, out here, Ox Woman, your cousin."

After a long pause. the squaw answered in Sioux: "Who is it out there calling me friend and cousin? And by my true name?"

"It's me, White Stripe. Kirby Randolph, the wagon scout. I'm coming in. Make no more noise."

"Come ahead, *wasicun.* Ptewaquin waits. And her gun is ready."

"Shut up," hissed Kirby, crawling out of the darkness. "Get the gal out hyar. Thar's a hundred Comanches a mile across this stream. They mean to hit the camp at dawn and steal her. The Spaniard plotted it with them. . . ."

"Which Comanche?" interrupted the squaw, keeping the rifle on him.

"An-gyh P'ih. And put that damn' gun down," snapped Kirby, turning to pull the tent flaps. Aurelie, already awake from the whispering, beat him to it, her tousled hair glinting in the starlight, her green eyes, smoky with sleep, showing in the opening as Kirby reached for the canvas. Sleep-smoky or star-dimmed, those eyes needed just one look at that gaunt, half-naked body. "Kirby." The shaky whisper had only time to wander off the parted lips before the hard-bearded mouth was crushing them into silence. Eyes closed, hungry arms straining, Aurelie came into that fierce kiss.

The watching Ptewaquin had blinked three times before the scout released the half-breed girl, began rasping the tight string of his adventures since leaving her at Arkansas crossing.

"Ye kin believe whut I say and come along with me," he concluded, "or ye kin set up a holler and get me kilt. Whut ye say, Aurelie?"

"Oh, Kirby, Kirby. I'm coming with you, man. I'll never leave you again, *wasicun.*"

"How about ye, *Tahunsa?*" The question, quick and harsh, went to Ptewaquin. "Is your heart open to this *wasicun* now?"

"My heart is open," said the Indian woman, following the response with a soft-spoken Sioux phrase that hit Kirby flat as the broadside of a swung axe. *"Etan' han yakaga witan'de!"*

Etan'han yakaga witan' de? Brother Moses! How did that translate? "From this time on thou makest my daughter's husband." What a hell of a time to drop a rock like that on a man! *"Iho'hun,* well, mother, listen. Ye go get the Spaniard's stallion. He's on a picket back of his tent. Get him and bring him to them piñons yonder. We'll get the gal's mare and meet ye thar. *Da' wi howo!* We must go right now!"

With the squaw gone, he and Aurelie made tracks for the piñons, the girl's paint filly quickstepping behind them. In five minutes Ptewaquin showed up, leading *Don* Pedro's black stud.

"Foller me," growled Kirby. "And fer Pete's sake hold onto yer hosses. We're goin' to wade the streambed half a mile to get downwind of the Comanche camp, then foller the bases of them hills south a ways."

The three of them had hand-led their nose-wrapped mounts for an hour when Kirby brought them out on the main road three miles below the hostile encampment. "Mount up," he ordered, "and hold to a rollin' lope fer two mile. After thet we kin open them up fer keeps."

XV

At noon they reached Ocate Creek crossing, where Kirby planned to turn east and run for the Mexican Customs Guard at the Canadian River Ford. While the women watered and grazed the horses, the mountain man scaled a hundred-foot escarpment and took a short look up the back trail.

The look was short because the elevation, the clear day, and the scout's good eyes quickly told him what he wanted to know. Far to the north a tiny dust haze hung over the Bent's Fort Road, snailing its thin way south even as Kirby watched.

He slid down the granite slope, his mind jumping ahead of his scrambling descent. If they could beat the Comanches back to the desert route, they had two weasel-slim chances: the first, that the Customs Guard was at Canadian crossing; the second, that Laredo had brought the wagons safely across the Jornada, lambasted the mules all the way up the Cimarrón and down to the Canadian, and arrived, just about now, at the Point of Rocks country. Come a time like this, with maybe fifteen miles between you and an idiot bunch like Big Foot's, you didn't tarry much over the cut of your chances, either.

Back at the creek he ordered all the extra weight off the horses, abruptly told the women to follow along and save the questions. Right now following along meant another half mile of hand-leading the horses down the brawling center of Ocate Creek. After that they pulled out on the south bank, mounted up, and swung due east, following the stream.

When Aurelie and Ptewaquin had brought their galloping mounts alongside Blue Bell, Kirby gave it to them straight. From here, they made their big ride for it. With all three horses in good shape and with the gain they could hope to get while Big Foot picked up their tracks back at Ocate crossing, they had a pack rat's chance of beating the hostiles to the Santa Fé Trail around Point of Rocks. After that it was up to the higher powers. In any case, they weren't scalped yet.

Late afternoon brought the fugitives to the mile-long race of

Ocate Creek Gorge. Here the Ocate trail left the waterside to climb over the shoulder of the deep-cleft channel, giving the mounted traveler a five mile view of his back trail and letting him see ahead to the distant thread of the Canadian and the Point of Rocks country. By the time Aurelie and Ptewaquin had brought their laboring mounts up the last rocky footing to join him in his hand-shaded, westward squinting, Kirby had seen more than he wanted. "Take a long squint at thet bunch in the lead, Ptewaquin," he said. "Tell me, can ye single out any one of them thet looks special to ye?"

The Sioux woman narrowed her eyes, holding her strong hands around them like copper-wrinkled binoculars. Shortly she turned, rubbing her eyes from the far-sighted straining. "One man big. Bigger than Ptewaquin. He rides in front, on a *sunkele ska.*"

"Trust An-gyh P'ih not to send a boy on a buck's errand," breathed Kirby.

"What White Stripe say?"

"Your eyes are longer than the eagle's, mother. Who else could see a pony's true color across so much land? Big Foot rides a spotted horse."

"*Ha ho?*" grunted Ptewaquin, highly pleased. "Thank you. *Hoohakey,* let's get out of here!"

As they went, the faltering hammer of the hoofs just behind him tightened the scout's wide mouth. Between his own aching knees he felt the rhythm of Blue Bell's tiring stride beginning to go rough. Ahead were still three hours of broad daylight, many a long mile of open trail. Time and three tired horses were running out on Kirby Randolph.

Two hours later they sighted the Santa Fé Trail. Taking a last look back as the stumbling horses left the long downslope to plunge into the rocks flanking the trail, Kirby saw the Comanche dust cloud rolling a scant three miles in their rear. Minutes after that they were through the rocks and out onto the main wagon road, walled in by saw-toothed, granite outcroppings. They would see the Comanches no more until they were looking at them over rifle barrels.

On the level and going up the packed ground of the wagon road, the staggering horses seemed to find some last ounce of bottom, steadied up a hopeful mite. And they had only three miles to cover to the Canadian crossing.

One way and another, kicking, beating, and cursing their breaking mounts, they made it. But behind them, as they rounded the last rock-walled turn hiding the near side of the crossing, the granite ribs of their back trail were echoing the crazy, high-pitched, wild-dog yammering of the closing Comanche pack.

The far side of the stream was screened by the river brush, but the near side, where the Mexican Customs Station should have been, was bare and clean. Not a tent. Not a single cook fire ash pot. Not a solitary horse apple younger than last month's. There wasn't a Mexican Customs Officer within forty miles of the main Canadian crossing.

The slobbering horses stood spraddle-legged, heads hanging, thick tongues slack between yellow teeth, lungs heaving, roaring. Their riders sat them like slumped statues—able to see, but not yet able to believe. "Come on," said Kirby dully. "We'll cross over, anyhow. Stream's only knee-deep, ye kin see. We'll hole up in them rocks acrost thar. I aim to ram me a galena pill down thet damn' Big Foot's gullet if it's the last dose I deliver."

"If you miss him, I won't." Aurelie's curving mouth set hard on the promise.

"Good baby." The scout's dust-bearded, drawn face softened. "Looks like we've hit the end of the trail together, after all."

"*Hopo!*" snarled Ptewaquin. "You can say good bye in those rocks over there!"

The squaw first, Aurelie next, Kirby last, they drove their horses toward the ford, rounding the screening timber just as Big Foot's yelping horde broke out of the trail head three hundred yards behind. The next seconds spun around Kirby so fast he couldn't grab more than the first handful.

Big Foot's triumphant war whoop was drowned by Ptewaquin's exultant Sioux scream, her cry in turn echoed by one from Aurelie, the three simultaneous yells covered by a fourth, piercing challenge that electrified the weary scout. There was only one sound like that in the whole damned world—and only one black-bearded horse skinner on the entire frontier to bellow it just that coyote-wild, West Texas way!

The next instant Blue Bell lunged him past the river timber, brought him the sight that had set Aurelie and Ptewaquin to yipping the Ogallala panther howl. Across river, the top sheets of its Conestogas white in the deepening shadows, squatted the tightest-parked, most God-welcome wagon corral any Comanche-shagged mountain man had ever dreamed. Aurelie and Ptewaquin had already made it across, had their horses stumble-running for the wagon square when Kirby finally got his own yell working. "*Hii-yeee-hahh!* Laredo! Laredo, old hoss!"

"Laredo, old hoss my backside!" the wagon boss bellowed, Hawkens muzzle waving frantically. "Yuh-all looked behind yuh lately? Get on ovuh heah!"

Ten seconds later Kirby was inside the square and Big Foot's braves were breaking around the edge of the cross-river timber.

The Comanches were halfway across the shallow Canadian before they realized what they had galloped into. By the time Big Foot had haunch-slid his red paint to a water-showering halt in midstream, the first ten-gun volley from the parked wagons had crashed into his packed followers, emptying five hostile saddles. Deep voice splitting with fury, the Comanche chief screamed at his braves to break and run for it, setting them the prime example by driving his pinto back through their piling ranks.

Kirby, cursing wildly, snapped a shot at the disappearing back of the Comanche giant, cursed again as he saw the chief spin in his saddle, clutching low at his right side. Damn! A man could tell by the way the big son twisted that he wasn't drilled dead center. Worse than that. As Big Foot spun to Kirby's shot, another rifle *boomed* in the scout's ear, another curse joining his own as the second slug ripped across the river, *whined* over the slumped chief's shoulder, *thudded* into the arched neck of his plunging stud.

The horse went down, headlong, the wounded Big Foot thrown clear and still kicking. The next second, two of his fleeing braves had scooped him up and borne him out of sight around the bend timber, and Ptewaquin's delicate growl was burning Kirby's guilty ear. "Damn! You bad shot. Make Ox Woman miss!" Kirby's disgusted answer was lost in the crash of Laredo's second volley, delivered the moment the panicky turning of the hostiles showed the wagon boss he had no need to hold a reserve fire. From the half dozen high screeches as the lead hit among the last of the red riders, Kirby happily allowed there would be tall wailing in more than a few Comanche lodges before the week was out.

XVI

The too-quiet midnight built rumblingly into a blazingly beautiful electrical storm. Aurelie and Kirby, snug and dry beneath the bed of the lead wagon, deep-burrowed in their borrowed blankets and buffalo robes, came awake to lie and watch the lightning chain its crazy way across the blackened sky belly, and to listen to the drum-fire bounce of the hailstones rattling off the stretched canvas spine of the Conestoga above them.

Refreshed as only the young can be by a scant three hours'

sleep, the pair lay like truant children half the night through—hand to hand, head to head, blinking to the stab of the lightning, flinching to the crash of the thunder, talking in guarded voices of the trail ahead. Aurelie, proud in her knowledge of the remaining way to Santa Fé, spun away the familiar miles for the enchanted Kirby, her clinging lips breaking the description at every landmark to brush the scout's swart cheek, or linger briefly against his ear.

When she had finished, Kirby nodded thoughtfully, the retreating storm grumbling under his low words, his dark face lit by more than the fitful lightning flashes. "Sure, Aurelie gal. It sounds like a tolerably smooth haul the way ye tell it. But me, I got an idee Santy Fee ain't no trail's end fer me. Nor fer my kind."

"How do you mean that, Kirby?" Aurelie's question mirrored her quick anxiety.

"Like I said it." The scout's words stepped carefully into the silence. "Thar ain't no end of the trail fer a High Plains man. Not so long as he kin wrop his shins around a good hoss. And still see to run a line of tracks."

"Kirby, are you trying to tell me you still want to go on, alone?" The gaunt scout's great hand found her slim one, closed quickly over it. "Wait up a minute, Aurelie gal. Yer answer's out yonder, thar." Before she could speak, he was gone, slipping away through the dark toward the distant bobbing tinkle that marked the position of Popo's bell mare and the rest of the night-foraging wagon herd. Listening intently, she heard the muffled tones of the old *arriero*'s purring Spanish, the good sound of Kirby's rare laugh, the lonely whistle of a night hawk.

Presently her anxious ear picked up another sound, the popping *crunch* of a shod horse walking on hailstones. Before she could make anything of that, a departing lightning flicker disclosed the forms of Kirby and Blue Bell.

Tying the tall Spanish mare to the wagon tongue, the scout ducked back under the Conestoga's bed, rolled into the warm blankets beside the puzzled Aurelie. "Thar's yer answer, gal," he muttered gruffly. "Tied hard and fast, jest like ye wanted."

"Kirby, I . . . I don't understand. . . ."

"I allow ye've bin away from yer mother's people too long. Let me ask you somethin'. When a *shacun* travels without his travois in a strange country, whar's his teepee?"

"Why, any place," said the girl, frowning. "Under a tree. Back of a cutbank. A hole in the rocks. Anywhere he is. Why ask that?"

"And it don't have to be a regular lodge, no matter whut? Jest so it covers thet particular *shacun* thet special night?"

"That's right. You know that. What's the matter with you, *wasicun?*"

"Could be even a Conestogy wagon bed?" The scout was grinning, not looking at her. "Happens it was hailin' hard enough?"

Aurelie's month dropped as far as her eyes opened. "Kirby! *Wasicun!* You don't mean it!"

"Hell I don't. Ye're a *shacun*, ain't ye? And this hyar wagon's yer teepee, ain't it?"

"Yes! Oh, yes!"

"And thet's my mare, ain't she?"

"Oh, Kirby, Kirby . . . !"

"And she's tied out thar, ain't she? Why fer Pete's sake, gal, I. . . ."

"Kirby, Kirby! I love you, man!" The girl's slim arms came around the mountain man's sun-brown neck, her lips burying themselves in his shoulder.

He took her close with a wide-mouthed smile. "It's like I said. Santy Fee ain't the end of the trail fer *me*. It's the beginnin' of the trail fer *us*."

Aurelie clung to him, wordless, the tear-wet lashes burning his shoulder. When she looked up, the tears were gone, the old snow-bright smile was flashing. "*Wasicun,* I'm going out there and feed that pony right now!"

"No, ye ain't. Right now ye ain't goin' no place."

"Kirby, it's the law! When a brave ties his pony in front of a girl's lodge, she has to go out and feed it, or else. . . ."

"Or else, hell!" said the mountain man, grinning. "From now on I'm the law in this teepee. Ye kin feed thet cussed mare in the mornin'. She'll never know the difference. Right now it's me that's hungry."

"And me thet's sleepy," murmured the girl, sinking back into the warm robes. "Lie down, *wasicun.* Here, where you belong. By your woman's side."

"I'm down." Kirby sighed gratefully, feeling the soft warmth of her move into the lean cradle of his shoulder, closing his eyes to the drowsy fragrance of her stealing its sleepy way up and around him with her reaching arms. "And this time, honey gal"—his trailing words slowed with the easing rhythm of his breathing—"I'll stay down. A long, long time. . . ."

There was quiet then in the oak-wheeled wagon bed lodge of Kirby Randolph and Aurelie St. Vrain. Quiet then, and for a long time after the last of the muttering thunder had tiptoed its growling way across the starlit crests of the distant Sangres.

★ ★ ★ ★ ★

A Bullet for Billy the Kid

★ ★ ★ ★ ★

I

When the child was coming, the mother glanced beyond the filthy-handed midwife tending her and saw the shadowed form of Asaph standing in the door.

"Who's there?" she asked, and the midwife, turning, saw no one.

"Shut up," she said, "and work."

But the man nodded and said softly: "I am Asaph. I heard your cries. I want to help you with the child."

The mother nodded, sighed, and lay back. "Thank you," she said. "You're a stranger. I don't know you."

"I am a stranger," answered Asaph, "but you know me."

The woman upon the rumpled bed began to cry. The baby was breech, and the hurt of it within her was very great. Asaph came to her side.

"Don't be afraid," he said. "Your son will come alive."

He laid cool and slim fingers on her brow, and the woman grew quiet.

"You said my son," she murmured. "How do you know it will be a boy?"

"Shut up, curse you!" growled the midwife. "Stop that crazy talking and twisting. I just had him by the ankles and he got away from me. Now lay still or I'll belt you one."

"You say it's a boy, too," groaned the woman. "How do you know that?"

"I can tell by the bottoms of the feet. Now shut your mouth

and bear down. I got my floors to scrub yet."

The mother looked up at Asaph, and the stranger nodded to her as if to say yes, now is the moment. She closed her eyes, and in a burst of agony the baby came. It was a boy, short and wide of body, big of head, and very homely.

"Call him Billy." Asaph smiled, and, when the mother nodded in agreement and opened her eyes to thank the stranger, he was gone.

"What are you going to name him?" asked the midwife, holding the ugly infant by the heels to slap the breath of life into the rasping lungs.

"Didn't you hear?" said the woman, frowning. "Billy."

"Better make it Beelzebub." The slattern scowled. "He sure took the devil's own time getting here."

When the boy was three the father, a drink-raddled rogue, moved his family from New York westward. His urge was to improve his fortune, but he died along the way or disappeared, and the mother continued drifting westward with the boy, making her own way. It was a far journey. Its directions came to her from time to time, and she followed them. Something told her where and when to bend her path, that was all. She thought often, along the way, of the soft-voiced Asaph who had helped her to bear young Billy. Many times she wished the gentle stranger would reappear so that she might ask his advice on what course next to take; the boy was growing now and needed a father.

Swiftly and with hardness the years wore on. The boy was eight or perhaps nine. Long since, his mother had taken another man. But the boy would have been better off with no father at all than Antrim, the dull-eyed lout the woman chose or who, more likely, chose the woman. From settlement to settlement the three wandered, and from sorrow to sorrow. The woman lost hope, the boy, happiness.

It was on a gusting autumn night, when the mother sat waiting long after midnight for her drunken second mate, that a knock came at the door of the shabby hotel wherein she and the brute and the boy existed. She did not think before she called out: "Who's there?" Yet the instant the words fell, she knew who it was and at once cried: "Oh, I'm so glad. Come in, come in!"

And it was he of course: Asaph, the stranger.

Now, however, in some way he did not seem so mysterious. She accepted him into the shabby room, warning him only not to awaken the boy who slept on a straw pallet in the corner.

"You know"—the stranger smiled—"you never told me your name."

"It's Kathleen, Kathleen Antrim now."

"And the boy? He is still Billy, as we agreed?"

"Yes. Some call him Billy Antrim. He calls himself Billy Bonney."

"Ah," said Asaph softly, "exactly."

There was a moment's silence. Asaph studied Kathleen Antrim.

"Take the boy," he said, "and go with him down into New Mexico. Here is money. It is sufficient to establish you. A boarding house would be good, I think. Yes, begin with that." He paused once more. "You will not like Santa Fé," he said, "and will end in Silver City."

"And you?" she said.

"I will meet you there. I have no choice."

"No choice?" She was puzzled, a little uneasy.

"It's the boy." He smiled. "Would you want me to forsake him?"

"No," said Kathleen Antrim. "You've been kind to us."

"How has the boy been?" asked Asaph softly. "He seems well, strong. There's something to him, too. He's not ordinary."

Kathleen Antrim looked down at the sleeping Billy. The youth's piggish nose tilted upward absurdly. Freckles spattered his impish face. Weak-chinned, the upper teeth protruding, rabbit-like, the eyes wide-set and angled for good humor, he radiated even in slumber the spirit of tough Irish carefreeness, the charm of the leprechaun and larrikin combined.

"You're right." She sighed. "And, ah, how lucky he is to have a man like yourself who knows his inner spark."

The boy stirred in his sleep, rooting in the sour blanket that twined his short form.

"*Shhh,*" cautioned Asaph. "Have you told the lad of me?"

"No."

"As well. Leave that to me. I will know the time for it."

The woman nodded. "When that time comes," she said, "will you also tell me of yourself?"

He caught her eyes, locking them. "Nothing has changed," he answered her. "You know who I am, and why I am here."

"No, no, I don't," she protested. "Honest to God!"

"*Don't say that again.*" Asaph rasped the words, white-lipped, then at once was gentle and kind as ever. "We've no need for oaths between us, Kathleen Antrim," he explained. "We're old friends."

"Then you still want me to take Billy and go to New Mexico?"

"I have given you the money to do so, have I not?"

She started to protest that he had *not* given her the money. But before she could, she realized Asaph was no longer in the room. Something else, however, was in that room that had not been there before the stranger's soft knocking at the door. In Kathleen Antrim's outstretched hands lay fifty $20 gold pieces.

II

In Silver City, life was a little better for them. Kathleen, living still with Antrim, worked as Asaph had instructed her, taking in boarders, and did well enough. But the boy, bright as new-vein copper, had some handicap of restless blood against the humdrum challenge of the schoolroom. Ignorant, raffish, rootless, he drifted the streets of Silver City like some runty brown-haired coyote whelp. And like the little brush wolf that he was, he learned the lessons of life from a sharper teacher than the weary headmaster of the camp's wet-pine and canvas schoolhouse.

Not yet nine years old, he understood that men drank themselves sick and stupid; that women sold themselves; that money was power, greed universal, gambling profitable to the dishonest; and that of all the virtues necessary to survival in that harsh time and place the greatest two were cunning and raw courage. In the bars, the bistros, the parlors of the mining camp the boy studied with a hero's application. He ran errands, carried messages, made assignations, racked pool balls, cleaned spittoons—whatever needed doing that would earn him the company of older men and women. He became welcome where the ordinary child would have been dusted out the swinging doors with the swamper's broom. And in all of this he managed, by the magic of his buck-toothed grin, his eagerness to toil, his rash courage and undoubted Irish gifts of blather and of blarney, to win the championing not only of the seamy set but of the very proper citizenry as well.

Where he passed upon the streets, old ladies smiled at him. They did not remember his name but had felt his sturdy hand in help with some heavy burden, or in crossing a crowded street, and they remembered *him*. All women, in fact, were his particular devotion. And of all women his mother was the major passion of his chivalry.

Some records say the Antrims lived in Silver City a sum of four years. If this is so, it does not agree with the ledger kept by Asaph who had it reckoned but three seasons. Yet, by either reckoning, the boy was twelve or thirteen and the year 1872 when the stranger kept his word and came again, and in the night, to the appointment he had made in Silver City.

It was a raw night. Gusts of wind whipped a fine rain through the mud gutters. Down Main Street, late in getting home, came Kathleen Antrim. With her was the boy, Billy. In the shadows of the alleyway separating the saloon from the livery stable stood Asaph. It took two looks to see him, then a third to be certain he was there.

Asaph, seeing Billy and his mother, turned his attention from them to the saloon. As his glance fell upon the slatted doors, they burst apart and a drunk stumbled forth to stand, swaying on the boardwalk. He had to give way for Kathleen Antrim, but, as she passed, he made an insulting remark that Billy heard.

The lad was at him like a ferret to a bear, so wrong was the pairing of sizes. But, armed with a cobble from the roadway, the boy might have brained the weaving sot had it not been for Asaph. The latter moved from the alleyway in time to lay his hand on Billy's back-drawn arm.

"Wait," he said in his soft voice that so compelled the listener to obey. "I will help you."

The drunk by now had recovered from his fog enough to stagger over to Billy. And in the same moment Kathleen Antrim had recognized Asaph. She opened her mouth to say his name, glad in her heart to see him, when he lay the slender long finger to his lips in the remembered gesture, warning her to be quiet.

"You sniveling guttersnipe," mumbled the drunk to Billy. "Pick up a rock on me, will you?" He steadied himself to seize the boy. Asaph glanced again at the saloon doors. And again they opened to bring a second customer, but not an unsteady one, out upon the boardwalk. Ed Moulton, a good man, took the sodden drunk by the collar and flung him into the muck of the gutter. He then tipped his hat to Kathleen Antrim and went his separate way. If he saw Asaph, he did not remark the fact.

More peculiarly, even, young Billy paid no heed to the soft-spoken stranger. He simply took Kathleen Antrim by the arm and said: "Come along, Ma, we'd best get shut of here." And when she held back to question Asaph—she had heard him speak to Billy—Asaph only put his finger to his lips and smiled.

"It's not time yet," was all he said.

"Ma, come on. Don't stand here worrying and muttering about that drunk. That mud and water will sober him up just fine." Billy gave her arm another tug, and she went along with him, shaking her head. At the corner she looked back. The boardwalk in front of the saloon was deserted. Only the lamp shine and the slick of the rain occupied it. Asaph was gone.

III

"Bottoms up," said Ed Moulton, raising his shot of red-eye whiskey. His companion nodded and downed his drink. The noise and crowd in Joe Dyer's place was about the same as it had been the night three weeks earlier when the drunk had insulted Billy Bonney's mother. There was this difference, however: the drunk had two friends with him this time and was sober. He came into the saloon, and Moulton did not recognize him or his companions. They were able to get behind the friendly Silver Citian. Had not Ed's drinking pal seen them circling, Moulton would have been unwarned of their attack. As it was, these were bad *hombres,* all three, and Ed no fighter. He had time to wheel about and get his hands up, then he was on the floor getting his ribs kicked in.

The crowd closed in as such crowds will, not caring who was being hurt so long as someone was spilling blood—not theirs, of course, and the winner would undoubtedly stand a round on the house. No one saw the small boy who burrowed through the circle of cheering oafs. But the boy, reaching the inside of the circle, was in time to see the brute who had passed the foul remark to his mother sweep up a chair and poise it to crush the skull of Ed Moulton from behind.

Someone saw Billy then because of the flash of the bared knife's blade in his hand, as he leaped in toward the hulking sneak who threatened Moulton from the rear. Several saw the bright arc of the blade as the boy swept it upward into the vitals of the bully, once, twice, three times, ripping on each thrust. And all there heard the grunt of shock come out of the man, saw the color drain out of his face, saw his mouth move with no sound coming from it, then saw him sag and turn to tallow in the knees, sliding down upon the sawdust of the floor.

"It's the Bonney kid!" someone shouted. "Stop him! Where'd he go?"

"Out the front," answered Asaph, sitting at a table in a darkened corner by the bar. "He went by me only this instant."

The crowd surged out upon the boardwalk, the barkeep, even, following the exodus. On the floor writhed the bully, dying, and his two comrades, peering down, saw this in the rotten color of his face, and they went out the back way of the saloon very quickly.

Asaph lifted the soiled cloth of the table where he sat. "All right," he said to the fearful boy crouched beneath the table, "out the back way after those two. Quick, before the crowd spills back in from out in front."

He led the way for Billy, ducking down below the bar, following it to the alleyway exit behind Joe Dyer's place, and the boy went after him closer than a shadow's shadow. Outside, Asaph pulled the lad into a dank hiding space between beer barrels, empty whiskey cases, and piled street refuse.

"Listen," he instructed him, "my name is Asaph. I knew your mother in New York. You could ask her, but there is no time. You can't go home again, boy. From here you follow me. Or, if you please, I follow you. It's in the viewpoint."

"I don't get you, mister," panted the lad. "You want to help me, or what? Why'd you get me out of there?"

"That man is dying, Billy boy. He will be dead before the people are all returned from the boardwalk. You killed a man in cold blood. The owlhoot places wait for you, and nowhere else will you be safe. Do you understand that much?"

"Yes, sir," Billy gulped.

"Now, boy," Asaph said, "there is no time for anything but flight. There is a place where we will rendezvous . . . Camp Bowie . . . do you mark it in your memory?"

"Yes, I've heard the name and I can find it. How come you to help me anyhow?"

"We're traveling the same road." Asaph smiled. He touched the boy on the shoulder, pointing down the alleyway to the south, where the town's few lights winked quickly out and only the black sagebrush waited. "Go that way," he said. "Here come the people from the bar. I will give them another bad direction. Run, Billy, run!"

Billy was gone, then, and in a moment Asaph was telling the first of the drinkers from Joe Dyer's that he had seen the boy run north, going toward Main Street and his mother's boarding house, no doubt.

When some of the men, disgusted, returned from their brief search to demand some further information of the stranger who had twice sent the hunt astray, the latter was nowhere to be found. Only the wind whistled up and down the empty alley— and even seemed to laugh a little on the way.

For three days Billy wandered without shelter or food. On the fourth day, toward evening, he came across a Mexican lad of his own age. The dark-skinned youth took him home, hiding him in the loft of the family goat pen. It was out of the wind there, and, smell though it might, it was warm in the soft prairie hay, and the friendly bleating of the animals kept their visitor calmed. The Mexican boy brought him tortillas and cold bean mash from the *rancho* kitchen, even some steaming coffee in a tin can. When Billy went on from that place, he took with him the loyalty for the dusky children of the *monte* that was to become a dedication with him; "my people" he would call them, and they would name him fondly "our Billito".

Drifting on, skirting all settlements, he worked his way toward Camp Bowie. He found a new friend, another frontier waif such as himself, also wandering the wasteland. The other boy would not tell Billy his name, and so Billy, never one to be daunted by such details, said, laughing: "All right, we'll just call you Nameless Joe, and leave it lay at that."

The two boys, astride a sore-backed mare stolen from a white squatter's stock pen—Billy would not steal from Mexicans—came at last to Camp Bowie. There they waited for Asaph, but he did not come. Some soldiers, though, befriended them. Much impressed by the bravery of the lads to be striking out alone in such a hard country, the troopers furnished them a rusted rifle and pistol, with some verdigrised ammunition, and warned them to "keep an eye out for the sneaking Apaches," as the Indians had been bad recently.

They were in Arizona, now, their path leading onward deeper into that neighboring territory.

On a bright sunny morning two days out of Camp Bowie, they came upon three Indians. Although Apaches, they were friendlies, and Billy knew enough of Indian talk to understand plainly their identity. He laughed with them, trading smile for smile, warm word for warm word. When the Indians thought they had gained the confidence of the boys, they gave them a generous gift of pipe tobacco and rode on happily, singing the Apache morning prayers of thanks for a fine day. The bells on their twelve pack animals loaded with fur pelts for the post trader at Camp Bowie tinkled and made a most pleasant music in the clear and tangy sunshine.

"Nameless Joe," said Billy, "do you suppose this old cannon will shoot where it is held?" With the question he pulled the rusted gun and leveled it and fired it pointblank into the back of the chanting Indians. The gun hit where it was held. The braves, all struck in spine or skull, toppled from their mounts and lay quiet.

"By jings!" crowed Billy. "We have struck it rich. We are in the fur business, Nameless Joe."

Nameless Joe nodded and said nothing. But he was thinking very hard. A white man knifed into the sawdust of Joe Dyer's saloon? Three friendly red men dead of gunshots in the back, fired with a laugh and no regrets? This was a good friend? A business partner?

Billy had used four bullets only on the Apaches. He had two shots remaining in the rusted gun. Nameless Joe kept thinking of those two moldy green bullets all day long. That night, when only the stars watched, he fled the camp on foot.

Next daybreak Billy, finding him gone, merely laughed and called him "Faithless Joe", and forgot him. But turning to fetch his horse, he heard behind him the rattle of a pebble. Whirling, he fired at the mounted man who had come up so silently. As he did, and through the smoke, he recognized the rider and stammered out hoarse apology for the mistake.

"No harm done." Asaph smiled, getting down from the gaunt and pale horse he rode. "I'm pleased to see you so alert."

"I'm glad I missed you," Billy said, but was uneasy in the claim. He had not missed that easy pointblank belly shot. He knew he had not missed it. But he could see no hole in Asaph's coat or vest where such a shot would have centered. Nor did the soft-voiced stranger offer explanation of the odd condition.

"I mean," said Billy, "seeing you're a friend of my mother's and . . . well, you know."

"Yes," agreed Asaph, "I know."

He regarded the homely, half-defiant urchin of the Owlhoot Trail with some bemusement.

"If you travel on in this Indian country with those horses and the peltries that they bear," he said, "other Indians will see you, and I need not describe the rest for a boy as smart as you."

"What do you suggest?" said his small listener, blue eyes watching him sharply.

"I'll buy them from you," said Asaph. "I know a place near here where they may be disposed of quietly."

"Hah! There's five . . . six hundred dollars' worth there!"

"Easily," said Asaph. "Nor do I propose to cheat you." He took a doeskin money pouch from his coat, hefting it. Tossing it to Billy, he said: "Here's a thousand dollars. You've made a good start. Buy yourself an outfit of the first order. Everything you need. But travel on. Don't turn back to Bowie."

Billy looked into the pouch, saw the dull winking of the minted gold, knew better than to count the ancient coins.

"Until the next time." Asaph smiled, turning his pale horse.

"Wait!" Billy called. "I will fetch my nag, and we can ride together for a ways. There's things I want to ask of you . . . and maybe say some others for myself."

He ran around the clump of mesquite scrub where his mustang stood picketed, with saddle on, the way all horses stand where riders slumber along the Owlhoot. But when he kicked the little beast into a gallop to spur back and join Asaph, he saw a thing that brought him to stop the pony and sit staring off, badly startled.

Asaph was riding away, leading the string of Apache pack animals that he had purchased from Billy. This was as it should be, for he had not answered Billy that he would wait for him.

But the boy still sat and stared and shook his head, and muttered under his breath. That was Asaph, sure enough. And that was Billy's Apache Indian pack string following him. But Billy had not been thirty seconds pulling picket pin and scrambling to saddle on his own mount. Yet Asaph and the Apache ponies were already disappearing past the crest of Mescalero Ridge, a rocky outcrop on the trail fifteen miles to the east.

IV

Billy lived eight years from those first kills and never spared the gun, and in all that time, beginning with the friendly Indians, he never shot from the front or straightaway, the legend notwithstanding. If he called out a man, he called him so with his trigger finger already closing, his small hand already gripped about the walnut handle of the Colt self-cocker .41 that had become his favored weapon in those latter desperate days.

When faced as several times he was by men of equal skill, Billy always quit. He would grin and give way and make as if the whole thing had been a joke from the first hard word. Later he would curse, alone, where none could hear his ugly oath to dry-gulch yet another poor devil who had offended his private code, which was whatever he wanted it to be, so bent to fit each crime. He never killed a man he did not swear deserved the death.

Yet Asaph, following him patiently, watching the way his life ran, as he had promised Billy's mother he would do, saw no killing any court would call justified or label, in the legal term, as self-defense. Asaph grew jaded with the chore. Kathleen Antrim, dead since 1874, could never know the full bad color of her runted son, and, if the gentle stranger quit the trail now, when she was gone, what harm in that? Would that warped life begun in the New York tenement run any different skein should Asaph drop its ugly stitch where presently it spun across the

Arizona sands? Ah, but that was not the question. This was no boy of Kathleen Antrim's here; this was child, Billito. He would not abandon him.

The numbers of the notches grew from four to five, the fifth a soldier blacksmith at Fort Bowie, the same place called Camp Bowie when Nameless Joe and Billy Bonney rode that way in 1872. When the blacksmith lay staring at the sky, eyeballs blank and glazing, there were again no witnesses—or there was none who cared to come forward.

"The rascal cheated me," claimed Billy, "and was to boot a sullen bully. If, as they say, I shot him short, then let the liar front me with it to my face."

But he was talking to the wind, or to the dust that stirred beneath it, or to the cold and blinking stars. For men no longer smiled back at him, although women still defended valiantly each ambush by the buck-toothed boy who, in his turn and just as senselessly, championed their sex against all charges. That was one of his two remaining loyalties in life: to protect the female kind. But men, looking down on evidence of murder mirrored in the open eyes of other men shot from behind, were not amused by amorousness or proof of mother love.

Billy found Arizona's climate warming unseasonably after the Fort Bowie affair. No more did he feel comfortable in the land of the Chiricahuas and the U.S. Cavalry. Surely, things would be better for Billito back in New Mexico, where he would be with his people, with dark-skinned Carlos, Juan, Roberto, and their steadfast clan. So determined, he rode at once and swiftly for the territorial line. But quickly as his pony ran, another paler horse was there before him.

Billy was heading for Animas, across the line, and over Antelope Pass. With the Peloncillos range behind him he would feel at home, and he could see the saw-toothed spine of that familiar rampart only miles ahead as his mount brought him down to the Cochise crossing of San Simon Creek, on the Arizona side.

It was here that he found Asaph watering his bony white. "By God," cried Billy, "this is luck!"

"Be still!" ordered Asaph sternly. "I don't like oaths."

"Oaths?" The youth laughed. "You don't like oaths? That's a hot one! You don't mind fencing Apache peltries robbed off dead Injuns, but you wince at cuss words, eh?"

"I didn't say cuss words. Just don't use that oath again."

"All right, hell, who cares." The blue-eyed fugitive grinned. "Here I am running from the cavalry and meet up with an old friend of my mother's just in time to swap him my blowed horse for his fresh one, and we're talking oaths!" With the grin, he produced the famed .41 Colt. "Now, old friend of my mother's," he said, waving the weapon, "get off that bone pile horse of yours and hand him over to me, easy like. From here, me and you leave different tracks. You take my nag, and, when the soldier boys catch up to you, just tell them I stole your plug and left you mine. Now, hop it!"

Asaph made no move to get down. "I doubt," he said, "that you would want to ride this steed. He goes a gait not many men sit happily."

"Get offen him!" snarled Billy, the time for smiles long past. "I missed you once, blast you. It won't happen again."

"No, it won't," agreed Asaph softly.

He swung down from the gaunt-ribbed white and handed up the reins to Billy, still mounted on his own rangy bay.

Billy moved to take the reins and, in the motion, his hand touched that of Asaph. He recoiled from the contact, his impish face a fleeting picture of startlement.

Asaph stood looking up at him. "What is it?" he said.

"Your hand," answered Billy, scowling now, recovering. "You got a hand like ice!" He broke off, defensive anger replacing the

221

moment's panic started up within him by the touch of Asaph's hand. "Go to the devil." He grimaced, waving aside the proffered reins.

"A reasonable suggestion," said Asaph, amused, "but I've little mood to humor it. Come along, boy, this time we'll ride a way together. The soldiers are too close for us to risk different paths."

Billy knew the troopers to be hard behind him. Yet, of a sudden, he did not want Asaph with him. "Listen," he urged, "I don't mean to draw you into this pot. You didn't call for no cards in the hand. No use declaring yourself in at this late date, *amigo*. I killed a man back yonder."

"I know," said Asaph. "I was there and saw you do it."

"You was? The hell! I never seen you."

"You shot him in the back of the head and turned his pockets out." The other shrugged. "He cheated you, all right. He had no money on his person."

"Son-of-a-gun," said Billy Bonney uneasily. "Let's go."

Asaph remounted, and together his white horse and young Bonney's bay splashed over the rippling shallows of Cochise crossing. But there was something odd about that fording. Two horses went into the stream and two came out of it on the far side, yet only one line of hoof prints appeared in the damp sand of the exit, to lead away from water's edge toward New Mexico—those of Billy Bonney's bay.

V

"Now," said Asaph, "I must leave you."

They sat their horses, not upon the trail to Animas but south-turning, through the Alamo Hueco Mountains and into Chihuahua, old Mexico. Billy nodded. He was still tense, still apprehensive. Yet Asaph had convinced him.

"Well," the young killer admitted, "I can't rightly dispute it with you. If you say I'd ought to go down there to Chihuahua City, then I'll go. I ain't forgot you told me to stay away from Fort Bowie, and look what happened."

It was Asaph's turn to nod. He thought how simple most men were. Did it not occur to this blue-eyed boy of his that Asaph understood he would do what he was told *not* to do, and that therefore the reason for so telling him was served precisely? No, never. This was what made it so easy for Asaph in the world. He had never had to sweat and toil to make his way, but only to direct and misdirect others to the end that they perspired and labored in his cause. In a way, this Billy Bonney lad sought the same conveniences. He would not take steady work, or work of any decent kind. Of the many unmentionable things he would do and had done, honest work was never one. Shady travail he would seize eagerly upon. He would run his lungs out on an evil errand, or peel his fingers to the tarsals, should the chore promise ill-gotten gain. But to hew to the line, sun to dark, for pay? Hah, not Billy Bonney! Well, the pity was that the lad, with all the appetite for wrong, had not the head to handle his stomach. The lack of brains was ever Billy's problem.

"All right," Asaph said, breaking the pause, "it is good that you have learned so early. It will make the rest an easier thing for both of us."

"What the hell are you talking about?" Billy scowled. "What rest of what?"

Asaph calmed him with a smile. "The rest of *us*," he said good-humoredly. "It seems we continue to meet along the trail, lad. Why not imagine we shall meet again, and continue thus to meet throughout your days?"

"My days?" Too long in the brush and on the lam to miss slight trail signs, Billy frowned again. "What about your days? Or ours? Why just mine?"

"Why not just yours? Do you know anyone else's more

important to the plan?"

"Cuss it all, what plan? You talk like a man with mush in his mouth. I ain't got no plan with you."

Asaph laughed aloud. It was a strange sound, not unmusical, however, and indeed attractive in a nameless way. "I mean to say, what life is more important to you than your own? Is it mine?"

"Well, not hardly."

"Exactly the point, wild boy, and who has been more tender of your days than I?"

Billy chewed his Irish upper lip and scowled. "Well, if you say so. I reckon now with Ma gone, and barring my Mex friends in the chaparral, you're all that cares for me or gives a hoot."

"Precisely."

"I'll do it then, Asaph. Chihuahua City it is, and I will stay there till you send for me."

Asaph nodded quickly. "A messenger will come in my name," he said. "Wait for him."

They parted, the deal agreed. But Billy Bonney was of wily mind, if limited. No sooner was he out of sight of Asaph than he wheeled his horse once more to the west. Instead of going by the left-hand trail to Chihuahua, he went the right-hand road toward Sonora.

VI

Martinez was the dealer's name. What town it was in old Sonora is not remembered. But Billy was there and the game went against him, or so the Mexican witnesses said. For Billy's part, he later insisted, faithful to his pattern in such affairs: "He peeled them from the inside of the pack. A Spanish deck is still a Spanish deck, to be dealt from fair and square. I was being robbed right there in front of everybody. More than that, the crazy fool laughed at me. Nobody laughs at Billy Bonney, not and steals the pot from him, by jing! Sure I shot him. And it's a black lie if they tell you I didn't give him no more chance than he did me. I called him and he laughed, and I let him have five rounds under the table. He could have played it fair and been alive today."

Whatever Billy's story, he was in deep trouble, far from the border and having killed his first Mexican. Now the last of his two loyalties was no more, and, when the word came up out of old Sonora that Billito had killed Martinez *beneath the table,* then the old security he had always known among his brown-skinned people was a thing of the receding past. From that day the Mexican folk were not so sure of their beloved Billito, even if their women still believed in him, and Billy could no longer count on disappearing into the *monte,* when the humor suited him or the sheriff was too close behind.

Indeed he might never have left Sonora alive, but for the timely interference of one Malquierdes Segura, a Mexican youth of his own age and his equal, as well, in wild daring. Segura it was, who, seeing Billy flee the dim *cantina* with his Colt .41 still smoking, beckoned him into the darkened doorway of his sweetheart's home, admitted him into that house, and hid him there until the hue and cry had died away.

When the excited townsmen rushed on by and vanished down the dusty street, shouting after him in Spanish to wait and be hung or, better, be shot while escaping, like a decent fellow would do in the same guilty straits, Segura turned to Billy with a grin as lunatic and scary as his own.

"*Ay, Chihuahua!*" He laughed. "That was a near thing!"

"Yes, indeed," responded Billy, bowing with mock gravity. "*Muchísimas gracias.* Permit me to present myself. I am Billy Bonney."

He of course spoke flawless Spanish, and, when he had told Segura who he was, the Mexican youth's dark face lit up.

"Why," he said, "that is a wondrous thing. I have been look-ing for you. I was told I'd find you here."

"You? Looking for me? How is that, *amigo?*"

Quick to take suspicion always, Billy was immediately on guard.

"Asaph sent me," was all Segura said, yet in those three words, or with them, he might as well have struck a knife in his listener.

"Asaph," breathed Billy. "That circling buzzard, why does he trail me so? He . . . wait, you lie. He told me to go to Chihua-hua."

"That is so. He said as much to me, also. However, that is not my affair, *compañero*. Asaph sent me to get you out of here, and that I will do. *¡Basta!* Come on. That crowd of barking dogs will be yelping back this way before you know it."

"But, blast it," protested Billy, "I'm not sure of you."

"*Bah,* why worry about me? Would you want to bring shame on the house of my sweetheart, a poor defenseless girl?"

"No, God forbid. I would never harm a woman. Let's go."

Go they did, and quickly, following narrow paths and secret trails through the hills that only wild cattle trod, traveling toward Chihuahua and the city to which Asaph had originally instructed Billy to proceed. Billy was much taken with Segura, and he with Billy. But the Mexican would not talk about Asaph, vowing that he knew too little of the latter to warrant a conversation, and saying, too, that it mattered not the least in any way. The important thing was that he and Billy Bonney had found one another and would make an outlaw pair to bring fond memories to the dark eyes of all the *chiquitas* twixt Agua Prieta and Guada-lupe.

"By jing!" vowed Billy, touching up the trim gray mare, La Chispa, that Segura had provided for him. "Me and you will bust the bank for sure, providing you can pick a lock or a hide-out house or a pretty girl as good as you can a horse."

"That mare," shouted back Segura, "cost Asaph five hundred in Spanish gold! I saw him pay it, for it was I who told him where she was for sale."

Billy laughed with pure good hellish feeling. The lights of the town lay far behind, and with them all noise of any play for vengeance over the monte dealer, Martinez. What luck to find a sidekick like Segura, and a mount the order of this hot-blood iron gray that moved beneath him fluidly and wildly swift as mountain water in cascade or quicksilver beading bright in racing pearls. *Santa* María! This was more like it was in the good old days. It was certain he owed Asaph more than any man could pay. But he would find a way to do it. For Billy Bonney settled his debts, whether with lead or gold, and he would see that he did not stand short with that cussed stranger when the last pack had been cut, and dealt, and all cards turned face up for cashing out.

"I guess," he said aloud, and after some delay, in answer to Segura, "I owe that Asaph dude aplenty. This here mare's a holy terror. She don't run, she *transfers* through the air."

"Something like that," said Segura, and laughed softly as he said it. "You know, Billito, that mare, she is the half-sister to that pale bone pile Asaph rides."

"A lie!" cried Billy. "Damn you, that's a lie!"

Segura turned his dark face from the moon. Billy could not see it, shadowed so. But he could hear the words that came, lisping with the Spanish laugh.

"A lie you say? No kin to Asaph's steed? Ah, *amigo,* so much to learn, so little time in which to learn it, eh? Do this. The next time that you see that horse of Asaph's, mark the track line that he leaves. *Then* tell Segura that he lies."

Martinez was the sixth man Billy killed. It seemed his death gave other ideas to the latter. Chihuahua City also had a monte game, but this time the dealer was not charged. It was the keeper of the bank who was waylaid going home in the black hours of the dawn. If he were killed, no one could ever prove, nor could theft of the money he was carrying be noted to Billy's account. The man *and* the money simply disappeared from the middle of the town and were not seen again. But there was a witness.

"The rascal cheated Billito and . . . well, who better to repay the loss than the banker of the game? If he disappeared, what difference, so long as the debt was discharged? Did anyone hear Billito complain past that night of being shorn in Chihuahua? Never! He was always fair about such things."

So said Malquierdes Segura, who told a good story then and later, too.

The Chihuahua banker was number seven and, like number six, a Mexican. How Segura balanced this account is business that he never jotted down. Seemingly he was a child of universal blood, the same as Billy Bonney. Besides, he had done no crimes, only transported Billy in these matters, guided him, or furnished horseflesh none could catch, such trivial things, no more.

Billy, past that year of 1876, was likened by some who knew him from Silver City, and the firming influence of Kathleen Antrim, to a trusty stock dog that has taken to killing sheep. The taste of the victim seemed to swell his appetite, not diminish it. And, like a dog gone wild, he commenced to kill senselessly, to strike at anything that moved or made a shadow or uttered a faint bleat along the trail he rode. In this manner the dead ones, eight through twelve and past twelve to pushing twenty, piled up behind him.

There were lies told of the list, of course. More men were added to it than deserved the fate. Circumstances surely were not always such as to place full blame on Billy. Indeed, as always with such warriors of the Owlhoot tribe, far from it. He became a hero in his own time according to the legend. He killed to protect the poor. He killed in defense of frightened woman-hood. He killed the wicked in the name of the good. He was generous. He gave away his bloody wealth. He traveled with no gold saved for himself. Had he a bone, he would share it with a hungry dog. Had he no bone for the poor brute, he would go to the kitchen of the nearest rich man and fetch him one. No little man need fear with Billy near, nor need his sister cringe in ter-ror, nor his old mother know want. These were Billito's people, these *pobrecitos* of the *monte*. If, to support them, he had oc-casional need to kill, well, one could not live a hard life without its penalties. So the legend grew with the dead.

But also, with the dead, another factor grew, and this one was no folklore fostered by the buck-toothed gunman's kindness to old ladies or his charms for younger ones. The responsible, quiet men of the territory were talking in covert meeting places. These were the cowmen, the merchants, the townsfolk of Lin-coln, Sumner, Fort Stanton, and the other settlements of the land Billito had returned to haunt. Gradually their decisions drew together. A man was needed who knew the wolfish outlaw boy and was, at the same time, unafraid of him.

Finding the man took a bit more doing. That was because he was so close all the while that no one recognized him. It took a soft-voiced cattle buyer from the East, a stranger to that part of New Mexico, to nudge the final choice. This took place when the buyer rode into town one afternoon in the company of famed local rancher, John Chisum. A gentle fellow with a ready and engaging smile, the stranger stopped his horse and said to his companion: "Mister Chisum, sir, who is that lean man yonder with the broad mustache? The tall one, with the ice-gray eyes, lounging there before that store, all easy and long-coiled like a cat?"

It was a peculiar description, and it caught at the mind of John Chisum. He turned to see whom it might be the pleasant buyer inquired after. When he did see, his eyes narrowed and he halted his own horse. "Friend," he said to the buyer, words low and tense with some excitement, "why do you ask?"

The Eastern buyer smiled quickly. "Oh, it was nothing definite," he said. "A stray thought took me riding by. No more than that."

"What thought?" pressed Chisum, watching him.

"Why, only that I would not care to have that man after me." The buyer shrugged. "Now I suppose you think that's rather random, sir, if not outrightly foolish."

John Chisum shook his head, excitement growing. "Not at all, sir," he replied. "Wait here a moment, if you will. And take my thanks beforehand."

He turned his horse and rode over to the hitching rail of the general store. Halting the animal, he nodded to the owner of the place, the same long-coiled, cat-like fellow described by the cattle buyer.

"Pat," he said without amenities, "you are the man." Then, turning back, he joined the pale horseman waiting in the road. "Thank you, Mister Asaph, sir," he said. "You have conferred a service here that none shall know officially, but one we local citizens may enter in the ledger of good luck, and thank the stars for sending you this way."

"I doubt the stars had much to do with it." Asaph smiled. "Nor luck the same. But if it humors you to think it so, then I am flattered. In my business, men are not often happy to be served my wares, much less to hail me on my way. A good day to you, Mister Chisum, sir. I'll think about the cattle."

That was in 1880. The place was Fort Sumner, New Mexico. The man in front of the general store was Patrick Floyd Garrett, a lean expatriate Alabaman gone West to improve his fortunes in the post-war 1860s, like a thousand others from the South before him. And what John Chisum meant by the blunt greeting just bestowed was that Pat Garrett was the man standing so close to history he had not been seen. He was the man to hunt Billito down, to kill the killer.

VII

For Billito and his coyotes of the chaparral, last earth was near. The Lincoln County War, so famed in song and myth, was fought, but it will not be waged again in this account. All who follow Billy's life know of that sordid struggle between Tunstall and McSween and the Murphy-Dolan faction for control, real and political, of Lincoln and its county. Billy fought for Tunstall as a gunman. They say he slew eight or nine or seven men, some say ten, but Asaph's record, whence this counting stems, says that the total number of the notches on his .41 that year when Garrett came to dog his trail stood at nineteen, two less than the years of his life. And Asaph's record, cast ahead as only he could cast it, showed the final entry to precisely match that span, which then was twenty-one—a man for each year of his life.

There were thus two more men to die. They must die quickly, too, for Billy's time to kill them ran now on a shortened rope, and tightening. Asaph already had selected the men.

But first came Garrett on the trail and closing, fast. He trapped Billy and four desperate companions in an abandoned ranch building at a place called Stinking Springs. Pat had an efficient posse with him, men who all knew why they were there. On the other hand Billy had often boasted that he would never be taken alive by living lawmen, and Pat Garrett in particular. Thus when the Lincoln sheriff—he wore that star officially now—called aloud for Billy to come out, hands high and walking slow, the gauntlet was down.

In the ancient house, Billy had his saddled mare, the noted gray La Chispa. Did he now spring on this splendid animal to carry out his claim, dash through the silent door onto the waiting riflemen, leap the mare and race her past the deadly guns of the quiet townsmen? Did this legend of the little folk of the *monte* ride thus through glory and gunsmoke to freedom far and dear? He did not. He first sent Charley Bowdre out to test the wind and shooting light of bullets meant for him. Bowdre, a man as tough and true as whang leather, walked out and took seven shots, all centered in his stomach, then still walked far enough to see Pat Garrett standing there and say: "Good morning, Sheriff. I am dead . . . good day."

After that came Billy. He showed up in the door, hands high, as told to do. The gray mare followed him, her head still high where his was not, her step still sure where his faltered with the white-lipped, sickly smile and whine: "I'm all done, Pat. Don't shoot!"

The chase to corner him had been long and hard. It had carried beyond Las Vegas, and the posse's horses were all done. The result was to take the train and ride the cars back home, the captured outlaws, with their craven chief, trussed in iron cuffs but granted the freedom of the smoking car. At each exit stood a deputy with badge of office, his waiting Winchester.

Fearing that at Las Vegas the hostile mob of lookers-on might try to take the outlaw for their long-due own and stretch him on the spot, the vigilance was doubled. A crowd did show up and did threaten. But Pat lounged to the platform with his thumb hooked in his vest, the coat turned back enough to show the walnut handle of the Colt worn low and buck-thong-tied, and the crowd shrank away, its nerve failing.

From Las Vegas the train sped west to Santa Fé. From there, by secret ways, the renowned killer was borne to District Court to hear Judge Bristol admit the evidence, then, staring coldly from the bar, intone: "Swear the prisoner in."

The charge was murder, first degree, for the death of Sheriff William Brady in the Lincoln County War, wherein Billy had shot the lawman down, unseen, from behind a breast-high adobe wall. It was the act of a mad dog, now so judged.

"On the Thirteenth day of May, Eighteen Eighty-One, at the county seat of Lincoln," droned the clerk, "you will be hanged as fully deserved and as your many crimes insist . . . not just this single one . . . and by the neck, and publicly, till you are dead."

That afternoon a visitor came unannounced to Billy's cell. It was Asaph.

"Ah, boy," he said, "think back to carefree days you knew when such as Jesse Evans rode your side and brave men like Segura risked their lives that you might win again and take it all, as was your way. Why, in those days, no man stood taller in his mind than you. What happened in between to bring you to this lonely cell where ought of friends or visitors you have are those which come to gnaw at night, the bedbugs and the rats?"

"Damn it all." Billy scowled. "Lay off that singsong stuff! It gives a man the creeps. If you've ought to say of help, then say it. Elsewise, leave me be. Jailer!"

"Tut," said Asaph softly. "No need to make alarm. Not that I blame you, boy. The rope's a nasty thing to face. But I have come to help you, as you say. I've brought a gift of prophecy. Will you hear it out?"

He let a moment's silence intervene, black eyes peering into Billy's face. And Billy nodded, somehow afraid, and said he would hear the tale.

Asaph's thin lips parted. "The last two men that I shall send to die beneath your guns will bear the names of Ollinger and Bell. I name them thus that you will know my tongue is true when the future brings your paths together, and the blood spills as I say it must."

"Stop!" cried Billy. "You're hexing me. That there's heathen mumbo jumbo. I don't need to set still for such daft talk. Jailer!"

But now a strange thing happened. Billy opened his mouth and the yell for the turnkey came out, but no sound was heard. The boy wheeled, white-faced, on Asaph.

"You are witching me, blast you. Let go my tongue."

Again he formed the shout, yet not one syllable of sound disturbed the eight-foot cell.

"If you wish to call it witchcraft," shrugged Asaph, not smiling but still gentle, "that is your affair. But you will listen to my augury all the same. When a man makes a bargain with me, he keeps it. You claim that rule yourself."

It was true. One of Billy's most frequent vows was that he would always do what he promised to do, keeping his word.

"Go on," he told Asaph wearily. "Mebbe there's something to your spell, after all. I ain't nothing to lose, nohow."

Asaph sat down upon the cell's rude cot. His dark glance lifted to the single narrow window, staring far away. The soft voice resumed its hypnotic murmur. Swiftly it foretold the fate that waited just beyond that cell for Billy Bonney. Almost before the listening boy realized it, the grim tale was done. Asaph's vibrant voice fell away. Billy shook his head. It seemed to him that he had merely dozed. Yet it was dark in the cell, and still as the grave, and Asaph was no longer there. Of a sudden, Billy was not sure of anything. Shakily he lit the stub of candle he found tallowed to the window's sill. Seizing up the light, he cast its feeble ray about. The cell was empty.

No, not quite. On the rude table by the cot a black book lay that had not been there before. Billy picked up the volume. He regarded it fearfully. He knew that it was Asaph's account book, and he believed that he knew the dread list that it contained. Or did it? And, if the list were there, did those two last names appear upon it in the manner Asaph had said?

No, it wasn't even Asaph's book. It was some prison Bible left there by the jailor as Billy drowsed. But no Bible had that snake-like skin for cover. The black book was actually coiling in Billy's hand. He could feel it move. The boy opened the book, peering with the candle. His stomach turned cold. The two names were there:

Bell, J. W., deputy sheriff, Lincoln town.
Ollinger, Robert, deputy sheriff, Lincoln town.

Then, noted in a fresher ink that did not match the other, Billy saw a third and final name, and his voice grew low and whispery. "Oh, no," he said. "Not that name, not *there*."

Asaph's prophecy was borne out with chilling speed. Billy, transferred to Lincoln town, was held in the old Murphy-Dolan store building. Assigned to guard him were deputies J.W. Bell and Bob Ollinger, as foretold by Asaph or, as Billy began to assure himself, by Asaph's ghost. For now the fugitive youth was believing what he wanted to believe. He had not seen Asaph since the jail cell visit, and the black book had vanished in some arcane fashion, meanwhile, and happily.

Accepting this as proof that he had dreamed the whole thing, the doomed prisoner at once began to dwell upon the problem of his escape. But when he arrived in Lincoln and was assigned deputies Bell and Ollinger as guards, he thought no more of dreams. The desperate light in his hazel-flecked eyes grew wilder still. All right, Asaph's augury was coming true. He, Billy, would play it as it seemed to go, and see what happened. He already had a foretold way in which to steal Bob Ollinger's sawed-off deadly scatter-gun. If that stolen shotgun part of the prophecy worked out and he got free, as the augury had said, then he would look up Asaph—or his ghost—and get the rest of the plan. All of it. Including that last name in the black book. The

one that came past Ollinger's and Bell's, and written in a different, fresher ink. But no. That last name was a mistake. It was an
addition of Billy Bonney's imagination. Surely it was not
Asaph's work to write it there.

Forcing the uneasy thought to fade, young Bonney shot down
Bell and Ollinger with scant concern, knowing from Asaph's
augury that he could not miss them with the stolen gun, nor
they harm him in any way. He was free and standing laughing
on the second-floor balcony of the old store building, the smoke
still curling from the muzzle of Ollinger's shotgun, when the
first chill doubt assailed him.

Damnation! The augury was ended. He was free, just as it
had said he would be free, but he was free in the middle of Lincoln, trapped on an upper balcony with an empty gun, still
shackled with the leg irons upon which deputy Bell had counted
so fatally to restrain the prisoner.

Curse the luck, where was Asaph now? Now, when a man
could use him? In the name of the Lord, why didn't he show
up? The seconds, the minutes were ticking away. If his mother's
strange friend were to make it in time, he would need to be
wondrous quick. The minutes became five, ten. But shadowy
Asaph did not appear, and Billy began to snarl like a cornered
animal. The devil with Asaph—or his ghost, whichever. When
the time came that Billy Bonney needed anybody, or anybody's
spook, to show him what to do when guns and horses were to
hand, then that would be the time to get the shakes. Right now
the game was his to play, and he would play it as he always
had—to win. Wheeling about, he left the balcony.

In Sheriff Garrett's deserted office room, where he had seized
deputy Ollinger's shotgun, Billy now armed himself with a
Winchester and two six-guns that he found there. *Clanking*
down the hall and the stairway of Dolan's store in his leg irons,
not looking down at his old friend, Deputy J.W. Bell as he was

forced to step over his bullet-torn body, he made his way to the street. There was no attempt to hide himself. Billy the Kid had guns to hand again and feared no man in Lincoln. Not, at any rate, with Pat Garrett out of town.

From above, he had seen the man he wanted most, coming down Main toward the store. Now, as the fellow limped past, Billy shadowed out of the doorway and hailed him.

"Hello there, Mister Geiss. Come in, come in, I've work for you."

Old Geiss, as he was called, was the German-born blacksmith of the town. A tough graybeard and strong as a salt cedar, he was old not only in years but in the ways to stay alive in that harsh climate. When informed that Billy Bonney needed shackles removed from his ankles and was willing to pay a bullet in the head to the blacksmith who refused the business, Old Geiss just nodded and replied—*"Ja, ja."*—and went on down the street to his shop and got his chisel.

Billy returned to the second floor of the store. There Old Geiss followed him and went to work on the leg irons while the Kid sat on the window sill of the front room talking with old friends below, who tarried in the street to inquire after his health and what they might be able to do for him. Billy's cool suggestion to these citizens was that they not try to leave town ahead of him, and, incredibly, they obeyed. The sly boy with his protruding overshot jaw, weak chin, bright eyes, and mad, quick grin had such a hold on the imaginations of the community that he was safe in Lincoln, even freed, and in fact and by the testimony of a dozen reliable witnesses he lingered two hours in the town, *after* old Geiss had cut him loose.

It was nearly twilight when at last he departed. He had a good horse, the stout bay saddler of William Burt, a customer of Old Geiss. The blacksmith had just shod the animal, and he was full of oats and ready to run. So, too, was Billy Bonney. His trail, when last seen by the Lincolnites, lay toward Fort Stanton. The only actions of pursuit adopted by the cautious townsfolk were the dispatches of private warnings to any enemy of the Kid's who might think him still safe in Dolan's store. It was actually two full days before Pat Garrett could get back and gather a posse, the killing of the guards being on April 28th, Garrett's start from Lincoln with the posse given as April 30th.

The track, cold now on the barren dusty ground, ran due west four miles, then veered north to disappear in the direction of Las Tablas. But the Kid was gone. Fort Sumner, Cañaditas, Arenoso, and Tayban, and a hundred arcane cow-trail and sheep-track camps hid him well in those following weeks. Wherever he was reported, he was somewhere else by the time Garrett could arrive. Traps were laid, a score of positive sightings run down and dropped in disappointment. Nothing hard was learned. Billy had vanished.

His *pobrecitos,* his "poor ones", had welcomed him back and were telling no man with a star where Billito rode or slept. But Billy was afraid. Something had changed. He trusted no one now.

May, with its brief flowers, passed into June with its little rain. July sweltered next, its dust devils whirling toward August. Pete Maxwell's place, and Curington's, goatherds and cattle drovers, water tanks, and railway switch tracks, lonely haunts and lonely men, saw much of him those fleeting final weeks.

And slowly the word crept back to Garrett. Billy, who knew all the range from Taos to Tucumcari, was circling back. He was going in a wide and wary swing out around the scene of his last kill. But like the wolf and coyote that he was, he could not help himself; he was heading back for Lincoln.

It was about this time that the sheriff had a letter. It came to him from a contact named Brazil, a rancher whose place had many times been used by Billy on the dodge.

Our bird is back, the letter ran, *and covied up nearby. If you will meet me at Tayban, perhaps we'll flush him soon.*

Although it was midday, and hot, Pat shivered. Where could he find two men, just two men, who would side him walking up on that bird? Men he could trust to hold their fire until the flush, then not turn and run when the quarry broke covert? The outlaw had a thousand friends, or a hundred at the least. But the sheriff had to think the better part of the day to scrape up in his memory the names of two men he could depend on going after Billy. Even then, he had no certain way of knowing that these two might not, when told the nature of the game, get word to Billy and back out themselves. But brave Brazil had chanced sure death to write the note. Garrett must sound out his aides.

First was John Poe. Poe was a good man, hard to bluff, an employee of the Stockmen's Association, experienced in trailing elusive prey. Poe would not turn tail or belly-up when called. He would stand and deliver. All right, then, Poe was one. Next, T.K. McKinney. Tom McKinney was likewise a working gun. He had been where the owl hooted and come back from there. He would do.

Garrett contacted them late at night on the roadside beyond Lincoln's lights. "Now, boys," he said, the careful words slow-spaced, "this is a chancy trip. You know the Kid. If either one of you wants out, just say the word and travel. Stay with me and we ride tonight for Roswell. That's where he is."

Both listeners nodded and neck-reined their horses to side Pat Garrett's. "Let's go," they said as one.

The three men rode away, Garrett tall and proud between his deputies. A mackerel sky striped the moon's white face, shadowing the sage at roadside. Out of the gloom thus made rode a fourth horseman, a stranger on a pale mount.

Halting the gaunt animal, Asaph stared off after the Lincoln sheriff and his hard-eyed henchmen. There went three good men, the kind that Asaph shunned for lack of profit in the breed. To such as them the law meant something, enough that they would die for it. To young Bonney it meant nothing, not the law, or the lawmen riding out in its just name. Of all the trashy lies men told in the behalf of Billy, none was so false, so ludicrous, so bald of proof as that which declared the buck-toothed weasel to be the good pal and boon companion of Pat Garrett, or the other way around. Pat Garrett knew the Kid, and nothing more. Past that, the two were scarcely of the same race. Pat was a man. Billy of the crooked grin, the protruding fangs, the dirty freckles, and the wild eyes, now green, now blue, now gray, but always wild—why, Billy was a boy, no more, and rotten to the sapwood of his spine.

At no time since he knifed the drunken man in Dyer's place had he been anything but the outlaw thief and bandit chief who cheated, stole, laughed, lied, cringed, and killed, for money. Yet Asaph, watching his executioners ride forth into that moon-streaked July night, felt a moment's strange compassion for the boy. He detested him, yes. But what rose in the stranger's mind, as now he knew the end drew near, was pity. Not disdain, not contempt, not censure. Just simple pity. What a wonder it was that a bright boy like this, true to himself and to others once, could have fallen so that he could be tracked and trailed and stalked like an animal gone mad, that must be cornered and destroyed because it now struck out in senseless viciousness at all who passed it, or drew near, or even took its name in vain, or called in sympathy for it to come forth.

Who had helped him on this way? Anyone? Asaph, perhaps? No, it wasn't Asaph, it wasn't anyone, it was Billy. Men are born to be bad, and men are born to be good. In the meanwhile, neither saints nor sinners are made by good or bad advice. It takes two to make a partnership in crime: one to propose, one

imagine that the words . . . 'Pete Maxwell's place' . . . popped all unaided into their heads, and in a perfect sequence of suggestion, so as to bring all four into conjunction at that spot in one same hour?" Asaph laughed softly. "Strange," he said, "and just a little sad."

He sat yet another moment, looking off through the moonlight to where the three figures of the distant horsemen dwindled on the trail to Maxwell's ranch. His voice took on that rhythmic cadence that Billy had cursed as singsong but which another ear might have labeled as a form of speech far older than any man then living.

"I set them on his trail," he said, "and yet I cannot say I feel well for it. Indeed, I bring them to him haltingly. Admire him, I do not. Who cherishes the coward, thief, and murderer? Not I, despite the things men say of me. It is that Billy has within him elements of all the sorrow and despair of man, wrapped in a cloak of happy dignity. Where he has killed, even lurking in the shadows or behind some leafy wall, he has known remorse, or call it conscience, if you will. He still would stand above the corpse and murmur down . . . 'Now, blast it, Bob . . . or Joe or Jim or Jack . . . I'm sorry as all glory.' What he stole of horse or gun or food, or even of some maiden's virtue, he always sent a message back avowing full repayment. What matters it, as heroes go, that never in all that time of vowing did he once make good his word? When he lied, he lied to good effect, such as to save his life or sacrifice that of another, perhaps that of some friend who loved him as a brother, or a son, and would have died for him, unasked, and so no real treason done. Ah, thus the charm he's borne. It has been, withal, remarkable. Sheltering him from winter's wind and summer's sun, alike, for twenty years, and thus far part of twenty-one. Which part now is run, alas, leaving Billy and his charm undone."

The bony white horse whickered inquiringly, expecting more.

But Asaph had finished.

He arose from the rock. "Do you know," he said, the soft laugh falling once more, "that I have so engrossed myself with his past that I've forgotten where he's going now. Another moment, yet, patient friend."

He took from inside his coat the slender black book and, holding it to the moonlight, squinted frowningly.

"Ah, yes," he said, the smile restored. "Pete Maxwell's place." Then added, softer still, and mounting up with haste: "Come on, old ghost, it's all been said . . . let's go."

"This will do." Pat Garrett reined his pony in. "We'll go in from here afoot," he continued. "This old orchard's our best cover. Tie your horses. We don't want them wandering."

"It's funny Pete would put him up," said McKinney.

"Not funny to Pete, likely," added Poe. "The Kid no doubt asked for board and bed, Mex style, with his gun or knife."

"Walk up soft, now," said Pat Garrett. "Hold your pistols cocked. Don't shoot until you hear me say . . . 'That's him.' "

They went through the orchard trees, gnarled and dim-seen, the moon having gone behind cloud. They could see the main house of the Maxwell ranch ahead. There was no light in it. There was not, either, any sound of human voices from the main building. But a square Mexican adobe hut lay between them and the ranch house, and from that source they did hear voices coming. The tongue was Spanish. Neither Garrett nor Poe or McKinney recognized any of the speakers, of which they made out three, at least, for number.

This failure to identify one of the voices put the sure lie to the legend claiming Pat and Billy to be friends. For the third speaker was the Kid. Garrett, had the myth been true of his great fondness for young Bonney, would certainly have known that bucktoothed lisp in any tongue. But he did not know Bonney that well, and he did not recognize his voice that night, nor did his two companions, Poe and McKinney.

But now Garrett paused, hearing those soft tongues of the *monte* from the hut. He saw three shadows squatting near an adobe wall, close by the door of the small house. These must be Maxwell's Mexican hands, his *mozos*, servants, something. One of them arose and, yawning, said he was going to bed. He went into the adobe, lifting its cowhide door flap and disappearing from view. The watchers saw a lamp turn up inside the hut.

Then they did a strange thing. The man who had gone in to retire was the one with the lisp, the bucktoothed boy, Billy Bonney. Yet the lawmen still did not know him, still turned away from that small house, where there were both light and voices, and went on to the big house where neither lamp nor sound was evidenced. Why? Did Garrett, when he signaled with his hand in silence for Poe and McKinney to follow him, know something he had not told his deputies? Was there a trap within the trap? Did he leave Billy in that hut on purpose? Did he go on to the main house knowing something? If not, why had he failed to order the surround sprung on the outlaw at the hut, where they had him dead to rights and caught cold in a one-roomed shack with no escape?

The legend goes that Billy grew hungry after deciding to bed down, that he got up and told his Mexican host, Maxwell's hired hand, that he was going down to Pete's and get a slice of beef from a fresh quarter he knew to be hanging on the ranch porch. This was Garrett's story, told in retrospect and after the grim fact of Billy's being taken. It did not match with Asaph's.

The soft-voiced stranger knew better. He stood in the same shadows of that adobe hut that sheltered the crouching lawmen from Lincoln. And he stood in those shadows after those lawmen had crept away, on down to the main ranch house, and were ready there. Then he heard what truly passed between

Billy and the Mexican hand. It was not Billy Bonney who said—"I am going down to Pete's."—but the Mexican servant of Maxwell who ordered, no, who suggested to the outlaw: "Billito, *amigo*, Pete, he says he wants to see you. Go down to the house."

Did Billy Bonney go, or was he *sent?* Asaph knew but never told. He saw no need to say that Garrett lied. A lawman never tells all that he knows, or, if he does, he soon finds himself the victim of his own honesty. Pat Garrett was a brave man, good and true. He went where his sheriff's star directed him, needing no testament from such as Asaph in the going.

At the main house, Pat stationed his two henchmen in an ambush of the covered porch, twenty feet from Maxwell's room. Maxwell lay on his bed, but wide awake. He also knew something.

When Garrett had first seen Billy that night, when the Kid went unrecognized at the Mexican's hut, Billy had worn his hat, his boots, his gun. His pony had been staked nearby and saddled. Would that have been the posture of a welcomed man at ease among companions he could trust, a man who knew no hint of the deadly danger around him, a man who had never been taken by the law, unless through traitors softened with the touch of silver on the palm? Why then the change? Why the sudden decision to go in the adobe and undress, and then, half clad, to come down through the dark to Maxwell's house, unarmed, save for the butcher knife borrowed from Pablo to take his cut of beef? For fools this story may suffice. Men with harder minds will say that Billy was betrayed—that someone took a bribe. Yet Garrett never spoke of bounty paid. Nor did Maxwell leave a memoir of his price. Neither did the Mexican, sly Pablo, advertise his pay among his people. The trap, no matter, was ready set.

In through the open window of Pete's room, Pat Garrett

went like a mountain cat's shadow. Pete saw him come and still made no move to leave his bed. Getting behind the bed, putting his lean back to the protection of the thick adobe wall, Garrett waved his pistol, spoke fast and low.

"Where is he?"

Maxwell was a big man, and tough with years. In the daylight he feared few others. But this was different. They were not alone in that room; both knew it.

"Where is Billy?" repeated Pat, his tension growing with the bedroom's eerie midnight quiet.

"I don't know," whispered Pete. "He's here, but I don't know where."

"Maxwell, I was told you'd have him *here.*"

"I will, I will, just wait."

With Maxwell's muttered promise, Garrett stiffened. Outside, the sound of muffled footsteps and a cheery whistle, known by ear to Pat Garrett, approached the porch.

"That's him," hissed Garrett.

Again outside, the sound now of muffled voices, Billy's voice asking of the evening from Pat's two guards, Poe and McKinney playing their parts well, answering him in the Spanish language of the land, posing as passers-through much like himself.

Now the whistle resumed. Less cheery, guarded, showing more breath than melody. The bootless footsteps crossed the porch, entered the main *sala* or front room, glided down the short hallway to Maxwell's door, pausing there.

Garrett tensed and raised his gun. In the doorway the small figure seemed slight, almost boyish. The light behind it was growing, as the moon slithered out from underneath its cloud. There could be no doubt of the fact that the newcomer was unarmed as to any gun. The question was as to whether he even still carried the butcher knife. Maxwell, rigid on the bed, saw nothing in his hands. But he knew the graceful boy-like form, and so did Pat.

"Pedro," called Billy thinly, whisper high with some unease. "*¿Quiénes son estos hombres afuera?* Who are those men outside?"

Pete, fearing to be shot by Garrett, said nothing.

Billy slid on into the room, still looking back over his shoulder toward the porch. "Pete!" he repeated sharply. "Answer me. Who's outside there? Those two men on the porch? Answer me!" His lisp was snake-like now, the alarm in it high and wild.

He came to the side of Pete's bed, bending over it. It was then his eyes made out the tall shadow standing beyond that bed, against the wall. He straightened.

"*¿Quién es?*" he whispered fearfully. "Who is it?" The tall shadow not replying, he turned again in panic to Pete Maxwell. "Pete, in God's name, who's there?"

This time his answer was not silence. Another shadow came into the room, spoke at his elbow. "It is I," said Asaph softly. "It is I who awaits you here."

And the thunder of Pat Garrett's gun broke loose. Two times its lightning lanced the gloom. The first shot, the range so close the flaring ball of powder gases ignited Billy's shirt and burned the flesh beneath, went in directly over the heart. It severed the main aorta and both its branches, rupturing out the blood and the life alike. The only sound that Billy made that was remembered by his human witnesses in that darkened room was a simple, gasping: "Oh . . . !" Then Garrett's second shot, missing wide, screamed off the wall and brought the final silence in behind it, thick and hushed.

Oh, *what* had Billy meant to say, in dying? Oh, Lord? Oh, shame? Oh, curse the Fates that lured me here? Only Asaph knew, and he would not say because the words held in them that name which made him pale. They were: "Oh, God, please help me, Mother!"

But let the legend have its way. He died without another sound, it says, except to struggle once or twice and strangle some, as Garrett put it. This ending would suffice for Asaph. When he had touched a man and said to come, that man went with him. He cared not for legends or for lies, or folklore, left behind. He was Asaph the Gatherer. When he had harvested the grain, the chaff might blow forever where it would. Thus he took Billy Bonney's hand and they, not hurried then, went out of that smoke-stinking room and mounted up on Asaph's pale horse, waiting beyond the lamplight now flooding Maxwell's ranch, its yard, and all around.

They rode, not swiftly, Billy thought, yet soon were halted far away. Here, Asaph, looking back toward the ranch, asked Billy if he wanted the answer to his whispered—"*¿Quién es?*"—in that dark room before the thunder of the gun. Would he wish now to know the name of the gunman who had killed him, and the names of those who waited on the porch to back him up? Or would he rather wait to ask eternity?

Billy thought it through. He was never the one to rush his play before the hand was dealt. He glanced at Asaph, blue eyes unafraid but filled with all those nameless things that haunt the eyes of men who look at that companion. At last he answered, high voice firm, sturdy shoulders squared. "No, friend," he said. "That . . . *¿quién es?* . . . was not for them, but you. I saw you all the time. I knew you were there. I only spoke to hear you say your name, and call mine after it."

"And now?" said Asaph, waiting still.

"Now?" said Billy, grinning widely. "Why the devil, pal . . . now let's go. You know the way, and so do I!"

Asaph nodded, and they traveled on to that far bourne from which no man returns. But as they went he noted that his comrade's step was light, his head unbent, the laughter that had been his life still ringing softly back across their footprints through the dust of time.

ABOUT THE AUTHOR

Henry Wilson Allen wrote under both the Clay Fisher and Will Henry bylines and was a five-time winner of the Spur Award from the Western Writers of America. He was born in Kansas City, Missouri. His early work was in short subject departments with various Hollywood studios, and he was working at M-G-M when his first Western novel, *No Survivors* (1950), was published. While numerous Western authors before Allen provided sympathetic and intelligent portraits of Indian characters, Allen from the start set out to characterize Indians in such a way as to make their viewpoints an integral part of his stories. Some of Allen's images of Indians are of the romantic variety, to be sure, but his theme often is the failure of the American frontier experience and the romance is used to treat his tragic themes with sympathy and humanity. On the whole, the Will Henry novels tend to be based more deeply in actual historical events, whereas in those titles he wrote as Clay Fisher he was more intent on a story filled with action that moves rapidly. However, this dichotomy can be misleading, since *MacKenna's Gold* (1963), a Will Henry Western about gold-seekers, reads much like one of the finest Clay Fisher titles, *The Tall Men* (1954). His novels, *Journey to Shiloh* (1960), *From Where the Sun Now Stands* (1960), *One More River To Cross* (1967), *Chiricahua* (1972), and *I, Tom Horn* (1975) in particular, remain imperishable classics of Western historical fiction. Over a dozen films have been made based on his work.